ENDER OF WORLDS

KIT HALLOWS

ENDER OF WORLDS

By Kit Hallows

To Rhiannon, Pip & other hellions

DARK COVENANT

Get your free copy of Dark Covenant, the explosive prequel to Dark City, as well as exclusive access to my mailing list for author updates and free Urban Fantasy stories by visiting: https://kithallows.com/DarkCovenant

Red and blue strobes flashed like lightning across the misty rain and the puddles at my feet. The very air around me pulsed with color and I braced myself as another wave of gunfire thundered into the cop car I was lodged behind.

The entire vehicle rattled, glass exploded from the windows above me and fell like glittering ice on the wet road.

I glanced back along the jagged row of black and white cars hastily parked in the middle of the street. The rhythm of their red and blue was almost hypnotic. Then the cops returned fire, their guns blazing in the rain as the rounds pelted the facade of the bank and I quickly looked away as they ducked back down.

The door felt smooth and cold against my face as I pressed up against it, then another salvo of bullets blasted out the rear window. I kept my head down, catching my reflection in the dark oily puddle. The police uniform I *wore* made me look like a real professional. Focused, disciplined even. It could have been a good look but in reality it was just an illusion. Samuel had done well, but the spell would only hold for so long and the last thing I needed was a jumpy cop spotting my ratty old coat and the sword stashed under it.

I winced as another hail of bullets rocked the car and clenched my jaw as I waited for the lull.

There.

I glanced through the shattered window toward the bank. It was a wide building with a tall portico supported by broad pillars, and polished granite walls riddled with bullet holes. Two robbers were holed up behind those pillars; somewhere inside was the third culprit, and he was wielding magic. Hence the rushed and scrambled phone call summoning me to the scene.

"Rook!" Haskins squatted beside the car next to mine. His face was a twisted mix of fear and excitement, and in that moment he once again reminded me of a gargoyle in a raincoat. "To me!" He glanced over the hood of his bullet riddled squad car and fired half a dozen rounds. The rest of the cops joined in and I used their cover to scurry over to him.

"Can't you do something?" Haskins demanded, his voice gruff. "Like now!"

"Do what?" I called as the robbers fired back. Splinters of glass exploded around us, splashing into the puddles at our feet.

"You know, some of that hocus pocus shit."

I nodded to the dozen or so cops around us. "Sure. If you want me to draw even more attention to *our world*." I couldn't use magic, not with so many blinkered witnesses. I'd have to get inside, where there was more cover.

"What the hell is that?" Haskins shouted as a bright, colorful pulse soared over us.

It was a wyvern formed of fiery light, its elongated head ablaze as it swooped over the cars, lashing its spiked tail, flapping its scaly wings and freaking out the cops behind us. It

2

was illusion magic. *Powerful* illusion magic, and it was more than just a terrifying distraction, it was mapping out our positions for its master.

I grabbed a crystal from my pocket and used its energy to drain the wyvern's power. It turned ghostly as I stole its color and magic, and fell in a hail of cinders that sizzled on the asphalt.

This was a bad development. Our kind had always kept themselves hidden from the blinkereds, even the criminals, because we all knew that when push came to shove, if the blinkereds caught wind of us, we'd be finished. That as evolved as they seemed, they were just a hair's breadth from going savage. And that they had lots and lots of weapons at their disposal, weapons that could decimate everything around us and turn the world into a smoking crater.

But the bastard brashly wielding magic in the bank didn't seem to give a damn about any of that. Which meant I had to shut them down, and fast.

I grabbed the enhanced scope from my bag and swept its charged crystal lens toward the walls of the building, revealing the fiery red beating hearts of the two robbers holding their position at the entrance.

They were clearly scared, amped up, and prepared to deal with anyone that approached them. I'd have to take them down before I could get inside. Once I was in, I'd need to be quick, eliminating the magician and as much evidence of his handiwork as possible before the cops caught sight of it.

I reached into my bag and pulled out a handful of crystals. They glimmered in my palm as I drew my fingers around them.

"What the hell are you doing now? A frigging faith healing?" Haskins demanded. "Quit with the flaky hippy bullshit and do something!"

"I am." I shivered as the magic coursed through me and I focused its energy into creating a line of illusory cops at the end of the street. Samuel had shown me the trick and it was convincing as hell, but it took a lot of energy and I wasn't exactly an expert yet.

The crystals grew hot in my hand as I harnessed their power and maneuvered the row of ghostly cops toward the bank, drawing the robbers' attention and gunfire while I prepared to make my move.

"What are they doing, who gave that order?" Haskins squinted at the fake cops.

"They're not real," I said, "listen, I'm going in. Wait for my signal and when you see it, tell your boys to hold their fire. Got it?"

He nodded numbly as I raced through the rain. Gunfire continued to roar out from behind the pillars but the blinkered criminals were still focused on the illusions.

I slipped past, almost reaching the bank without being riddled by bullet holes, when a bolt of fire shot out toward me like a blazing spear.

2

I ducked the flames as they roared over me and seared the side of my face. The spell's trajectory led back to the bank entrance where a man stood, a staff of power in hand.

His features were stony below his wild ash-grey hair, and he was dressed in dark archaic robes. Our eyes locked, and he raised the staff again, unleashing another deadly bolt.

I pulled my coat up over my head, its armor-like enchantments dispersed the worst of the heat, but I still felt like I'd tumbled into the fires of hell. I peered out as the man shouted to his accomplices and strode back into the bank.

Within moments the pair leaped out and fired, their bullets ricocheting off the ground and the wall around me.

I ran hard as the cops fired back, forcing the robbers to take cover. Their onslaught bought me enough time to leap up the steps and dive behind a pillar.

One of my targets, a dead-eyed man about my age, spotted me and fired. Chunks of stone exploded around me as I ducked away. I glanced back as the cops returned fire, riddling his arm with bullets. He fell to the ground clutching his wrist as he inched toward his fallen weapon. I shot him before he could grab it, then his partner leaped from behind his pillar and tried to stumble inside the bank, but another hail of gunfire peppered him with lead.

"Hold!" I shouted and gestured to the car where Haskins had taken cover.

An eerie silence fell across the place as I broke cover and ran to the front doors. They slid open as I cast a simple spell over the threshold to stop any cops from following. At least for a while.

I summoned the rest of the crystal's magic and used it to reveal the fire magician's footsteps. They burst into light like a winding path of flares leading back to the vault. Cries and whimpers echoed across the foyer from the tellers and customers who lay sprawled out, their hands stretched before them. "Stay down," I said. "Got it?" A few nodded and cried garbled promises of compliance.

I'd almost reached the counter when a bullet hit me square in the chest, sending me staggering back. The enchantment in my coat stopped the round but it still hurt like hell. I glanced up the wide flight of steps toward the upper floor as someone ducked down.

"You're next," I said as I hunkered down behind a desk, grabbed a small mirror from my bag and angled it toward the stairs.

The man peered over the balcony as he took aim. Moments later a bullet whistled toward the mirror, nearly shattering the glass.

I swiped the mirror's surface and zoomed in on my target.

He was blinkered, and as our eyes met I befuddled him with a quick paralysis spell. He remained frozen as I ran for the stairs. I reached the top, seized his gun, and used the butt to knock him out cold.

I glanced down as footsteps echoed across the marble floor below. A man emerged from the vault, his gun held before him. I leaped onto the balcony rail and dropped, taking him down hard.

Two more robbers appeared, their black canvas bags stuffed with cash. Between them was a man that had to be the bank manager. He had the look; thin and jittery, a perfectly tailored suit and preoccupied eyes framed by silver designer glasses. I'd been turned down for credit by jerks like him more times than I cared to mention.

My reflexes were faster than the thug beside him. He raised his gun toward the manager's head, trying to get leverage over me. I shot before he knew what had happened, taking him out with a bullet to the heart.

I pulled my coat around me as his partner returned fire. Bullets pinged around me and a few struck me hard. I waited for the click of the empty magazine before firing back. His gun fell from his hand as the round struck his shoulder, then I punched him, sending him crumpling to the ground.

Only the manager's girlish whimpering broke the silence that had fallen over the building.

Something was wrong. I'd failed to catch something.

I glanced at the thugs sprawled on the bloody polished floor. They'd been sent out as a distraction. What had I missed?

A moment of time…

…and something else.

But what?

3

I wanted to tear through the place, search every nook and cranny, but I forced myself to concentrate on the things I'd overlooked in the heat of the fight.

The magician...

... he'd strode past as his thugs engaged me, several black canvas duffle bags draped over his shoulder, each enchanted to be as light as air. He'd moved outside my field of time, but only just enough for me to miss him.

I started toward the front doors but stopped. He was long gone. He'd slipped out of the building and down the street leaving spent gun shells, some dead goons and an empty vault in his wake. "Who is he?" I demanded of the shooter squealing like a pig on the ground, his jacket soaked with blood as he clenched it to his wounded arm.

He shook his head. "I ain't telling you shit."

"They always say that." I sighed.

"Who?" He spat on the ground.

"Criminals. Thugs. Idiots. But I break them all, just like I'll break you. Now give me the name of your pal who just walked out of here with all the cash and left you behind holding the baby, loaded diaper and all."

"Go fuck yourself!"

I pressed the gun in his wound until he roared with agony. And then I held it to his head. "Who is he?"

He gazed at me for a moment, and it almost looked as if he was going to talk, then his eyes turned hazy and took on a strange, milky hue. Before I could react, he reached up and pressed my finger to the trigger.

The gun roared, the air misted red and most of his face vanished to gore.

"What the fuck?"

Shock passed through me in a bludgeoning wave and my ears rang with the din. It took a moment to discern the whimpers coming from the people lying on the cold floor with their hands over their heads.

I glanced through the distant glass to the wet grey world beyond. The cops hadn't made it to the door. Presumably Haskins was holding them back, but I doubted he could keep it up for much longer. When they got in, there'd be questions. And not just about the corpses, they'd want to know about all the weird shit that had taken place too. The line of illusionary cops, the fireballs, and that frigging wyvern made of light.

I pulled out my phone and called Erland.

No answer. Again.

I hadn't spoken to him since my battle with Elsbeth Wyght and even then, the call had been brief and he'd been beyond evasive. My announcement to him of Wyght's demise had been met with scant relief, then he'd growled at me to keep my head down and lay low for a while.

His number rang on a loop, but just before I hung up I heard a click.

"Humble."

Humble... it took a moment to realize I was talking to one of Erland's partners. A man at The Organization I'd never laid eyes on, let alone spoken with. Something in his voice sent a cold shiver through me.

"Humble!" he said again. This time there was a trace of anger in his tone. And then he said, "Rook?"

I hung up.

What the hell was going on?

The thudding from the entrance dragged me from my reverie. The cop hammered on the doors with his fist as another tried to pry them open. I called Haskins and watched him through the glass as he answered. "I'll let them in, but keep 'em away from me. I need to get out of here."

"You're involved now, you can't just leave!" Haskins glared my way.

"I can and will. If you want me to catch the bastard who did this, let me go about my business and you go about yours. Right?"

He stared at me for a moment before ordering the cops to step back. I walked to the door, discharged the enchantment that had held them back, and strode through, tipping my illusory cap as I went.

4

Rain drops spattered the sidewalk as I crossed the city and headed for the magical quarter. The air was thick, charged, and full of static from the storm threatening to unleash itself. It had been building for days and the breaking point was close. Just like the city. I could feel it all; the tension in the streets, the fear, the sense of things coming to a head, or even to an end. Something had to give, and I was pretty sure that when it did, I'd be smack bang in the middle of it.

A car roared by, drenching the sidewalk as I made my way onto Lunar Avenue. I wanted to grab a crystal and send a curse after the driver but thought better of it. Onwards. I was looking forward to catching up with Astrid and Samuel.

It had been days since they'd stepped through my bedroom mirror and set out for the Hinterlands. Allegedly they were heading off to look for clues as to the whereabouts of Endersley, but I was pretty sure the timing had more to do with giving me some space after my battle with Elsbeth Wyght, as well as time to deal with the tempest of emotions that had followed. The savage, victorious highs and the desolate feelings of emptiness. Losing the foe I'd been on the trail of for years, coupled with the curious silence of my dark other had been one hell of an adjustment. I'd slept for days, and when I'd woken the apartment had been empty and the cats subdued.

I slowed as I reached Nika's Diner, looking through the windows for a sign of Astrid or Samuel. Nothing. Not even in the gloomy booths toward the back. I pulled my phone out and called the burner phone I'd given Astrid.

"You're late," Samuel said, through a tumult of shouts and braying laughter in the background.

"Where are you?" I peered down the street as people huddled through the growing torrent of rain.

"We decided ale was in order. And that revelation led us to a charming little establishment called The Lucky Coin. You should join us."

Great. I glanced to the tavern, just a few doors down from Nika's. It was possibly the last bar I'd have chosen in the quarter, and that was saying something.

I stood before its flaking emerald green facade and peered through the bullseye glass in the window. The bar room was as dark as the clouds sailing overhead with only a scattering of candles illuminating the thuggish patrons within.

The battered front door looked like it was about ready to fall off its hinges and the beer coasters taped to its tiny window seemed to be the only things keeping the glass intact. I did my best to overlook the stench of yeast and piss that loomed at the threshold as I stepped inside.

Music blared through dusty black speakers. The singer, who or whatever it was, sounded like they were standing on a distant hill screaming through a megaphone while a band of mad Vikings charged at them playing thrash metal. It was something I'd have expected to encounter in Dauple's car, and

I had to wonder if he was now moonlighting as their DJ. The place was packed, mostly with undesirables. Brutish men, brutish women, a troll or two and a group of pale sickly warlocks. More than a few dagger-like stares were thrown my way as I crossed the sawdust strewn floor. I ignored them. I hadn't come to fight, I'd come to find my friends and hopefully get them the hell out of this place.

Loud, hearty laughter boomed through the murk, and I followed it to find Samuel regaling a dodgy-looking congregation. Astrid sat beside him in the booth, leaning against the wall. Was she asleep? If so, I was impressed.

"Morgan!" Samuel called as I approached. The group turned my way and I recognized a few creeps I'd come to blows with over the years. One gave me a hateful look and his hand strayed toward whatever he was concealing below his manky winter coat.

"Morgan, meet my new friends. Good men and women all!" Samuel clapped a hand on my shoulder and everyone around him seemed to soften a little, caught as they were in his spell. "Now, if you don't mind," Samuel said to them, "I need to talk to this man in private." A chorus of mutters and tuts filled the air but slowly the group disbanded and wandered away.

"I see your charms work on rats as well as people," I said as I took a seat across from Astrid.

"Now, now, Morgan, those were fine upstanding citizens," Samuel grinned. "And it's always wise to mix with people from every strata of life. You never know when such alliances might come in handy. Now, how's about I get this empty pitcher filled with something dark and frothy." He grabbed it from the table and strode toward the heaving bar as Astrid opened her eyes.

It took her a moment to focus on me. She looked exhausted

and I wondered if she'd fully recovered from the healing rituals she'd performed on me after our battle with Wyght and her coven.

"Hello, Morgan." She gave me a slow, soft smile and sat up. "How are you?"

"Better for seeing you."

I returned her smile, it was impossible to hold it back and I was thankful we were tucked away in a shadowy bar as my cheeks reddened. For some reason, whenever she complimented me it made me feel like I did back in high school, off guard. Exposed. I was about to try and summon a suitable response when Samuel appeared, pitcher and empty tankard in hand. He filled it for me and shoved it my way then topped Astrid's glass along with his own. "So," he said, "what's been happening? You look like you've just fought your way out of a room filled with overly amorous ogres."

"Not quite. But yeah, I guess I just had an interesting experience," I said and took a sip of beer. It was surprisingly good, deep and nutty with a hint of pine. "We just had our very own official bank robbery."

"The first? Really?" Samuel looked doubtful. And then he looked… interested, and I could almost see the wheels turning in his mind.

"No, not the first. And before you get any ideas, the banks here are not easy pickings," I said. "No, I meant the first time someone from the magical community openly robbed a bank without even attempting to hide their abilities. The guy was wielding some serious magic, as if he didn't have a care in the world, right in front of an audience of blinkered cops." I took another drink. "Which is perfect seeing as the media's already been a hornet's nest after Wyght's little stunt in Temple Park."

"How did you explain that away?" Astrid asked. "There were so many dead. So much destruction."

"The Organization combed over the scene pretty intensely. Then Haskins put out a disinformation campaign calling it a terrorist incident," I said. "It seemed the blinkered authorities swallowed it for the most part, or maybe they were paid off. But this robbery isn't exactly going to help matters."

"I don't understand, why a robbery? Why would anyone from the magical community need blinkered cash?" Astrid asked. "Especially when there are so many other ways to acquire whatever you desire."

"I don't know either," I admitted. "But under the circumstances, the magician's not likely to be on the loose for very long. Maybe he'll shed some light on his motives before he gets hauled off to Stardim, but right now I'm more concerned with Stroud and his plans. Are you any closer to finding Endersley?"

"No," Samuel said, "but we did manage to round up some new folks that'll be keeping an eye on the Hinterlands in case he tries to pass through there again. They're not what I'd call ideal, but they'll get the job done as long we're paying them. Which was something else we had to take care of."

Astrid coughed and I saw her give a slight shake of her head. Clearly they'd been up to no good while they were away, not that I cared. I policed the blinkered world as best I could, not theirs. At least I knew they had a code of conduct, even if it was shot through with many shades of grey. "Before you left," I said, changing the subject, "you mentioned bloodsuckers hiding Endersley. Did you mean vampires?"

"Yup," Samuel said, with a slight shiver, "horrible things. We tried taking them down, and we got a few of 'em, but in the end there were just too many."

"And while we were fighting them off, Endersley slipped away," Astrid added.

"Right," I said. "Well, it sounds like tracking them down's

the best lead we have right now. What did they look like?" I asked, before finishing off the rest of the beer and pushing the tankard aside. There was work to do.

"Sharp teeth, starey eyes-" Samuel began.

"They were very... tight," Astrid said. "Coordinated. At first glance I thought we could eliminate them before they could so much as blink, but things didn't turn out that way. They had a leader, a vampiress. White hair, but she was young and there was a scar running down the side of her face. Does she sound familiar?"

I shook my head. "I've been out the loop with the comings and goings of vampires since this business with Stroud began. But Talulah might know something about them seeing as she's of that persuasion herself." I pulled my phone out and was about to call *Books, Nooks, Oddments, and Glamors*, when I noticed more than a few of The Coin's patrons glancing our way. "Excuse me," I said as I stood and strode outside.

"Morgan Rook," Talulah said as she answered. "You just caught me on my way out. What do you need? A cure? A tonic? Information?" I could hear the smile in her voice. "You still owe me, you know."

"I haven't forgotten," I said, "but you're right, I do have another favor to ask. I'm looking for a vampire. Or a vampiress to be more precise."

"Well, it looks like you just got lucky."

"Not you, Talulah, magnificent though you are. No, I'm looking for a young lady with long white hair and a scar on her face. Do you know her?"

"I can't say that I do. But then I tend to fraternize with all types, not just my own. My grandfather on the other hand is far less cosmopolitan and likes to stick to his own crowd, so you'd probably have better luck asking him."

I shuddered. The last time I'd dealt with Talulah's

grandfather was just after I'd been stricken with a particularly horrendous curse. I remembered him lurking in the back of Talulah's shop; a creepy, ancient vampire with horribly appraising eyes. "Can you give me his number?" I asked.

Talulah snorted. "Grandpa doesn't do phones. Hates them even more than I do. If you want to talk to him you'll have to toddle along and see him. He lives on Hopswytch, number seventeen. Tell him I sent you and to keep his eyes off your jugular."

"Will do."

"Watch yourself, Morgan. He can be... unstable."

"Perfect," I said. "Well thank you... I think."

"No problem, I'm adding it to your tab."

I took a deep breath, filling my lungs with the cold air as I glanced down Lunar Avenue. Night was closing in and it seemed even darker than usual. The moon was just a sliver hidden by a steady ragged bank of rainclouds and the atmosphere felt even more charged, if that was possible. It put me on edge, made me jittery. Like things were about to go south. Big time.

5

Hopswytch Street was a grim line of gloomy shops that had apartments stacked upon their second or third stories, and straddled the border between the magical quarter and the blinkered city. The air was sour and carried an irrepressible sense of imminent danger, a deliberate deterrent for blinkereds who might otherwise wander down roads that weren't made for them. We walked on, ignoring the odd stares and questioning glances from the hookers and crystal dealers lingering along the sidewalk.

We came to a stop outside a shadowy doorway next to a butcher shop with an ornate gold seventeen painted on the glass. I glanced through the window; the place didn't look like it was doing much business. The cold cases were empty and the counters clear but for a few knives and long sheets of stark white paper. "Nice," Samuel said, as he peered in through the window. "Seems like an ideal cover for dismembering and disposal."

"And you haven't even met Feist yet. You're in for a real treat," I said as I rang the bell.

The door swung right open and I saw Feist lurking by a

darkened stairwell. There was just enough light from the nearby streetlamp to make out a few details, like the old white shirt he wore and the suspenders that held up his long trousers but could do nothing about the cuffs that sagged around his gnarled feet. He'd worn the same outfit the first time I'd met him. He stepped forward and I noticed that the liver spots on his face had multiplied and his straggly beard was longer. All in all he looked about ready for the grave, yet his eyes were as bright as a newborn babe's as they flitted over me. "Yes?" he asked, his voice gruff. He glanced from me to Samuel and then to Astrid, and his tongue flickered over his dry, cracked lips.

The last time I'd met him I'd caught a glimpse under the magical cloak he'd disguised himself with and I could still remember his true and ancient form; that skin the color of moonlight and the long, long fangs. "Good evening, Mr. Feist," I said, offering a faltering smile.

He continued to stare then stepped forward, sniffing me. "We've met before," he said, his accent thick, possibly Eastern European. He licked his lips again and peered out to the street behind us, before offering a cold, unpleasant grin. "Yes, I remember you."

"Sure, I'm Morgan Rook" I said, "we met at your granddaughter's shop a while back."

"Yes, I remember that too. You were…dying. So tell me, why have you come?"

"Talulah sent me."

"Did she?" He asked. The air flickered and before I knew it, his cold bony hand was resting on my shoulder. Astrid stepped beside me, one hand beneath her cloak. Feist nodded. "Then you are much welcome. Come in. You and your charming friends."

I glanced at the doorway and wondered if there were any

rituals for entering a vampire's house, and if non-vampires had to be invited over their thresholds. Either way I wasn't exactly enthusiastic as I stepped into the gloom and waited for Astrid and Samuel to join me.

We stood in awkward silence as Mr. Feist appraised each of us then slowly closed the door, plunging us into darkness. My hand strayed to my gun. What the hell had I been thinking...

"This way," Mr. Feist said, his breath frosty and bitter in my ear. I heard him ascending a flight of stairs. Slowly, and awkwardly, the three of us followed, climbing up into shadows. As we neared the top a door creaked open, casting a dim light onto the final steps.

"Come," Feist said.

We entered his tiny living room. It was sparsely furnished. A crumpled sofa, a lone chair set before a dining table, a dank empty fireplace, and a few scattered old photographs of severe-looking people staring out from gilded frames.

"One moment please," Feist passed through a door in a corner of the room and returned with a bottle of vodka and a coffee mug marred with muddy-red stains. "Drink?" he said, as he filled the cup, took a long sip and handed it to me.

"I'm okay thanks," I said.

"You?" he asked, offering the cup to Astrid. She shook her head, and even Samuel turned it down. "Suit yourselves," Feist said, as he walked over to Astrid and Samuel, sniffing the air above their heads. "Is good," he said. "Your scents. Succulent." He moved in closer to Astrid but she stepped away and before I knew it, there was a dagger in her hand.

Mr. Feist exploded with dry, rasping laughter. "I will never hurt you! This man," he nodded to me. "This man is friend of my granddaughter. This means he, and those who walk with him, are my friends too. Trust me, my dear, I'm man of honor." His eyes twinkled as they found me. "Now tell me, what brings you to my home on a stormy night such as this?"

"We're looking for some people."

"People?" Feist asked.

"Well, you know, people of your kind."

"Vampires? Don't be afraid to say this word out loud, it won't bite." He smiled, but his gaze lingered on my throat.

"Yes, vampires," I said. "We're looking for a gang run by a young-looking woman with white hair and a scar-"

"Helena Castle." He turned and spat into the empty fireplace. "That bitch!"

"You're not fond of her then," Samuel said.

"Samuel!" Astrid gave him a withering glare.

Feist shook his head. "I kill her."

"You killed her?" I asked.

"Not yet, but I will. I kill her, I swear it. She is old enemy." Slowly his face softened and I could see the machinations passing through his eyes. "You're looking for them? You want fight?" He stood taller, more alert. "We attack them, yes?"

"If we have to," I said. "But right now I just want to talk to her."

"There's plenty of them. Too many for me to defeat alone," Feist said. "But together, me and your finely scented friends, together we smash them." He walked into the kitchen and returned with a meat cleaver, its blade glistening in the dim light.

I suppressed my sigh. "Like I said, we're planning on talking to them first."

Feist shook his head like he was dealing with a disagreeable child. "They won't talk to you. You want information, you crack heads open and snatch it out with bloody fingers. I help you. Now, follow me."

I heard a faint scratching upon a small door on the other

side of the room. "What's that?" I asked. Samuel and Astrid looked similarly alarmed.

"Little dog," Feist said. "She likes cupboard, frightened of strangers and storm. The darkness pleases her, makes her feel safe."

I chose to believe it, but as we descended the stairwell and emerged onto the street I was struck with a low, ominous feeling. What was it? My nerves? Faint stirrings from my dark other? Had the darkness or some unspoken threat in Feist's grim apartment woken him from his slumber? A part of me hoped not. My life had definitely been simpler without him.

"Come," Feist said, leading us down the street, "we have job to do." We followed him back past the dealers and hookers and I watched them avert their eyes as Feist strolled by, cheerfully swinging the meat cleaver in his bony hand. "Is good, yes?" he asked, and when he turned back toward me his fangs were notably longer than they'd been.

6

We gave Feist a wide berth as he led us along. He was clearly unhinged, even for a vampire and it led to several moments of discomfort, mainly as we passed bright young things on the sidewalk. I shivered when I caught him staring at their throats and saw his fingers twitching restlessly by his side. Then there was his humming, the long drawn out dirge-like melodies accompanied by his relentless, chipper smile.

Thankfully, the people that we passed seemed to keep their distance, possibly on account of the meat cleaver. Or maybe it was the browning blood stains on his starched white shirt.

"You have curious allies," Astrid remarked, as we followed Feist across the magical quarter into the blinkered city. I nodded. It was a fair point. The night grew later and later as we passed through one quiet neighborhood then another and it soon seemed like the entire city was asleep, except for us. Soon the residential blocks turned to timeworn buildings and warehouses, and we found ourselves at the dead end of a narrow street, facing a chain-link fence. Behind it was a yard, a few small shed-like structures and a tall, wide redbrick building. The battered old sign on the fence read:

Fink and Sons Meat Packing

It looked like the place had gone out of business some time ago, but there were still a few rusting trucks parked in the lot. I glanced up as a light flickered in one of the darkened windows and Feist turned to me, an expectant gleam in his eyes. "They are there,' he said. "Hiding like rats. We'll catch them by their tails, and then they'll see." He licked his lips. "First we must look for sentries. Help me to find them."

"So," Samuel said, "Just to be clear, we're staking out a gang of vampires. Staking…" He grinned. "Get it?"

I made a mental note to unplug the television as soon as we got home. "Yeah, I got it." I said, "sadly."

"There's someone on the roof," Astrid whispered.

"There's *someones* on the roof. I see two of them," Feist said. "They will be armed." He pulled his shirt from his trousers and hiked it up, revealing a series of angry red welts on his belly, as if someone had poured boiling water over him. "Do not underestimate these rats. I learn this, last time I was here." He scowled, his fangs even longer than before.

"I can make my way to the roof and take at least one down before the other notices," I said.

Samuel removed his bow from his shoulder. "I'll take care of the other one the moment you strike."

I turned to Astrid, and she nodded as if reading my mind. "I'll stay here with Mr. Feist," she said, "and make sure nothing goes wrong."

"Thank you," I said. Because there was a good chance that plenty could go wrong where Mr. Feist was concerned. He glanced my way and tightened his fingers on his cleaver. I ignored his gesture, pulled a scope from my bag and took a close look at the roof.

One of the vampires lounged on a deck chair while the other perched by a chimney gazing into its phone. Neither of them seemed very alert. It was as if they'd figured no one on earth was crazy enough to attack their lair, and I hoped we could use that to our advantage.

"Right, I'm going in," I said. I strode along the chain-link fence toward an area obscured by shipping containers, scaled it and dropped unseen to the other side. I made my way through the jumbled maze of long metal boxes, clasped a crystal and willed myself to become unseen. Or at least as unseen as I could be under a vampire's heightened senses.

The old trucks in the lot served as good cover as I ran toward the building. Sprinting low, I made my way to the rusted ladder that ran up to the roof, shivering as my fingers brushed the wall behind it. It buzzed with the ghosts from the past, echoes of the animals that had been slaughtered there. The place was steeped in their panic and terror as well as the slow descent into decay and despair that arose after a new corporate-backed operation set up shop just two blocks away, putting Fink and Sons out of business.

It was little wonder the vampires had been drawn to this mournful place, and soon after they'd moved in the terror and blood ran anew, but the slaughter was focused on an entirely different species now.

I climbed the ladder slowly, to prevent my sword from rattling against the rungs. The vampire's senses were far more acute than mine and even the slightest mistake could catch their attention.

An icy breeze stirred as I stepped out onto the roof and heavy clouds obscured the sliver of moon. The vampires hadn't budged since I'd spotted them from the street.

I crept toward the one in the chair. He was short, stocky and the scars and bruises on the back of his neck told me he'd been in plenty of scrapes. It would be easy to run him through with my sword, but such cowardice wasn't in my blood. I pulled a cosh from my bag, lined with fragments of silver and iron to knock him out and take care of any magical protection he'd placed over himself before nap time.

Before I struck, I glanced back into the darkness below. There was no sign of Astrid, Samuel or Feist. I hoped that was a good thing, and that Samuel was watching as I brought the cosh down over the back of the vampire's head. He gave a short hiss and sank deeper into his chair.

His friend gazed up from his phone and growled. The bloodsucker's eyes flashed as he pulled a knife from his belt and took aim to throw it. He froze as an arrow whizzed by its head. Samuel's arrow.

He'd missed.

Shit.

The vampire lunged and slashed his knife at my chest. My coat repelled the blade but I staggered as I brought my cosh down on the side of his face. He tottered back and opened his mouth to call out a warning, but the only thing that slipped past his fangs was a strangled gasp as a glistening arrow pierced his throat. I lowered the dead creature to the ground quietly and waited.

Moments later Samuel appeared silently at my side. "Astrid and the old freak found the door to the warehouse around the back," he said. "They'll wait for us to clear any hostiles from the upper levels, then we'll strike the heart of the lair together. There's a large gathering in an open space on the ground level. They seem preoccupied with drinking and smoking from what I could tell, so they should be easy to take out."

"Providing your arrows fly true," I said, smiling to show I was joking.

"Sorry about that," Samuel said. "It's pretty dark, and I think I may have sobered up. Which never helps."

We made our way to the access door. It was unlocked and moments later we crept down a flight of wooden steps.

Music blared as I glanced down over the landing to the ground floor. Ramshackle tables had been arranged into a rough square and eight or so vampires were sitting around drinking beer, wine and what may have been absinthe, while the pungent scent of weed wafted through the air. It seemed they weren't as disciplined as Astrid had initially thought or, more worryingly, they were damned confident. I hoped it was the former.

I glanced to the head of the table where a woman with silvery hair leaned back in her chair reading a paperback. A long scar ran down the side of her cold, pretty face. "I take it she's the one you ran into last time?" I asked.

"Yup. How do you want to proceed?" Samuel whispered.

I nodded to the second floor landing just below us. It was a large open plan office and, except for the elderly vampire watching an old-fashioned television at one of the desks, it appeared to be empty. "I'll get rid of him," I said. "Take a position and get ready to thin out the group below. Except for her of course," I glanced toward Castle as she turned another page of her book.

"Got it." Samuel vanished into the shadows as I made my way down the flight of steps and slipped through the office. The vampire didn't notice. He was engrossed in a documentary about the Galápagos Islands, which seemed like a bizarre point of interest for a vampire considering all the sunshine. I ducked through the room as he marveled at the salt-sneezing iguanas and bashed him over the head. Once I was certain he wasn't going to be getting up any time soon, I returned to the landing.

I had a better vantage point of the room below, and a bird's eye view of the greasy haired vampire below me. He was stooped over a teenage girl sprawled out on a butcher's block and her glassy eyes stared up at me as he fed.

Rage roared through me and I felt my other stir, as if drawn to my fury. "Fuck it," I whispered as I grabbed a knuckleduster from my bag and strapped it on. I climbed onto the rail and crouched to steady myself.

I dropped, smashing my fist into the back of the vampire's skull as I hit the ground. The crack that rang out was sickening, but he deserved every bit of the pain. I placed my gloved hand over his mouth as he collapsed to the ground and yanked his head to the side until his neck cracked.

The girl on the chopping block lay still, her eyes lifeless. I pulled a dusty old sheet from the floor and draped it over her as I glanced to the landing above to find Samuel poised in the shadows. He had an arrow notched and aimed at the table below and he nodded to me. I scoured the rest of the packing room until I spotted a glint of steel. It was the dagger, clutched in Astrid's hand. She began to mouth something to me but stopped as Feist strode past her and stepped boldly into the room.

Brilliant.

Tables and chairs squealed as the vampires jumped to their feet.

"Fuck you vermin," Feist shouted, his voice echoing around the room. He shook his meat cleaver toward Castle as she set her book down. "I told you I'd be back. And here I am you filthy bastards."

"Didn't we make things clear enough for you last time?" The vampire beside Castle asked. He raised his beer bottle to throw it at Feist but an arrow pierced his chest and the bottle shattered on the table as he collapsed to the floor.

"You see!" Feist called, as Castle and the others peered up at the landing, searching for the archer. "I didn't come alone. Now I have army!"

Idiot.

Feist slapped the flat of the cleaver against his breast and for a moment his mask slipped, revealing the repulsive creature beneath, his preternatural flesh glowing grotesquely in the gloom.

"Perfect," I muttered as I stepped from the shadows and called to Castle. "We just want some information, that's all." I glanced at Feist. "We're not interested in your vendettas, just answers."

All eyes turned to me, but I ignored their hypnotic pull and kept my focus on Castle as she said, "Morgan Rook."

I'd never heard of her prior to Samuel and Astrid's encounter, but it seemed she'd heard of me.

"You're with Feist?" she asked.

"No. Like I said, I'm just here for answers."

"I heard about your tangle with Tudor," Castle said, and gave me a crooked smile. "A lot of people are upset about that. Personally, I think you did us a favor. The Crimson Eye has long been a thorn in our side. But, it seems you've set your sights on us now." she stared as she pulled a small ax from the table, "You're crazy if you think you can waltz into my place with that doddering old husk, demand answers, and expect to walk out alive."

"I told you they wouldn't talk!" Feist sounded elated, and then he lunged for the closest vampire and grabbed him by the scruff of his shirt. With a grimace, Feist hacked the cleaver into the vampire's throat, adding a fine spray of blood to the gruesome stains on his shirt. "Come!" he cried. "Let's finish this!"

I pulled my sword as a vampire charged me, bottle in hand.

Before I could strike, the blood sucker broke apart, then reassembled by my side and cracked the bottle over my head. I stumbled back and swung my blade, lopping its hand off before it could shank me with the broken glass.

A violent uproar filled the place and everything became a whir of motion.

I glanced back as another vampire lunged but before it could raise the bonesaw in its hand, it fell with an arrow quivering from its back.

Bang!

The round ricocheted off my magical armor. The vampire that shot at me looked confused, then she raised her gun to my head and tightened her finger on the trigger.

7

I leaped aside as the gun roared. The bullet shot past my head and struck the wall behind me. Before I could get my bearings the vampire's eyes went wide and Astrid was standing behind her, her brow creased with effort. The vampire convulsed as blood painted her lips, and then she fell to her knees and slumped to the floor.

"Astrid!" I shouted as another vampire swept toward her in a cloud of motes. He slashed at her with his knife but I fired, taking him down before he reached her.

Astrid vanished into the gloom but I could see the silvery flash of a throwing dagger as she pulled it from the sheath near her ankle.

I turned back as Feist roared and charged into the fray, his meat cleaver hoisted high over his head like a demented knight of old. Helena Castle was hot on his heels, ax in hand. She moved toward Feist with quick, purposeful steps.

I ran to cross the room to impede her attack, but before I could reach them Castle swung the ax. Then she dropped it, an arrow protruding from the back of her hand.

The dark green fletching quivered as she glanced up to

where Samuel stood perched on the railing, notching another arrow.

I spun round as a huge vampire with leathery wings swooped in toward Astrid who was fighting off one of its brethren. I fired, taking it down, while she dispatched the other with her blades. She nodded to me and a slow, silent calm began to fall over the place.

Castle's face grew somber as she took in the scene. Her entire brood was either dead, or dying. Feist stepped triumphantly over the writhing bodies, pausing only long enough to finish them off. "Let's talk Helena," I said, pulling out a chair for her.

"Coward," she replied. She winced, gritting her teeth as she pulled the arrow from her hand. "You're all cowards. Attacking from the shadows-"

"Are you suggesting that you gave all of your victims a sporting chance," I said, nodding to the teenage girl slumped over the butcher block. "That doesn't look like a fair fight to me."

"Go fuck yourself, Rook. You and your Organization. You don't run things, not anymore."

"I'll crack her head open if you like," Feist said, "and you can scoop out her secrets like sweet golden yolk."

"I might just have to take you up on the offer, Mr. Feist," I shoved Castle and she fell into the chair behind her. "Or she could just tell me about Endersley."

A flicker passed through her eyes. Fear? Maybe. But within moments her contempt resurfaced. "Do whatever you want, Morgan Rook, let's see how tough you really are."

"I'm not one for torture." I nodded to Feist. "But I'm pretty sure he is. Please, Mr. Feist, do what needs to be done. But keep her conscious, no yolk scooping."

I joined Samuel and Astrid at the far side of the room. As

they conferred a series of short, brutal screams rang out behind me and I saw Samuel wince, then Astrid glanced my way with disapproval in her eyes. I shared it. This wasn't something I condoned, but the clock was ticking.

"Okay!" Castle finally shouted, her voice hoarse with agony. I turned back to find Feist holding her wrist to his mouth, his chin slick with blood. Castle's eyes were rolling and she was almost as colorless as her hair.

"Enough, Mr. Feist," I said. "For now."

He dropped her hand and shot me a furious glance. And then he backed away, licking his fingers as he hunkered down beside the last twitching vampire and began to feed on it instead.

"Let's talk about Endersley," I said to Castle. "Why are you protecting him?"

"That's what he hired us to do. He tracked us down, said he'd heard we could get things done," Castle said. "I didn't exactly take him seriously at first but he had a flask of blood with him, blood the likes of which I'd never tasted before." She gave a slight, ecstatic shiver. "It was not of this Earth. It was so pure! Like it had been drained from a fresh born." She gave me a rueful smile. "And just like any other dealer, he was aiming to get us hooked. A sample and a promise of more if we provided him with protection and safe harbor while he conducted his experiments. So we agreed and whisked him away to one of our more discreet lairs." She glanced at Astrid and Samuel. "Then they turned up and Endersley fled."

"To where?" I asked.

"Who knows?" Castle shrugged, "But he said he'd be back, and that we'd be paid handsomely for looking after his keepsake."

"Keepsake?"

She seemed as if she was about to respond, then her eyes

were drawn to the gaze of the dead vampire slumped over the table across from her. She trembled and as I glanced over it was as if someone had thrown a bucket of iced water over me.

The eyes that gazed back at us did not belong to the vampire. No, those cold, bright green watchful eyes belonged to someone else. They flitted from Castle to me and as they did, I felt my other stir.

"Emeric?" The sound spilled as slow as tar from the dead vampire's mouth, and as I heard it I knew where I'd seen those eyes before. They'd peered out from a painting as I'd investigated the crime scene of the Hexling's first victim, and I'd run into them again in Galloway Asylum. They were Stroud's eyes and it seemed I wasn't the only one to recognize them, and that my other knew them too. And seemingly, much better than I did…

"No!" Astrid cried.

I broke Stroud's gaze and glanced back to find Castle gripping a shard of brown glass so tightly her fingers ran red with blood.

8

Before I could move, Helena Castle slit her own throat and a fountain of blood streamed from her neck.

I clamped my sleeve over the wound, but the cut was too deep. Her mind was fixed to some far off place but her eyes were locked onto the dead vampire's as her entire body began to spasm. There was nothing I could do but hold on as her feet kicked out in shuttering jerks, and then she finally fell still in my arms.

When I glanced back to the vampire's corpse, its eyes were lifeless once more, Stroud was gone, his grim plan apparently accomplished.

"What happened?" Astrid asked. She looked as shocked as I felt.

"Stroud," I said. "He was here, watching us through that dead vampire's eyes."

"That would have taken a lot of power. He's growing stronger," Astrid said.

"Clearly he didn't want us finding out what Endersley's keepsake is." Samuel said as he covered the vampire's face with a coat he'd whisked off the back of a chair.

"Which means we'll have to search every inch of this place. Hopefully, whatever they were keeping for him is still here," I said.

I combed the offices above while Samuel and Astrid covered the ground floor. All I found was files and ledger books that extended back decades, and it seemed anything of value had long since been removed. Finally, I heard Astrid shout, "Here!"

She was standing in a back room filled with rusting equipment, holding a tarp in her hands. Under it was a trapdoor, and I caught the glimmer of magic. Some kind of hexed barrier or deterrent. She held her hand in the air above it and there was a bright flash followed by a muffled crack. "Move aside," Astrid said as she pulled a dagger and used the pommel to batter the padlock.

"I could have picked that open with my magic fingers," Samuel said.

"I know," Astrid said, "but where's the fun in that?" She tossed the broken padlock aside as she bent over to lift the hatch. It creaked open onto a flight of stairs that plunged into the darkness below. The place reeked of mildew, damp and… terror. As we descended I shone my flashlight into the corners and almost jumped as the beam illuminated a man chained to a wall. He looked like someone that had been living out on the streets for decades and his eyes flashed with panic as they met mine.

He began to shriek, his words unintelligible as they emerged in a long hoarse stream. Sweat gleamed on his forehead and it looked like most of his mousey grey hair had been ripped from his scalp.

"Good gods." Samuel shook his head. "Should I turn him loose, or do you want to check him over first?" He seemed genuinely unsettled.

The man's voice slowed as he repeated a single word, over and over again. "Please!"

I carefully placed my hand on the side of his face as I attempted to read him and find out how he'd ended up in this horrendous place.

There was nothing. Literally nothing at all. Where I'd usually get glimpses of a blinkered life, all I saw was endless empty darkness. "He's...dead," I said. I was about to pull my hand away when the man screamed, "Please!" and with that cry came a vivid snapshot of his life.

Harold had been perfectly content bundled up his blanket in his regular spot beneath the overpass, at least until the man had found him. The man in the long dark coat. The man with the crazy salt and pepper hair and the drawn, ratty face... and those eyes... God how they'd bulged with fire, madness and festering insanity. Harold had seen plenty of mania over the years but nothing quite like that.

He'd watched, frozen with panic and indecision, as the man had dug into the bag at his feet. It looked like a doctor's bag to Harold, one of those old fashioned ones... the kind they had in the old Jack the Ripper movies. "Shhh," the man had whispered as he held out a tiny ornate bottle of golden amber liquid. "Open it," he'd said.

Harold unscrewed the cap and the scent! Like honey. No, mead, and... something he didn't recognize. But whatever it might have been, he knew it was potent. A clear promise of oblivion lurked within the scent, an oblivion he hadn't reveled in since his good and terrible old days of meth and sweet hateful crack.

Caution jabbered at Harold like a shrew, but before it could sway him with good counsel, he'd gulped the liquid down.

Never once questioning why a stranger might give a man like Harold such a gift...

Beautiful empty darkness had swaddled him in soft warmth. And when he'd woken it was to find himself on a cheap, lumpy bed with a syringe buried in his arm, as the ratty-faced man stared down, notebook in hand.

The pain that followed had been horrendous. It had started with an invisible fire that tore through his gut, and then his heart. And from there it raged all through him.

Harold had screamed for help but the ratty man had ignored him, as had the others who stood watching. The pale ones with the long, long teeth. Harold hadn't liked them, hadn't liked any of it, but the straps that fastened his limbs and the gag over his mouth had rendered his protests useless.

I jerked my hand away as the scene in Harold's mind faded to black. I checked his scrawny tattooed wrist for a pulse, but there was nothing. "He's dead," I said. "And yet-"

"Please!" Harold screamed as he jolted back to life. "Please! It keeps starting and stopping. Over and over!"

"What does?" I asked.

"My heart!" He trembled, as the chains attached to his legs and arms rattled. "Keeps stopping and starting. Help me finish it please! Kill me!"

"Unchain him," I said to Samuel. He stooped over the locks holding Harold in place and moments later they clattered to the floor.

"I just want to die I just want to die I just want to die!" Harold hollered as he flew at me and then to the shadows. Heavy thudding came from the wall and I turned my flashlight to find him battering his head against the bricks. "Stop!" I tossed the light to Astrid and grabbed him, pulling him away. There was no blood in the wound, just red raw flesh. Harold began to shake and his limbs writhed uncontrollably. Then, he fell silent and stared up at the ceiling as if the heavens were pressing down.

"I've seen this before," Samuel said.

"Yes." Astrid crouched beside me and peered into Harold's eyes. "The ones who turn... the restless, they start this way."

"Only it's more rapid in our world," Samuel said, "and once they turn they don't come back. And they certainly don't speak."

"Maybe people in your world are made up differently than blinkereds," I suggested. "Maybe their blood is different."

"That must be the case," Astrid said, "otherwise the disease would have spread like wildfire by now."

"I'm sure Endersley's working on a solution to that particular problem," Samuel said, his face grim.

"No doubt," Astrid agreed, "which is why we need to- look out!"

I glanced down as Harold grabbed the gun from my holster, clamped it to the side of his head and fired. There was a loud explosion, and he slumped to the filthy ground. I recovered the gun from his twitching fingers and fired another round into his heart. "I'm sorry," I said. And I was. My brief journey into his life had shown it had been a hideously unhappy one and his deathly fate even more so. "We need to find Endersley," I said. "And fast. That makes two witnesses that have died by their own hands before they could finish telling their stories. Three counting the blinkered robber at the bank."

"Stroud was pushing Wyght and her coven to open a portal," Samuel said, "it looks like his aim was to bring the restless into your world but he can't do it alone. Maybe we need to go back to the place where you first encountered

43

Stroud to make sure that portal is fully closed," Samuel said, "and see what else we can dig up while we're there."

"The asylum?" I shrugged. I didn't have any better suggestions. "Did either of you understand that word the dead vampire said?" I asked. "Emeric? What did it mean?"

"It's a name," Astrid said, "an uncommon one." She gave Samuel a quick glance before returning her gaze to mine. "Emeric was the name of Stroud's son."

The room seemed to darken around me. "I don't understand."

"Neither do I," Astrid said. "Stroud's son died years ago, along with his wife and the rest of his cult. But Samuel's right, we should examine the portal you closed, try to find out how it was opened and who's working with him. If we can get to one of his allies, we might discover more."

"But I already know who opened the portal. Prentice Sykes. He was dying and wanted Stroud to heal him, that's why he brought him here."

"Sykes never had the means to open a portal like that on his own," Astrid said. "It would have taken great power, someone helped him. More than likely that person has a direct connection to Stroud and if we can find them, we can use them to find Stroud or Endersley."

"It's all we've got now," Samuel said, as he glanced down at Harold.

"Then I guess it's time to head over to good old Galloway Asylum," I said, trying my best to ignore the sinking feeling in my stomach. I hated the place, even more so after the last time I'd been there and would have happily burnt it to the ground, but somehow it seemed to keep calling me back. I pulled my phone from my pocket but there was no signal, so I made for the stairs. As I stepped into the main room Feist glanced my way, his mouth, chin and throat slick with blood as he continued to feed. I did my best to ignore him and called Dauple.

"Morgan," he said, "long time no hear."

"How are you?"

"Busy. But I always have time for you, you know that."

"I need some help. Can you to head over to Fink and Sons Meat Packing."

"And what treasures will I find there?" Dauple asked. He sounded just as eccentric as ever, but I detected a slight tone of guardedness in his voice.

"About a dozen dead vampires and two blinkereds. The one in the basement is going to need special handling. He might be infectious."

"We can do that. Both me and my new assistant." He sounded irritable and the last of his humor wilted away. "And by that I mean there's a second pair of eyes and I need to do things by the book. Including noting that you called this in."

"That's fine. I couldn't give a rat's ass."

"Maybe not," Dauple said, "but the Organization does, and so does the Council. They've instructed me to log and report every single interaction I have with you. Usually, I wouldn't, Morgan. But now I'm being shadowed and he..."

"Do whatever it takes to protect yourself," I said, " who's pressuring you? Erland?"

"No. Erland's away. I haven't seen him for days."

"Any idea where he went?"

Dauple paused. "None. But Mr. Humble's taken over his office. Look," he sounded perturbed and I could tell I was putting him on the spot. "I want to help-"

"I understand, I won't get you into any shit. Just get over here and get the place scrubbed as best you can, report this however you need to. Except the guy in the basement. Get him out quietly and take him directly to the incinerator. Quick smart. Got it?"

"Got it," Dauple said.

I hung up and made my way back through the warehouse. Feist barely looked up as he continued to gorge himself. "I'll take care of the mess," he said, wiping his mouth with the back of his hand.

"You've done more than enough already, Mr. Feist," I said. "A crew from The Organization's heading over. Which means you should probably be on your way."

He stared at me for a moment, sizing me up, but finally he nodded. "Very well, Mr. Rook." He climbed to his feet, tucked his bloody cleaver into the waistband of his trousers and strode from the warehouse, leaving me with the grisly remains of the dead.

9

I was glad to get out of that slaughterhouse and slip into the night, even if it was still raining hard and fast. We waited under an awning and watched as Mr. Feist sloped off into the shadows. I hoped it would be the last I'd see of him.

"So, should we head to the asylum?" Samuel asked.

"Yeah. But we'll need a car," I said. "It would be too risky to take a cab there or call for an Organization vehicle, it could draw attention. Plus I'm not sure where I stand with them so it's probably best to maintain radio silence."

"Well, this city's full of cars," Samuel said, "just pick one that takes your fancy."

I nodded. He had a point. Stealing wasn't my style, but time was of the essence and I was itching like hell to uncover the bastard that was backing Stroud. Heads were going to roll.

We rushed out toward the lot, pelted by the rain but there wasn't a drivable vehicle in sight. The streets that surrounded Fink and Sons were just as bad but once we reached the more residential neighborhoods I was overwhelmed by choice, and a guilty sensation as I sized up each car. That was until I spotted the BMW double-parked over a disabled space. "Perfect."

Samuel pulled a ring of skeleton keys from under his coat and rifled through them. He selected one and rubbed the tip between his fingers. Tiny bright green sparks glowed and wafted up like embers. He looked over his shoulder and slid the key into the lock, opened the door and gestured to me to climb in.

I leaned over to check the glove compartment for a spare key. Samuel and Astrid climbed into the back and helped me search, and then Samuel lifted his head and sniffed the air. "Here!" He leaned down and pulled something from under the passenger seat. A ring of keys stuck to a strip of duct tape.

The car purred into life and we headed across the city as the rain pounded the windscreen. The streets were quiet as we turned toward the on ramp, swooped up onto the highway and sped through the night. I glanced back to find Samuel and Astrid staring out the windows in silence, lost in their own thoughts.

The sky was free of moonlight, making it difficult to distinguish cloud from hill, but as we neared our destination a familiar twinge of apprehension told me we were in the right place. I suppressed a sigh as I took the exit that led to the back roads and glanced into the mirror to meet Astrid's watchful gaze. She gave me a soft smile that eased a little of my rising anxiety as we approached that damned, labyrinthine place.

The wheels crunched through the wet stones as we pulled up and parked outside the building. The place was deserted, its edifice bathed in a wall of almost impenetrable darkness.

I climbed out and checked my gun as Samuel and Astrid got the lay of the land.

The last time I'd been inside I'd absorbed a great deal of the pain and suffering that coursed within those walls. It had surged through me, that flood of malevolence, and woken my dark other from his slumber. I still carried more than enough memories of how I'd harnessed its relentless might and slaughtered the unsuspecting Nightkind trapped inside. Erland had mentioned numbers, but I'd blocked those facts from my mind. Of course they'd deserved to die, there was no question. But the morbid pleasure I'd experienced committing the massacre had made me sick to my very soul. Or at least the part of it that wasn't infected with malice.

I glanced at Astrid as she stared up at the asylum, then to Samuel as he took his bow out of the car and slung it over his shoulder. I was glad they were with me.

We walked up to the entrance. The double doors leading inside had ribbons of yellow crime scene tape strung across them. It hadn't been placed there by cops, there was no way they'd ever made it to the scene. No, the Organization had used it as a quick, simple, yet effective barrier for any would-be explorers. But should it fail, they'd also embedded magical binds over the threshold that would make anyone who came too near feel as if they were losing their minds. Which was apt.

I removed the binds, tore away the police tape and threw open the doors.

Inside, the scant light from the windows was faint to almost nonexistent. I took a moment to listen for any telltale sounds. Except for the persistent distant dripping from the rain soaked rooftop, the place was silent.

I pulled my flashlight from my bag and swept it over the lobby. The remains of the candles that had lined the corridors the last time I'd visited, remained. They'd burnt themselves out long ago and melted to the floor like waxy stumps.

Astrid placed a hand against the wall and shivered. The furrows on her brow deepened, and it took a moment for her to speak. "Such a dark place. So much suffering. Some old," she kept her eyes closed but turned her head my way, "some new."

Yes, that had been my handiwork.

"I can see the people who were originally here," Astrid continued, "they screamed and howled, so they were fed potions to keep them quiet. But some of them still weren't quiet enough." A shudder passed through her as she added, "he only chose the most disturbed."

"He?" I asked.

"The man with silver glasses. The weasel in the suit."

A dull thud echoed along in the passage before us. Astrid pulled her fingers from the wall and in a flash she had a blade in her hand. We stood, poised in silence, staring ahead as we waited. No more sounds followed.

"Which way?" Samuel whispered.

I nodded to the staircase then led the way up and through the door at the top, my flashlight cutting through the darkness. We passed the cells where I'd slaughtered Nightkind and liberated their blinkered victims. I shivered as I felt an echo of the fury that had overwhelmed me that day, and my other stirred. I waited to see if he had anything to add but he remained silent. Perhaps listening, observing and holding his tongue lest he give himself away. Why?

A rapping noise filled the corridors. Like one stone being tapped upon another.

"What is that?" Samuel whispered.

"It… it sounds like a signal," I replied, "there's a rhythm to it, like a code."

"For what?" Astrid asked.

"I don't know." I released the strap on my holster as Samuel pulled an arrow and slipped his bow off his shoulder.

We turned the corner at the end of the corridor and the beam of my flashlight skimmed over the cracked green paint and scuff marks as I trained it onto the double doors ahead. An odd sulfurous smell hung in the air and I pushed them open onto the long room that still reeked of burned paint.

A square patch of dappled light shone down amid black patches from the spell Stroud had cast to blot out the skylight. I gazed down at the melee of footprints. Mine, from the fight with the hexling and the shadow-like incarnations of Tom and Hellwyn.

And Willow.

My flashlight strayed toward the scorched painting at the end of the room, then to the door to the left of the canvas, the one the hexling had sprung from so many weeks ago.

Samuel produced a tiny ball of soft blue flames in his hand and held it up toward the canvas. Tracing a finger through the stiff ridges of paint, he leaned in close and took a deep sniff, before turning to Astrid. "You can smell it," he said. "Penrythe. It's faint, but it's there." He stood back and gazed up.

Astrid brushed her fingers across it. "Someone's tried to repair it, but they didn't get very far. The fire you conjured certainly did its job." She glanced at me. "Or should I say, the fire *he* conjured." She winced as she continued to run her fingers over it. "I can see the poor souls that created it. They were confronted with horrendous suffering and then forced to paint their anguish out under the guise of therapy. It was a ruse. Many died. But at least their torment is over now."

"So where does this leave us?" Samuel asked.

"We need to figure out where the asylum's records are

stored," I said. "See if there's any documents that might tell us who owned the place. I couldn't find anything online apart from an obscure entry on an urban explorer site. It's almost as if the asylum never existed." I took one last look at the canvas and was about to head outside when I caught the glint of eyes watching from the corner of the room. Someone had opened the door.

"Who's there?" I demanded. My heart raced as I bolted toward the threshold, drawing my sword as I went.

10

Samuel had my back as I approached the door. I paused to listen for whoever, or whatever had been lurking in the room but there was only silence.

Then I heard a faint scrape of feet and a distant thud.

The sword of intention bristled with fiery light, illuminating the footprints in the dust. There were dozens of them, but one set was recent and the toes were clawed. I slipped through the door in time to see something drop from the window at the far side of the narrow, empty room.

"What was it?" Astrid asked as I ran to the window.

It was barred, but a couple of the rusting rods had been hacksawed off and the others were bent out of shape, leaving plenty of room to squeeze through. I looked down the sheer drop. I saw no movements in the grounds or the woods beyond, and whoever had jumped seemed to have completely vanished.

I glanced back to Astrid as she joined me. "I don't know, they're gone." I sheathed the sword. "Come on, let's check the offices. See if we can find out who built this damned place and get the hell out of here."

We roamed the corridors until we found a sign marked *Admin*, followed it through a pair of doors that had been kicked in and emerged in a pitch black corridor. I trained my flashlight along the walls until we found the office door. It was half hanging off its hinges and the place was a mess.

A desk with an ancient bulky monitor stood against one wall. The computer below it had been gutted and its yellowing case was scorched and black. I followed its frayed cord to the plug that rested amid a scattered pile of floppy discs. "That's not going to be much help," I said.

Boxes of papers lay upended across the threadbare carpet. I picked up a handful and trained the flashlight over them. Invoices for laundry and food deliveries, nothing of interest.

"Here," Astrid conjured an orb of orange light and tossed it into the air. It hung there like a tiny sun, filling the room with light. I continued to leaf through the papers as she gathered file boxes from a storeroom and Samuel wandered out into the corridor.

None of the files in the boxes yielded anything of value. Most of the contents consisted of expense reports, inventory records, receipts and petty cash ledgers that drifted down through the decades. They ran the gambit from handwritten to typewritten, mimeographed to dot matrix. Now and then I spotted a long, looping blue signature. It was clearly signed by the same hand, but its curves were too faded to be legible. I glanced across the room to the shredder and the plastic bags beside it stuffed with twists of paper. Anything damning, useful or of value had most likely long since been removed, or destroyed. But all we needed was a clue, even if it was a crumb.

I checked a door in the corner of the office, it opened onto a makeshift break-room. A few mugs were scattered along the counter, their *humorous* slogans buried under layers of filth, and dingy notes with passive aggressive cleaning requests still clung to the wall from strips of ancient yellowed tape. I was turning to leave when I froze.

A small mirror hung beside the door and as I glanced at it, I almost cried out. A man stared back. A man that wasn't me.

Stroud.

He wore the same wine-colored frock coat and his black hair fell to his shoulders. But his face seemed older than I remembered, his eyes aged, cruel and furious, his stare nothing short of pure, unbridled hatred.

I stood transfixed as his eyes bored into mine. My dark other stirred and rose through me, almost forcing me out of consciousness.

Stroud frowned and his expression turned from hatred to reappraisal.

The door swung open, blocking the mirror for a moment as Astrid walked in. "Are you alright, Morgan?"

Get out bitch

The words almost left my lips as my dark other seethed. He tried to force my gaze back to the mirror, but I grabbed a mug from the side and threw it at the glass, smashing Rowan Stroud into silver shards and splinters.

Astrid leaped back. "What the hell are you doing?"

"I…" I had to use everything at my disposal to suppress my other. "I don't know what…I'm sorry." I gazed at the shattered fragments of mirror on the floor, surreptitiously checking them for a sign of Stroud, but he was gone.

As Astrid continued to watch me her cold haughtiness returned, and she only glanced away when Samuel called out. "I think he's found something," she said and nodded for me to follow.

Slivers of the mirror crumbled under the soles of my shoes as we left the kitchen. What the hell had just happened? That connection between Stroud and my other... like they'd recognized the evil in each other? A chill shot through me, as I tried to set my concerns aside and return my focus to the task at hand.

Samuel was waiting anxiously out in the corridor. He led us to a spacious private office and rushed over toward a row of dark wooden bookcases lining the masonry wall behind an expensive-looking desk with a shredded leather chair.

"Watch!" Samuel said with a big grin. He tapped a brick beside the bookcase and a small panel slid open. "It was hidden well." He pulled a metal box from the compartment and handed it to me. "But not well enough for me to miss it."

With a snap of her fingers Astrid summoned the light she'd conjured as we'd searched the other office and it bobbed into the room. I opened the box and set it on the desk. Inside were bundles of letters tied with a crimson ribbon, and a handful of rose petals that crumbled as my fingers brushed them aside to remove the parcels. At the bottom was an old, washed out color snapshot, I took it out and held it up to the light.

A portly man in silver glasses and a pin-striped suit stared out at me, but my eyes were instantly drawn to the woman beside him. Somehow the image of her had remained in vivid color and I could tell the picture had been printed long before digital photography tricks were so much as a pipe dream.

She wore a simple black dress and a double strand of pearls that held an iridescent glow. Her hair was a dappled shade of honey and fell luxuriantly to her shoulders while her eyes were a mixed shade of red and brown. They smoldered, captivating me and locking me into their gaze. I tried to look away, but it was impossible.

"A succubus," Astrid said. Her thumb descended, blotting the woman's face out as she plucked the photograph from my hand. I could see the man more clearly with the succubus obscured, his graying hair, doughy features and restless, piggy eyes. He smiled but there was no warmth or soul in the gesture. He just stood there, his face half turned toward the woman beside him. As if he couldn't tear himself away from her. As if he'd been thoroughly bewitched.

I pulled the ribbon from the letters and began to glance through them. The slanted writing was almost uniform in its perfection, and even though the ink used to pen it had faded slightly with age, I could still read every word.

They were the love letters she'd written to him, Joseph Charrot. The name didn't mean anything to me, and neither did the one signed at the end of each letter; Kitty Frostrup. Her script flowed like sweet wine, each line a testament of her love for Charrot. As if he were some kind of God or Emperor instead of a man of dough and pin stripes.

"What do they say?" Astrid asked.

"They're love letters. The man, Charrot, was blinkered and Kitty Frostrup was the succubus. It seems he owned this place, inherited it from his father. From what I can tell he'd built it to help people, the sick and weary. Charrot followed in his father's footsteps, for a while at least. My guess is Frostrup was sent to sway him, and re-purpose the asylum to house the portal."

"Well, I'm no expert," Samuel said, "but all this stuff looks pretty old."

"It is. I'm guessing by the photographs it's from the eighties," I said, "and by the age of Charrot in that picture there's a good chance he's already taking a dirt nap, so we're probably out of luck there."

"Quite," Samuel agreed, "Unless you have a way of waking the dead?"

I shook my head. "Not a chance" My last foray into the world of the dead, had been more than enough, not to mention the black crystals it had taken to get me there. "But the succubus, she might still be around."

"Indeed," Astrid said, "they don't age like blinkereds."

I slipped the letters into my pocket. "Can you hang on to the picture for me?" I asked Astrid.

"Sure. Why?"

"Because we're going to need it, and you seem to be immune to its charms. I know a succubus that might be able to help us identify her. She's one of the good ones. Or at least as good as you can get, with their kind. Maybe she'll-"

I paused and Astrid spun toward the door as the sharp sound of knocking stones echoed in the murky corridor outside.

11

"What is it?" Astrid asked.

"No idea," I said, as the knocking intensified. I stepped out and swept my flashlight toward the opening at the end of the corridor. Plaster and masonry littered the floor where part of the ceiling had fallen in and the doors leading to the yawning black darkness beyond had long been wrenched off their hinges.

Tap. Tap, tap.

Clack.

Tap. Tap.

Clack, clack, clack.

It grew faster, then slower, and then stopped. We made our way toward it, Astrid's orb of light bobbing along behind us, casting long, ominous shadows. She sent it into the room ahead, and it fizzled over me, throwing orange light over the floor as it led the way.

Judging by the tattered sofas and amateurish paintings on the walls, the room had once served as some kind of recreational space. I swept my flashlight toward the tapping as it resumed, illuminating the source.

A demon. Wiry with a mop of greasy mustard-yellow hair and golden scaly flesh, his eyes fizzled with bright silver light when they met mine and he smiled widely as he continued to knock two round pebbles together. Then he glanced at the heap of stones and fallen plaster beside him.

I pulled my gun and Samuel notched an arrow, while Astrid stood her ground, dagger in hand.

"Stop," I called.

"Stop what?" the demon asked, his voice high and wheedling. He licked his lips with a forked tongue and knocked the pebbles together once more.

I closed in, my gun trained on him. "Stop with the pebbles."

"These?" he asked, holding them up. "Okay." He dropped them and slowly, almost theatrically, reached into the pocket of his faded corduroy jacket and pulled out a glowing spark. "You want me to drop this too?" He tossed it aside before I could answer and the little spark bounced across the floor and vanished into the piles of rubble.

"What the fuck was that?" I demanded.

"Life." His smile danced upon his lips. "Death."

"Were you watching us upstairs?" I wanted to shoot the piece of shit there and then, but we needed answers.

"Indeed," he said, "As I was when you last entered the old master's chamber. You're the one who destroyed the portal, are you not?"

"You were there?" I asked.

"Oh yes! I saw *everything*, the hexling, the fights that still haunt you, the black fire and the blood you spilled." He paused to cackle and shake a finger at me. "You became quite the demon when you slaughtered all and sundry that day." His gaze fell to the floor as the spark he'd dropped crackled, buzzed and pulsed with life. A tiny whirlwind of dust rose from the pile and slowly, it built momentum, getting faster and faster. The surrounding stones and debris were drawn up around it and formed a stony grey mass.

"What have you done?" I trained the gun back on the demon.

"I made a new friend for you." He tugged his greasy forelock, stepped into the gloom and vanished from sight. Astrid sent the orb of light after him and it illuminated the shadowy walls and an open trapdoor in the ceiling. A pair of silver eyes blinked down at us, and then they were gone.

I glanced to the strange whirling debris, it had grown in mass, pulling in stones one by one and piling each upon the other.

"What is that?" Samuel joined me as I began to kick the stones away but as soon as they came to a stop on the grey linoleum floor they shuttered and swept back toward the pile. Dust swept up in torrents as the stones clacked together, almost blinding us. I threw my hands over my eyes as a gale surged and forced me back, then it slowed enough for me to peer between my fingers.

A huge, grey stone creature towered over us. Its bright red eyes stared down from dim hollows and its jagged mouth was lined with sawtooth shards of stone. A dusty cloud swirled at the center of its chest and within it sat the spark that had given the monster its life.

"What in the hell are we supposed to do now?" Samuel shouted as the creature lumbered forward, its head brushing the ceiling.

Before I could answer, it swung a fist and sent me flying back into the wall. Picture frames flapped and fell around me as I slid down and lay there, the air knocked from my lungs.

Samuel let an arrow fly. It struck one of the creature's eyes and it howled. With long stone fingers, it reached up and plucked the arrow out, reducing the orb from fiery red to milky blue.

I staggered to my feet as the creature roared and a surge of dust rippled back through the room in a wave. It lunged at Samuel. He darted away but the edge of its fist caught him, and he flew across the room, crashing through a card table.

Astrid was little more than a shadow, moving with such speed I could barely follow her. She leaped upon the creature's back, reached over and plunged a dagger into the hollow where its heart was. It lurched forward, flipped her off its back and onto the ground and gave a loud, rumbling bellow before stomping toward her.

I leaped in front of Astrid and swung my sword at its throat. Sparks flew and the sword of intention blazed, but didn't leave a scratch. Then the creature lashed out with a fist.

My coat saved me from the worst of the blow, but the momentum threw me to the ground. The creature lumbered toward me and raised a foot to bring down upon my head. I rolled away as the huge stone mass crashed beside me, smashing a hole through the floor.

Samuel loosed another arrow, striking its remaining eye. There was no pain in the creature's howl; just pure, unadulterated fury.

I scrambled to my feet as it pummeled its fists against its chest like an ape, and produced a rolling boom like muted thunder.

Samuel shot again, his arrow quickening towards the spark in its heart. The creature snatched the arrow from the air before it could strike and threw it down. How? It had no eyes... my gaze drifted to the hole on the side of its head.

It could hear. That was its strength, not its sight.

I snatched stones from the debris and ran toward the

hulking mass. It swung its fist, but I dived down, skidding across the floor on my knees.

It grabbed me and I let it haul me up toward the shards in its mouth. Then I clapped the stones to the side of its head, thrusting them as far as they'd go.

The creature dropped me and reached up to its ears as I rolled across the floor. "Your blade's beside you" Samuel called from across the room.

I leaped to my feet, seized the sword of intention and thrust it into the creatures chest, pinning the spark with the tip of my blade. "End!"

A final cry broke from its stony throat and as it lunged forward the sword roared with flames, enveloping its life-giving spark. It fell to its knees and wavered there for a moment before tumbling apart in an avalanche of stones and dust.

12

"Well, that was something new and fun," Samuel said, as he glared at the rocks and dust.

"Yeah, I can't say I've ever run into one of those before," I sighed. "Anyone got the slightest idea what in the hell it was?"

"Hostile," Astrid said, with a rare smile. "And now dead."

Samuel glanced to the trapdoor in the ceiling. "You want to find its maker?"

I shook my head. "No point. It probably knows this place like the back of its maggot-infested hands. I doubt we'd find it now." As I thought of the demon, I thought of Stroud. I had little doubt he'd posted it here.

"What's wrong?" Astrid asked.

"Uh. Stroud. He was here."

"Where?"

"The mirror in that little room. I only saw him for a moment…"

"The mirror you smashed?" Astrid demanded.

"Yeah. I'm sorry, I should have said something at the time."

"So why didn't you?" Astrid's eyes blazed at me. "We're

supposed to be working together. That's what you said."

"I know, and I'm sorry. It unnerved me. But I'm telling you about it now. It was weird. My other seemed to recognize him and Stroud seemed to recognize him too. How can that be possible?"

"You've seen him before. Right here, in this building," Samuel said.

"I did, but my other wasn't present for the confrontation, not until the end. He only rose to the surface after I tapped into this place's energy. That's when he summoned the black fire that destroyed the portal as Stroud fled. They didn't have time to focus on each other, not really, but when their eyes met in the mirror just now…"

"What?" Astrid began watching me closely.

It took me a moment to realize I'd been lost in my thoughts. "They truly seemed to *see* each other."

"Ask him what he knows about Stroud," Samuel suggested.

"It doesn't work like that," I said. "He comes and goes, wakes and sleeps, or does whatever the hell he does when he's not present. I can't access his thoughts and he can't access mine. It's like we're two people stuck in the same room, but in this case it's body and mind. We only really seem to come together when we're in mortal danger." I looked from Samuel to Astrid. "The first time I met Stroud he said I was familiar to him. What did he mean?"

"Well, we're certain that you're originally from Penrythe, even if you can't remember it. Maybe you encountered him there?" Samuel suggested.

"Maybe." I glanced at the stone creature's remains. "We should get out of here before the demon returns, who knows what else it's got up its sleeve. Let's go talk to Glory. We could do with some sunshine in our lives."

We left the room. "I'm sorry," I said as Astrid passed me.

"I know," she smiled, but it was half hearted and short lived. We left the asylum and recast the binds I'd removed from its doors. "Wait up, one last thing" Samuel said, as he added a magical booby trap for the demon lurking within the building, in case it tried to undo the spell. "There you go little guy."

As soon as we got near the car I called Glory.

Heavy bass boomed in the background and she answered with a shout. "Morgan?"

"Yeah. How's tricks?"

"Good. But I'm guessing this isn't a social call, it's almost five am."

"I'm sad to say it, but you're right. I'm on the trail of a succubus by the name of Kitty, ever heard of her?"

Glory paused and if it wasn't for the rattling thud of the music, I might have thought she'd gone. "Meet me," she said. "I'm close to our bridge. I'll meet you there at dawn."

I hung up and grabbed a couple of crystals so I could place a quick spell over our stolen car, in case it had been reported missing. Now, any blinkereds that spotted it would see just about any color and model combination other than the one it actually was.

"So we're off to meet a succubus," Samuel rubbed his hands together as he climbed into the passenger seat, and Astrid sat in the back. "I've never seen one in the flesh."

"Glory's cool," I said, "we've helped each other out over the years, quite a few times actually." I peered into the mirror and met Astrid's gaze. "She and Tom were good friends."

"Then I'm sure she's perfectly pleasant, despite their reputations." Astrid glanced at Samuel. "Just watch yourself, you know how easily swayed you are."

"Perhaps I should put a hot knife to my eyes," Samuel offered. "Blind myself to her allure."

"If you think it'll help." Astrid muttered, as the car swept along the driveway and away from the asylum grounds.

I parked under the bridge as the dawning sun rose behind us, painting the lapping waters and steely girders in soft pinks and reds. I climbed out of the car, stretched my legs and took a moment to gaze across the silver and grey city. It was colder than I'd expected, but peaceful at this early hour.

"You okay?" Samuel asked as he joined me.

"Mostly," I said. "I guess that incident at the asylum unsettled me. It's weird, carrying someone else inside you. Or maybe it's the other way round; maybe he's carrying me inside of him. That might help to explain his rage."

"Could be." Samuel gave me a slow, almost surreptitious glance. "You know, once this is over, *if* it goes our way, you might want to consider finding a way of resolving your split. We have a lot of learned people in Penrythe. Some of them are pretty powerful."

"I'd like to try," I said. "Just as soon as we've stopped Stroud from his wholesale destruction."

"You're optimistic."

"Aren't you?"

"Yeah, I suppose I am. Otherwise I'd probably just weigh myself down, jump in the ocean and go to a peaceful, watery grave." Samuel nodded toward the city. "You really like this place, don't you?"

"I do. I mean it's far from perfect but it's home. For pretty much as long as I can remember. And I like the people, for the most part, and I don't want them to get hurt." I turned to look behind me as a clacking sound echoed along the bridge.

Glory, walking in her stilettos down the concrete sidewalk. As ever she shone, and the rising sun behind her seemed to dim as she drew in all the colors of dawn, leaving the river dull and grey in her wake. Her golden hair was piled up on her head, perfectly complementing the short sleek violet dress that fit her like a glove. She smiled, her teeth pearly against her full red lips and I felt the warmth of her eyes upon me, even through those dark designer shades.

Astrid climbed out of the car, her face sleepy. She watched Glory's approach and I saw her hand drift toward one of her daggers.

"Morning, Glory," I said. Just like I always did.

"Indeed. *Early* morning." Glory pulled her sunglasses down and smiled at Astrid and Samuel. Her eyes shone crystalline blue "Is that a note of Penrythe I detect below the mud, blood, and exhaustion?" she asked Samuel with a wink. "Reminds me of Tom." She turned to Astrid. "And his good friend Hellwyn. I met her once. You're her kin if I'm not mistaken."

"You're not mistaken. I'm Astrid." She offered her hand to Glory and as the succubus shook it, a little of the tension loosened from her shoulders.

"Tom was very fond of your mother. He said she was as valiant as she was formidable, at least against her foes. We need brave people like that right now," Glory said, as she turned to me. "And Elsbeth Wyght. Ding dong, I'm glad the bitch is dead but you're looking awfully rough Morgan. "

"I'm glad she's gone too, but unfortunately our problems didn't end there." I sighed and laid out all the relevant details. Glory wasn't going to just roll over on one of her own kind, not without an explanation.

"And that's why you're looking for the succubus."

"It is. Someone's tried to reopen the portal to Penrythe, we think she might've had a hand in it."

"To bring Stroud through?" Glory asked and raised a perfectly plucked eyebrow over her shades.

"Exactly. And our river's run dry so we're following any leads we can get our hands on. So, that brings us to Kitty Frostrup."

She shook her head "Doesn't ring a bell, but in our little circle names can change. What else have you got?"

I delved into my pocket and pulled out the photograph from the asylum. Glory glanced at it and a slight furrow marred her brow. "Well, well. Would you look at that? Frostrup indeed. She must have left quite the trail of former identities, broken hearts and destruction judging by the age of that photograph." She handed back the picture. "You'll find her on the east side; Hattersley Street. Last I heard she was dismantling an old man who'd spent his entire life building up this city. Wrecking ball that she is." Glory shook her head. "Nasty, bitter old thing. Be careful, Morgan, she's dangerous." She pulled out a phone, tapped the screen and my cell phone buzzed. "That's the address. Her current beau is as rich as Midas and he ain't in the ground yet, so she should still be there, sucking him dry."

"Thank you."

Glory gave me a slow, seductive smile. "Of course if you'd described her when you'd called it might have saved you the trip. Then again, that would have robbed me of the opportunity to see you. It's been a long time, sweetie. Far too long." Her smile faded. "Call me if you need anything else. I want to help. I hate the shadow that's fallen over our city. I want to see it gone." Glory gently placed her hand on Astrid's shoulder. "It was a pleasure to meet you, Astrid."

"As it was to meet you," Astrid said.

"Samuel." Samuel extended his hand and gave her a big cheesy smile. "We weren't introduced for some reason." He cast me and Astrid a dark look. Glory slowly rubbed her fingers across his palm before she shook his hand and released it. "A pleasure to meet you, Samuel. I get the sense you're a fellow hellion."

"I... I can be." Samuel's cheeks reddened, and he looked down at his empty hand, as if mourning the loss of hers.

"I suppose it's high time I catch up on my beauty sleep," Glory turned and walked off, waving over her shoulder as she went.

"Can I give you a ride?" I called.

"Oh you could, I'm sure," Glory called back. "But I'll make my own way, Morgan. You have things to do and places to be. As ever."

"Well she's... fascinating," Samuel said as we watched her go.

"She certainly is," Astrid said. "Stop sniffing your hands, Samuel, it's creepy. And keep them out where we can see them."

Samuel shoved his hands into his pockets. "I was smoothing my beard." He cleared his throat and nodded to the car. "We going then?"

"Yeah," I said as I watched Glory turn the corner. I hadn't seen her since Tom's wake, indeed I'd hardly seen anyone since that dark day. I vowed, right there and then, to make sure to spend time with all of my friends when this shit was over. To go out and raise hell with them, and to keep them closer. "Come on," I said as I climbed into our stolen car. It was time to make some headway and put an end to Stroud's evil before it swallowed up everything I loved.

13

W e cruised past the long rows of townhouses that lined Hattersley Street. They were the gateway into another neighborhood in this city where people on the higher side of society lived, and a place I rarely visited. It was a different world, one I hadn't been given the key to, and likely never would.

As we climbed out of our stolen ride, Samuel took a deep sniff of the cold air. "This place absolutely reeks of money." He glanced at the houses. "We could probably amass a fair bit of treasure if we...start digging." He ran his hand over a wrought iron gate. "They believe this keeps them secure, how delightful."

"We're not here to pilfer," Astrid said. "No light fingers."

"Fine." Samuel said, but as we passed he gave the house a slow, lingering glance.

"Good man!" I threw my arm around his shoulder, gave him a sharp pat on the back and led him down the street, hoping to disrupt the plans percolating in his mind.

The road was quiet and still; the only sign of life at that early hour was a stressed looking man sitting by his window, eating breakfast as he stared into a newspaper. He glanced at me and then casually turned away, a sign that the illusion Astrid had cast, to disguise our relatively rag tag appearance, was working. In a place like this we'd have stuck out like a sore thumb without it, just like the house the succubus was inhabiting.

It was obvious long before I pulled out my phone to double check the address. Drawn curtains, overgrown garden and the abundance of flies buzzing round the filthy windows. They were all symptoms pointing to the air of evil murmuring through its walls and wafting over the tall iron gate.

"This place is infected," Samuel said as he peered through the bars.

I nodded as I reached for the black wrought iron handle. "It's locked."

Samuel rifled through his ring of keys, worked his magic and stood back with a satisfied smirk as I pushed it open. The hinges squealed and the bottom rung of the gate scraped over the concrete path.

Soggy dead leaves littered the front steps and the bell next to the large oak door was broken, so we knocked and waited, but there was no answer. I walked back down to the path and checked the windows but it seemed no one was home.

"Allow me." Samuel whipped out his keys, which definitely beat my method of dissolving pesky locks to rust. Within moments the door swung open onto a wide hallway dotted with furniture draped in dust covers. The place seemed deserted, like a musty summer house closed up during off season. I shut the door behind us and we started checking the place out.

The front rooms had been totally stripped of their furnishings; dents and impressions marring the thick shag carpeting told tales of where sofas and tables had once rested, and a trailing dark red stain drew my attention to a short dark hallway.

For all of its apparent emptiness, there was someone here. I could feel it.

"Is it blood?" Samuel asked as he nodded toward the rug.

"No. Wine."

We did a quick sweep of the ground floor, found a pristine kitchen without even so much as a single dirty cup in the sink, and another emptied room alongside a small bathroom. Then we headed upstairs, our footsteps stifled by the plush carpet.

The first room had a few pieces of furniture shrouded by paint-spattered drop cloths and the marks on the dust-laden dresser spoke of the objects that had once rested there. But the second room really piqued my interest and I strode to the far wall.

It was covered with photographs and there seemed to be no rhyme or reason to the arrangement of the images, but the theme was decidedly Kitty Frostrup; she was the focus of each and every one of them. No not the focus, the star. I glanced over them quickly to avoid the pull as she gazed out, her reddish brown eyes gleaming like rubies, her thin lips pouting, her soft honey-colored hair in an ever changing variety of styles. The locations and landscapes behind her spanned the globe, from deserts and tropic isles to exotic cities. Milan, Tokyo, London, Paris, Moscow and everywhere in between.

In some of the snapshots she posed with men. Most were well tanned, decked out in designer clothes and their smiles were straight, bright, white and confident. While their posture was always pure alpha, it was very clear that they'd all been brought to heel. But, as the photographs in the erratic timeline changed I found her men seemed to diminish in their stature until they almost appeared shriveled. But not Kitty, no, she beamed in every single image and if age had ever gotten a claw into her, she hid it well.

"Hmm. Looks like someone's a bit conceited," Samuel said as he joined me.

"Just a touch," Astrid agreed as she pulled a frame from the wall and looked into Kitty's eyes. "Still, if you look hard enough, you can see her true face. Not that I'd recommend it." She set it down on the floor, nodded toward the ceiling and turned to leave.

We checked the final room before heading upstairs. An oak bureau that held a few scarves stood to the right of the door and a wing-backed chair sat in the center of the floor, facing another wall covered in framed photographs. They were portraits of men carefully arranged in a grid and each one had a big red X crossed over it in lipstick, as if they'd merely been spent days on some twisted calendar.

We headed up to the third floor. There were two doors leading off the small landing. One door led to a gleaming bathroom stocked and outfitted with every luxury I'd expect to find in a house like this, except a mirror. And as I turned and thought about it, I realized there wasn't a single mirror anywhere in the place.

The space around the second door seemed to shift as I pushed it open and a chill passed through me as I spotted the emaciated figure laying stock still in the queen-sized bed. It was hard to make out whether it was alive or dead, but as I drew back the curtains it coughed, stirring dust that had wafted up into the dappled morning light.

The wrinkled old man, stared up at me as he reached toward the bedside table with a clawed, bony hand. I grabbed the empty glass he was seeking, strode to the bathroom to fill it with water and rushed back to him. He forced himself up and drank fast, the water slopping over his flaky unshaven chin. "Where is she?" I asked.

He cocked his head, as if trying to listen. His pale, watery eyes flitted over me, then to the corner of the room. "Kitty," he said, his voice a feeble whisper. "Kitty, is that you?"

"She's robbed him of his senses as well as his gold," Astrid said.

"And why wouldn't I?" a cold, clipped voice demanded.

Kitty Frostrup stood with one shoulder leaning against the doorway. She still had it, the sensuality, the pout, the wicked gleam in those reddish-brown eyes as they peered over her designer shades. The glamor was still there in the elegant cut of her jet-black dress and the twinkling jewels that sparkled above the swell of her breasts. But there was a hidden hint of ruin as well as the tragic jaded air of someone who knew they were well past their prime, yet refused to let it go. The resentful desperation of someone clutching at their lost youth with brittle, trembling fingers.

I caught a glimpse of the creature she was desperate to mask. Her scaly, demonic face, her dark almond-shaped eyes and the pair of black feathered wings nestled behind her bent bony shoulders.

She hissed and a forked tongue slithered over her thin parched lips, then she reignited the illusion and Kitty, seductive slayer of men's hearts and minds, was back. "Now who the hell are you?" she demanded, "and what are you doing in my house?"

14

"We're here to find out about Galloway," I said, "and why you made Charrot open the portal."

"And you assumed I'd have something to tell, did you?" Kitty gave a slow, creeping leer as she glanced from me to Samuel and then Astrid.

"No. We're *sure* you have something to tell, and we're prepared to go to great pains to inspire you," Astrid said, her thumb stroking the hilt of a dagger.

"Maybe even fatal pains," Samuel added. "Which has been known to happen when things don't go our way."

I drew my gun. "So tell us what we need to know and go back to whatever stone you crawled out from, or, we'll do this the hard way."

Kitty rolled her eyes and spoke as if addressing a child. "Stupid man. You want to know about the asylum?"

I nodded.

"Go fuck yourself." She glared at me as she whispered and placed a manicured finger on the jewel gleaming around her slender throat. Her entire form shimmered, and I watched in awe as all evidence of the passing years began to drop away and she suddenly looked like she was in her twenties once more. "Now," she said to Samuel, her voice a breathy purr, "come here, come to Kitty."

He looked confused as he glanced from the succubus to me. As if he knew me but couldn't remember why or how. I kept my eyes trained on a spot just above Kitty's head as I raised my gun toward her. "Stop the enchantment. Now."

"Stop what? Being beautiful? Young? Magnetic?" she asked teasingly, and softly parted her lips with the tip of her finger. "Help me." She turned back to Samuel. "That nasty man's threatening me."

Samuel leaped between me and the succubus, his face impassive, but I could tell he'd forgotten who I was.

"Samuel!" Astrid growled, "Come here."

He glanced her way but returned his attention to Kitty as she pointed at me. "Destroy that man, honey. Get him now, him and that sour-faced bitch. They're trying to keep us apart."

Samuel came at me, hands raised, eyes smoldering with fury.

"Samuel!" I warned. He threw a punch. I ducked, backed away, and holstered my gun.

He roared as he tore toward me, hit me hard and took me down. I tried to shove him off, but he weighed more than I'd expected and most his bulk seemed to be well honed muscle.

I tried to evade him as he seized my throat and bared his teeth. He began to squeeze, his eyes locked on mine, flames dancing in their reflection as if he was staring into an inferno.

Kitty had started a wildfire and if I wanted it to stop I was going to have to put it out myself.

I grabbed his hands and struggled to pry them back. He'd

cut off my air supply and my chest started to ache. I brought my head up hard, smashing it into Samuel's nose.

He shook his head before doubling down on his efforts and slowly choking the life out of me.

I reached behind me to find anything to batter him with, but there was nothing close. Pure wrath stirred within me and snaked its way through my pain and bewilderment.

My other. Rising to the surface of my consciousness like a long-submerged crocodile.

Black stars danced in my eyes, my back spasmed and my fingers seized within the soft nap of the carpet. I tried to smash my forehead into Samuel's nose once more, but he drew away and my head fell back to the floor with a thud.

Someone screamed, the sound garbled in my ringing ears.

A woman.

She sounded outraged, furious.

I knew in an instant it wasn't Astrid.

The flames in Samuel's eyes began to dim, and a furrow crept across his brow. His hands loosened just enough for me to pull them away and then I gasped for air and shoved him back. I staggered to my feet to find Astrid standing with the succubus's jeweled necklace gleaming on the end of her dagger.

Kitty had changed from seductress to a shriveled, crooked thing, her only concession to humanity the wig resting on her oily scaled scalp. "Give. Them. Back!" she screamed as she tore toward Astrid, her claws raking the air.

Astrid flicked the jewels from the end of the blade to me. I caught them and jolted at the blisteringly hot energy contained within the stones.

"We warned you," Astrid said, as she swiped her dagger, taking off the tips of the succubus's fingers. Blood arced through the air. Kitty shrieked and clutched her injured fingers as her wings flicked like an angry cat's tail. But her eyes didn't move. She seemed to be fixated on the polished blade of Astrid's dagger, as she if she was mesmerized.

I grabbed a small mirror from my bag and cast it toward the succubus as she tensed herself to attack.

She slowed and her pupils dilated as her eyes locked upon their own reflection. I glanced at Samuel as he joined me. He looked both revolted and embarrassed. "Grab her sunglasses," I nodded. He plucked them from the floor near her clawed feet as she continued to stare at herself, her body slowly rocking.

"You dropped these," Samuel said as he slipped the sunglasses over her eyes, dousing the power they were exuding. I tossed the mirror away and replaced it with the gun and pressed it hard against her leathery forehead. Gradually, her attention returned and a scowl crept across her face.

"Take a seat," I said, forcing her toward an armchair in the corner. She slumped into it, held up her hand and sucked at the stumps of her bleeding fingers.

"What do you want?" Kitty demanded as drops of blood freckled her chin and dripped upon the cream colored carpet. "Fucking human."

"I want to know about Charrot."

Her face wrinkled with disgust. "Awful, disgusting pig of a man. Reeked of B-O and cigar smoke. He was one of my first marks in this realm, but not by choice. I was in my prime and I could have netted far better than him. Believe me."

"So why didn't you?"

"I was forced to work my wiles on him, and turn him our way."

"Our way?"

"My master's way." Kitty's scowl deepened and a glow of light drifted out from under her sunglasses.

"Who's your master?"

Kitty paused, withholding the answer. And then she glanced at her bleeding fingers and clearly thought better of it. "Franklin Lampton. The jerk that summoned me into this shitpit of a world. The man who trapped me here, tore my heart out and pissed over its remains."

Lampton. Like the Lampton who served on the Council? The man who'd been undermining me from the moment I'd encountered Stroud? No, he had to have been a kid back when the asylum was up and running, but she could have been talking about his father or grandfather. "Why did he want you to seduce Charrot?" I already knew the answer, I was just priming the pump to see what she'd say.

"Charrot had all the loonies at his disposal, Lampton wanted to put them to work. Focus what was left of their shattered psyches on creating the portal."

"To Penrythe?"

"If you say so," Kitty said. "I was just the messenger, a liaison. I passed the instructions on to Charrot and fulfilled whatever vile fancies he cooked up while he completed my master's work. He wasn't hard to turn. When I met him his heart was full of God and peace and goodwill. But it didn't take much to corrupt him. It never ceases to amaze me how fickle blinkereds are. It's like there's an ocean of darkness bubbling below the surface, and all it takes to bring it flooding out is one little scratch."

"Where's Lampton now?" I asked.

"Probably at home, hiding. I'd know if the piece of shit was dead. He's a shut-in, a recluse. Hardly surprising given how many enemies he's made over the years, myself included." Kitty gave me a snaggle-toothed smile. "He has hounds roaming the estate as well as binds to keep us all out. Such a scaredy cat."

"Where does he live?"

"About ten miles east of Galloway, near Albany. *The old lodge* as he calls it. Not a place you'd want to visit, trust me," Kitty said. "But then again, it might be fun if you did."

"How well fortified is it? Tell me exactly what we can expect," I asked, but before she could answer my phone began to buzz. I pulled it from my pocket.

- Haskins

"Rook," I answered.

"I'm at the City Library," Haskins said. "We got a situation. A serious situation."

"I'm busy," I said, suppressing a shudder as I felt Kitty's eyes roving over me.

"This can't wait, Rook. It's going to bring all sorts of heat down onto your side of the fence, believe me. We're talking about a goddamned zombie for fuck's sake. And terrorized kids, and who knows how many news crews on the way."

"Okay." I glanced at my watch. "Give me twenty minutes."

"What do we do with her?" Samuel asked, nodding to Kitty as I hung up.

I crouched down close to her ear, doing my best to ignore the reek of her breath. "Are you going to leave the city, or are you going to be a problem?" I asked," 'cause I'm short on time and willing to put a bullet in your head if it'll solve this problem."

"I'm happy to move on to greener pastures." Kitty sneered as she glanced to the bed and the man she'd reduced to a pile of skin and bones. "My work here is done."

I glanced at Samuel and Astrid. "Can you create a little fog, make her forget everything? For as long as possible?"

"We can. Wouldn't last much longer than a week or two..." Samuel said. "And the spell could addle what's left of her mind."

"Good," I said. "Do it." I nodded to the man in the bed. "Please get him food and water as soon as you've got her out of here. I'll call you as soon as I can."

"Take care," Astrid said. I smiled at her as I closed the door and wondered what fresh hell Haskins had dug up for me.

15

The library was right in the middle of the city and not far from the bank where I'd encountered the magician. I realized I hadn't asked Haskins what his official cover story for the robbery was, there hadn't been time.

I crossed the plaza as cold rain struck the back of my neck. Winter was drawing in and it seemed this year was bringing a gloom and darkness worse than most.

A crowd of women and children gathered under umbrellas as they gazed toward the library, their faces shocked and concerned. I was outnumbered; there were at least thirty gawkers out on the sidewalk; too many memories for me to wipe with a spell. Which meant I should have called the Organization, but that wasn't going to happen, not until I'd heard from Erland and found out what the hell was going on.

"I wanna go home," a young boy whined as he tugged at the sleeve of his mother's raincoat.

"We will. I just want to make sure she's alright," she said. But his mother didn't really sound all that concerned; it seemed more like she captivated by the shock and awe. It was only as I looked again that I noticed that she and the others were carrying bags of groceries. Donations for the Winter Festival's food drive. The library was one of their collection points, I'd spotted posters for it plastered across the city, featuring families of sparkly jolly snow people with frosty smiles gleaming below blue skies that never seemed to come.

The festival was our seasonal celebration and a call for goodwill and charity, though I couldn't help but feel most the proceeds ended up in the coffers of the bureaucrats who oversaw it.

I grabbed a crystal and masked myself as I pushed through the onlookers, ignoring the waspish remarks that followed in my wake.

An ambulance was parked near the library entrance, its red lights flashing in the windows as a medic treated his partner who was profusely bleeding from her wrist. Both gave me stony glares, as if whatever had happened inside the library was my doing but I ignored them and slipped through the sliding doors as I looked around for Haskins.

The place was a book lover's dream, well lit and peaceful - apart from the thuds and muffled shouts coming from the far side of the maze of bookshelves. I made my way toward the ruckus, glad for the industrial heating and its dusty dry warmth.

"Back off!" Haskins shouted. He sounded flustered, angry and scared.

The racket grew louder as I made my way past the paperbacks in the romance section flouting oiled six packs and half dressed couples embracing in far off locales.

"It's about time!" Haskins barked as he caught sight of me. He was manning a door and his face rumpled into a grimace as he clenched its twisting handle. The door rattled and as the handle began to turn again, he forced it back.

"What's going on?"

"This kook's what's going on. She's lost her fucking mind and started acting like a zombie. Take over the door," Haskins said. "I still got stitches from that last loon you got me involved with."

"Yeah, the witch who got the drop on you, I haven't forgotten." I nodded for him to release the handle and grabbed it in his stead. The sound of muffled, labored breath emanated from behind the wooden panels, followed by a shockingly diverse string of profanity. "What's the situation? And can you give me a little more detail this time please," I asked as the door buckled and jerked.

Haskins shot me a glowering look. "The staff said she's been stark raving mad ever since she showed up for work this morning. Talking all kinds of crazy shit and breathing weird, like she was hyperventilating. They thought maybe it was a panic attack until she started running around like a bat out of hell, sweating and shrieking. Then she passed out, right in the middle of the health and wellness section." Haskins flinched as the door rattled in its frame. "So they called an ambulance, and when it arrived, Mrs. Thompson in there," he nodded toward the door and rolled his eyes, "sits bolt upright and sinks her teeth into one of the medics, like a rabid dog. So they call the precinct and the call gets rerouted to me because as you know, I take these kinds of calls, on account of you. So I listen in and think, yeah, this is right up Morgan Rook's alley. Proper screwball stuff."

I braced myself as her fists pounded the other side of the door and the wood began to splinter.

"So I called you up and grabbed that broom." He nodded toward the broomstick leaning against the wall by the door jamb. It had been painted black and adorned with fake cobwebs, a Halloween prop yet to be cleared away. "And used it to force her back into this room."

"Okay, I get the picture. Stand back."

"Suits me." Haskins inched away, his beady eyes locked on the door, as I let go and stepped away. The bangs and thumps continued to rain down, more frantic than ever. I reached out, twisted the handle, shoved the door open, and jumped back.

A thin, spindly woman leaped into the frame. She had to be in her late sixties. Her reading glasses were fogged over and dark streaks of mascara had run down her powdered cheeks. The pastel sweater, blue jeans, and a red furry hat that she wore were a million miles from the feral monster I'd imagined when she was pounding on the door and swearing like a sailor, but they made for a picture perfect librarian. "Are you okay?" I asked, as she stared up at me.

"I…" she took a step, her forehead gleaming with sweat. "I…" She peered around and held a hand over her eyes. "I don't feel well. My heart… it keeps stopping." She glanced at Haskins and gagged as if she was going to be sick. "I don't know what's happened to me."

I had a pretty good idea of exactly what had happened. Endersley. My anger grew but I did my best to stay calm. "Let's find you a seat," I said. I held my hand toward her and she took another tottering step my way, then her eyes seemed to lose focus and her lips drew back over her teeth.

"You know, I don't think she's-" Haskins fell to silence as the librarian lunged at him, with clawed fingers and gnashing teeth. I yanked her away before she could tear out his throat and she rounded on me with a husky, animalistic cry.

"Shit!" I shoved her back as Haskins grabbed his gun. "Put that away Haskins, for God's sake!"

The librarian charged at me, ducking low, her claws swiping at my eyes. I did my best to subdue her but she was too quick and evaded me with a low, throaty growl.

"Now what?" Haskins backed away as she prowled toward

him. He stopped as he bumped into a rack of books and sent them cascading to the floor. The librarian roared and pounced on him, taking them both down, the lurid books tumbling around them like an avalanche.

I pulled the librarian off Haskins, grabbed her by the arms, and kept her snapping teeth at bay as I dragged her toward a sofa in the reading nook. She snarled and roared, but soon her aggression fell to grunts and whimpers. "What's happening?" she cried, her voice full of pleading. "What's happening to me?"

"Sit down and try to take slow deep breaths." I reached into my bag and pulled out a small vial of healing waters that Bastion had sourced from a cavern in the heart of the Carpathian Mountains. "Sip this. It will help."

She took it from me and emptied it with a single swig. Her hands shook and as she returned the empty vial and I held them, watching closely as her pupils dilated and her breathing began to slow.

I read her and rifled through her memories as her hands relaxed in mine. Snapshots of her life flew by; the husband she'd lost, the three grown children who doted on her. I leafed through her recollections as if they were photographs, bypassing one after another until I reached this morning's.

The coffee shop. A table for two, the chair across from her empty. Until the man had set his coffee down, took the seat and smiled. Endersley. She'd returned his smile and considered what nice cheekbones he had, even if he did seem a little on the ratty side.

She'd returned to reading her newspaper, an article about the sherpa from Tibet who'd relocated to New York City. When she'd turned the page of her newspaper, the man had gone and his steaming coffee remained untouched on the table.

It was only after she'd got up and walked out that she'd felt hot. Boiling almost, despite the cold chill in the morning air. And then the jitters had followed, like she'd taken a triple shot in her latte, but she hadn't. She'd drunk decaf because… then the world had spun around her, grey, black and white, slowly growing dimmer.

Her recollections jumped. One moment she'd been standing on the corner of the block, the next she was staggering toward the sliding doors of the library. The little she recalled from the in-between consisted of jumbled angry shouts, car horns and squealing tires. Had she been there? Had any of it happened?

She'd wandered into the building, swaying like she'd had a snifter full of brandy, only half recognizing the concerned faces as they'd turned her way. Then the rows of books had spun like a tilt-a-whirl as the world came crashing down.

The last thing she remembered was the feeling of the ridged carpet against the side of her face as she'd slowly closed her eyes.

When she'd opened them, people had been standing over her, staring like she was an animal in a zoological exhibit. People she knew, people she didn't. One had been the man from the coffee shop. He'd watched her closely but as she'd caught his eye and lifted her hand toward him, he'd melted away.

Time passed again and her memories of it had been lost. Something bad had happened. There was blood in her mouth and it wasn't hers, but it had tasted good. *Very* good. She wanted more of it.

She remembered the man who'd trapped her in the office. A frightful man with a badge in his hand and a gun at his hip. He'd annoyed her on sight, even before he'd locked her in...

I let go of the librarian's hand, severing the connection. When she looked my way her eyes were filled with tears. "Are you alright?" I asked. She said nothing. "I'm, Morgan, and you are?"

She stared at me for a moment before shaking her head. "I don't know." The tears fell down her cheeks.

I glanced up as a woman appeared between two stands of books, recording video with the phone in her hand. The girl at her side was not much older than seven. "She okay?" the woman asked. I could tell by her tone that she didn't really care one way or the other; she merely wanted to capture a moment of someone else's hell on her ever-ready camera.

"Get her out of here, Haskins," I said.

"You okay, Mary?" the woman asked, ignoring me.

"She doesn't look well, mom," the little girl whispered.

Haskins began to stand. He looked rattled as several people walked through the library doors. "Hey, get out of here!" he shouted, brandishing his badge. "This is police business."

"This is a public place," a man replied, his umbrella dripping water onto the carpet. "I got DVDs to pick up," the jackass added as Haskins rushed toward him.

The librarian looked terrified as she glanced around. "Wait here," I told her as I stood and helped Haskins clear the people out. "Where's the kid?" I asked as I steered the woman with the phone out the door. She glanced down from her phone to the empty space beside her. "Shelley?" she called.

A cold pang passed through me.

I hurried back, Haskins by my side.

Shelley was with the librarian, her little face filled with horror as the once familiar woman bared her teeth and growled like a dog. Shelley broke away and began to run as the librarian crawled after her on her hands and knees, agile as a hound, her face starved and contorted with hunger.

16

B*ang!*
  The sound of the bullet was brutally loud as it tore through the librarian's chest, spattering blood over the books, shelves and her quarry.

I turned to find Haskins preparing to take another shot. "Stop!" I scooped up the screaming child and handed her to her mother, who'd rushed up behind me. "Get enough footage?" I asked as I grabbed her phone, deleted the files and shoved it back at her. I pushed them to the doors. "Take your kid to that ambulance, get her seen to and stay the hell out of my way." The crowd outside the doors watched the whole exchange, but looked elsewhere as I met their gaze and then they began to disperse.

"I... I didn't want to...but the kid..." Haskins was visibly shaking as he gazed at the horror show before him.

"It wasn't your fault," I said. "Now listen." He looked my way and nodded, desperate for someone else to take control of the situation. "Stop anyone from trying to get in here, and make sure that little girl sees a doctor. If anyone asks, we think the librarian has a rare condition, and it's being looked into. And it's definitely not contagious."

"Oh fuck," Haskins said. "Is it?"

"I don't know, that's the god's honest truth. It doesn't look like it but I'm working on finding out for sure, okay? You need to trust me and if you run across any more situations like this, call me immediately. In the meantime get your people to go over this morning's CCTV footage from Elliston Street. There's a coffee shop on the corner," I nodded to the librarian, "that's where she was infected. The man you're looking for has messy grey hair, a ratty face and bulbous eyes. It's not a face you could miss. You might find images of him here too, if these library cameras are working. We need to grab him, and fast, so keep me appraised."

"You think he's still in the city?" Haskins asked. "In *our* city?"

"It's doubtful, but we should still look. There's a good chance he might have slipped away to the other side, if you know what I mean."

"Your side," Haskins said. "This is all coming from your side." He bristled with anger.

"Cool it, Haskins," I said. "I'm all you've got right now and those two sides, you don't want them clashing, believe me."

"Then do something about it. That poor broad..." he gazed down at the dead librarian, "she was one of ours. I don't care what happens to your freakos. Got it?"

I bit back my first response. "I care about everyone, both sides, I don't distinguish. Now let's work together to get this shit shut down. Yeah, it's coming from *my side*, but I'm fairly sure it was yours that adeptly started two world wars all on their own. Let's avoid giving them any inklings or cause to kick off a third one, with us."

Haskins stared at me for a moment and slowly his jaw and fist unclenched. He nodded. "Sure."

"Good. Now, you know what we need. Get to it, and I'll get on with finding the man who did this. Okay?"

"Okay." Haskins glanced back to the dead librarian. "What about her? There were witnesses. Those medics-"

"If anyone asks, she's been taken to a lab for tests. It's the truth. I'm calling my people, they'll come here and clean this up. Hopefully they can find out what the hell she was infected with as well. Once they've run their tests, I'll see that her remains are turned over to your department so you can close your case, and her family can give her a proper burial."

"Right." Haskins holstered his gun, pulled his badge out, and walked into the thinning crowd outside as I called Dauple.

"Hello?" It was a high, scratchy voice. But not his.

"Where's Dauple?"

"He's driving. I'm Mortensen. His assistant."

Great. "Tell him it's Morgan and I need to talk to him. Now."

I heard a muffled conversation, what might have been a yelp, and then Dauple got on the line with a heavy sigh. "Sorry Morgan, I have a new intern. The Organization's expanding our department. Fast."

That didn't sound good. Were they expecting more bodies? "I need your help, Dauple. I'm downtown, at the city library. It's important. *Really* important."

"I can be there in half an hour, but I'll have company. If you know what I mean?"

This was probably the most lucid I'd known him to be. "Yup, I know what you mean. I'll be waiting for you. Just try your best to make sure this doesn't reach the Organization until I'm away from the scene."

"Will do."

I hung up, sat on the library desk and gazed out the window as Haskins cleared the crowd away and the ambulance drove off, its lights the only living color in the grey and brown morning.

Dauple pulled up in his hearse earlier than expected and parked outside the library's entrance. I watched as he rattled his keys and slammed the car door, his face tired and dour above his black winter coat. He looked like a crow today, an angry, seething crow. Moments later the passenger side opened and a younger man popped out. He was tall and slightly bug eyed with tousled blonde hair. He followed Dauple like a duckling, his face gleaming with enthusiasm.

"Morgan," Dauple said with a nod.

I was taken aback as I realized how much he'd changed over these last few weeks. I guessed the darkness that had been washing over the city was eating away at everyone, including him. Suddenly I wanted the old Dauple back, and a return to simpler, crazier times. "Thanks for coming," I said.

"My pleasure," Dauple said, but the tone of his voice told me it really wasn't. "You alright?"

"Kind of," I smiled, then he smiled too, and finally the ice broke.

"Hi," the intern said, and as I glanced toward him I realized he'd been studying me all this time. He offered a hand that was slightly less clammy than Dauple's usually was, but only just. "I'm Benny. Benny Mortensen."

"You're aptly named," I said. He looked confused. "*Mort*ensen. You know, with your chosen vocation."

He gazed up at me blankly and I couldn't find the will to explain.

"Um, this looks like a blinkered. What do you want me to

do?" Dauple asked, as he leaned on his haunches and assessed the dead librarian.

"Bag and tag? Burn and churn?" Benny asked, clearly pleased to be using Dauple's parlance as he stooped over and got so close to the librarian his nose almost brushed hers.

"We think she's contagious," I said, relishing the panic as he sprang up like a jack-in-a-box, lost his footing and fell on his ass. I turned back to find Dauple rolling his eye with disgust and frustration. "Can you check? Maybe run some tests and see if you find anything unusual in her system?"

"Unusual?"

I turned to Mortensen and gestured to the fallen books and blood-spattered carpet, "Get this mess cleaned up."

He nodded and sprang out to the car to get his gear, like an eager puppy.

"*Is* she contagious?" Dauple asked. "Is this the same condition the old man in the meat packing place had?"

"Yes, it's the same condition but we don't think it's contagious, not yet. I was just messing with your idiot assistant."

"I must say I feel a degree of relief," Dauple said.

"That's not to say the situation won't change. We suspect the piece of shit responsible for this is working on it. I'm looking for him now and the less you know about it the better."

Dauple gave a brief nod and gazed down at the librarian's corpse. "And what do I do with her?" he asked.

"Run tests if you can, and if you can't then cremate her. I'll give you my contact in the police department's details so we can at least get her remains back to her family."

"Will do."

"What about Erland," I asked, "have you heard from him?"

"Not a peep. He left town a few days ago."

"Left?"

"Vanished. No one's seen hide nor hair of him, and Mr. Humble's overseeing all his cases." Dauple glanced behind me and lowered his voice. "I've never liked that Mr. Humble, Morgan, he's… spooky."

This, coming from Dauple, was troubling.

"And," he continued hastily, as Mortensen burst through the doors with a bucket in hand and a body bag tossed over his shoulder. "You know they're looking for you, don't you?"

"They?"

"The other agents. I heard Humble's ordered them to bring you in. Off the record."

"Thanks Daup," I said as Mortensen came within earshot. Dauple held out his hand, and I shook it.

Once again I was in his debt, and I wouldn't forget it.

100

17

I called a cab and sat back in the seat as it sloshed through the streets toward my apartment. The rain pounding the sidewalks turned the world into a wet silvery blur as I tried to take stock of what had just happened. The fiasco at the library had really unsettled me. I felt terrible for the poor woman, Mary. The snapshots from her life played through my mind, Endersley targeting her in the coffee shop, then how her heart kept stopping and starting as she'd found herself caught between living and dying. It was a horrific fate for anyone and a clear demonstration, as if I'd needed one, of how far Endersley was prepared to go.

The cab stopped as it came up on a knot of traffic. I glanced out the window as blinkereds hurried by, their umbrellas shaking in the growing wind. The hard truth was, I'd never truly felt like I belonged among them. And when it was all boiled down, I had about as much in common with them as I did with a gloaming ghast. And yet I couldn't deny that I'd lived, loved and lost in their world, I'd built a meaningful life here and they were a part of it. Which was why the thought of them being picked off by some malignant manufactured disease, made me sick to my core. I took a deep breath as rage bloomed inside me and my dark other began to stir.

I had to find Endersley, and fast.

"I'll get out here," I told the driver. It would be quicker to walk home. I handed him a twenty, ignored his protests about safety regulations and used a quick spell to unlock the passenger door. The rain soaked my hair as I raced off, weaving through the throng.

"You look like a drowned hedgerat," Samuel said as he sat back on the sofa, a fug of pipe smoke hanging in the air above him. "It's a good look for you." I grabbed a towel from the bathroom, rubbed the back of my neck and hair, and returned to the living room.

"Care to tell us where you ran off to?" Astrid handed me her coffee. "Here, you look like you need it more than I do." I took a sip and gave them a detailed recount of the events at the library.

"Endersley's testing again, and it sounds like he's had success. That poor woman," Astrid said, with a shiver.

"It was bad. There was so little left of her humanity by the time I'd gotten there, barely a scrap. I don't know if we could have reversed things…"

"Definitely not" Samuel said. "Especially after your friend put a bullet through her."

"Haskins is a colleague not a friend. But he had no choice. The way she was looking at that kid, it was like she was two seconds away from tearing her throat out. Anyway," I said, "Haskins has a lot of pull in his department and he's working hard to help us track down Endersley. He'll let us know the minute he hears anything"

"So what are we supposed to do now, just wait for him to call us?" Samuel asked. "I mean, I'm happy sitting here smoking and watching this blinkered gibberish on your television all day, but we could probably serve better uses." He was being his usual snarky self, but I could see by the way he was drumming his fingers that he wanted to take action. And so did I.

"If you're up for a little interrogation, let's pay old man Lampton a visit. Might shed some light on how long the Council's been in cahoots with Stroud and confirm who the key players are. Hell, he might even choke up some firm evidence of a conspiracy. If we can blow the lid off this now, we might be able to rally some support among the uncorrupted Council members. If there are any left."

"I'm ready when you are. How 'bout you Ast." Samuel clapped his hands together as she nodded.

"Great." I finished my coffee and set the cup down. "I'll get cleaned up and ready to head out."

I left the room, showered and threw on some clean clothes as my phone went off. Hoping it was Haskins, I grabbed my damp coat, fished through the pockets and tossed it back over the radiator to dry as I checked the caller ID.

- Unknown Number

"Hello?" I waited for their reply but all I got was a low buzz of static and a torrent of rainfall. "I don't have time for games. Who the hell is this-"

"Morgan Rook."

A woman. Well spoken. Impatient. She instantly reminded me of… who? "This is Rook, and you are?"

"An ally, of sorts. I need to see you at once."

"What's this about?"

"A mutual friend who hankers for only the finest of threads."

She had to be referring to Erland. "I can meet you tonight at-"

"I won't be anywhere near this damnable place tonight.

Meet me now and don't dither. He's hurt. And he needs your help."

Shit. "Where?"

"Arthur Street."

"Is there a number?"

"No, but there's an alley. Make sure you come alone. You've got fifteen minutes." She hung up.

I pulled my coat on, checked my gun was loaded and shoved a few things into my bag. "Okay," I said, as I entered the living room, "slight change of plans."

"Who was it?" Astrid asked.

"I don't know, but she needs to meet me urgently. My boss... Erland..."

"The fae?" Samuel asked.

"Yeah, the fae. He needs my help."

"What about Endersley?" Astrid asked, barely masking her irritation.

"Can you and Samuel head over to the magical quarter, see what's going on there? Between Helena Castle and the incident at the library there's got to be some rumors or gossip flying around, at the very least. The chatter there's usually pretty helpful. I'll be done in an hour or so and I'll meet you here. This could be a lucky break, Erland knows pretty much everything worth knowing about in this world, chances are he'll be able to point us in the right direction." While all this was true, the most pressing thing on my mind right then was the fact that he was injured. But I wasn't going to admit that, not with the look Astrid had just shot me.

"Sure," Samuel said. "We'll do that."

I sensed he shared Astrid's irritation. They were fighters. They'd been pursuing Endersley for what must have seemed like forever. We'd just gotten back on the trail and here I was shutting them out and flitting off again. But there was nothing

I could do about it. The woman on the phone had made it clear, I had to go alone. "Good luck," I said, and hurried out.

I slipped past Mrs. Fitz's apartment, rushed out into the pouring rain and dug into my bag for a crystal. After a stealthy look around I cast a quick spell to shield myself from the worse of the torrent and ran up to the main road to hail a cab.

"Where to?" the driver, a grizzled man with a grizzled beard, asked.

"Arthur Street."

"Never heard of it."

"Can you look it up?" Or maybe I'll take your frigging cab and drive there myself.

"I guess." He sighed as he pulled over and dug into his glove compartment. He traced a stubby, grimy finger over the map and sighed once more. "It's all the way on the other side of town."

"Is that a problem?"

"I guess not." He started the car, and we drove through the streets to the soundtrack of his sighs and occasional belches. I glanced out the window as the rain continued to pound the city, *'And it rained all night'* played through my mind. It was only when we hit Third Street that I felt it. There were eyes on me. Eyes full of bad intent.

Someone was hunting me, and their magic was powerful. More powerful than anything I could summon. I searched the shop windows and doorways. There. A glint of eyes in a side street, a brief connection that was soon severed. But not quickly enough. I rolled down my window.

"Hey!" The driver yelled.

"Shut up," I replied. "Seriously, shut the fuck up." I stared at him until he looked away, then returned my gaze to the side mirror. I spotted her emerging from the side street. Ebomee, her sniper rifle magically concealed in a thin black case made for a pool cue. She flagged a cab. Shit. "How far are we from Arthur Street?"

"About a mile," the driver said, his voice mixed with anger and unease. Idiot.

"You need to take the next right and then you're going to drive as fast as you can. Got it?"

"I can only drive as fast..." He paused as I handed him a fifty, laced with a spell. Moments later his features set into grim concentration and he nodded. The charm was relatively weak, but it was more than enough to sway his mind. I glanced back into the mirror as the cab two cars behind continued to follow.

I reached for the grip as the driver took the turn and gunned the engine, the back of the cab skidding as we weaved in and out of cars. Ebomee's cab slid round the corner amid a screech of brakes and blue smoke, then it shot toward us, the slashing rain backlit by their headlights.

Arthur Street was only two blocks away now. I could make it on foot. I grabbed three crystals and shuddered as their magic shot through my veins. I performed a simple illusion spell, just like Samuel had shown me, before leaning down and leaving the ghostly illusion of myself sitting in the seat. It wasn't the greatest trick in the world but with the rain and the speed we were driving at, it should work. Or so I hoped.

The driver stared ahead, still under my control as he took the cab racing down the street.

"Make a hard right," I said, "gun it for at least ten blocks then pull over and let the woman that's following us get a good look inside the car. Once she's gone, head back to Arthur Street and wait there. Got it?"

He nodded absently, and as soon as he turned the wheel and shot around the corner, I opened the door and jumped, landing hard on the slick road. My coat spared me from a severe case of road rash as I rolled toward the curb and scrambled behind a parked car before the other cab came screeching around the bend.

Ebomee stared ahead as her car sped by, sloshing rain over me. I barely felt it, I was already soaked to the bone and plagued with cuts and bruises, but I could heal those later if it came to it. I crouched down and watched as the two cabs hurtled the length of the block and only once their taillights had faded, did I run.

I crossed the street, ignoring the family in matching rain coats that stood and stared at me as if I'd just descended from a space craft. "Nice day," I said and as I rushed by the mother grabbed her kids and pulled them in close. Blinkereds, may the gods bless each and every last one of them.

A bolt of lightning split the sky and a deep rumble rattled the city as I neared the next intersection. I hoped it was a good omen as I ran, my coat flying around me.

Arthur Street was at the end of the block. I'd made it; I turned down a narrow lane lined with apartment buildings and spotted the alleyway that ran halfway between them. The murkiness of the storm and the looming shadows amid the towering concrete walls were so dark and heavy it almost seemed like night had fallen.

I slowed as I reached the alley. It was still, the far end shuttered off by a high gated metal fence. I glanced round, checking each of the parked cars as I looked for my contact, but they were all empty.

A crack of thunder boomed above me as I reached the dead end, my heart racing from the run. Then I drew my pistol as a heavy, ominous feeling stole over me.

A feeling that told me, without a scrap of uncertainty that someone had just cut off the escape route behind me.

And they were closing in fast.

18

"Stop where you are. Don't move." It was the same voice I'd heard on the phone. Female, husky, with a trace of an accent that wasn't quite British, but wasn't a million miles from it.

I glanced down at the pooling water around my feet as a bolt of lightning flashed across the sky and caught the reflection of bright lilac eyes and long hair. Then her black leather boot shattered the surface of the puddle.

"Raise your hands up over your head," she said, as the echoing rumble boomed over the rooftops.

I did as I was told. If she'd meant me harm, she would have already made her move by now. Then a strange whisper began to fill the alleyway, her words too distorted for me to understand, her voice soft, melodious and calming. But it still troubled me. I bristled as she placed her gloved hand on the side of my face. She was reading me, or trying to. My defenses blocked her more invasive intrusions, but she must have uncovered whatever she was looking for because she stepped away and said, "You can turn around now."

I did as she asked and found myself face to face with a tall, willowy fae. The first thing that struck me was her long strawberry blonde hair and how it pooled in the folds of the collar on her elegant, forest-green coat. Her face was pretty, long and slender and her gaze was cold and even. A large silver hoop glimmered in one of her sharply pointed ears and the other was studded with three emerald stones. "Are you..."

"I'm Abigayle Underwood, Erland's sister."

"I never knew he had a sister."

"You'd expect him to confide something like that to the likes of you?"

I ignored the barbed remark. "Where is he?"

"Recovering." Her eyes turned a shade colder.

"From what?"

"An attack by vicious cowards. Common assassins."

"Is he okay?"

"We anticipate he will be." Abigayle reached beneath her cloak, pulled out a weathered map and handed it to me.

I expected it would detail some strange, mythical land, but it was just an old map of the city and its surroundings. "What's this for?" I asked as she handed me a slip of paper.

"Memorize this."

I unfolded it and read the hand-written coordinates, then the paper burst into flames. I dropped it. "Nice," I said, blowing on the tips of my fingers as it fell and hissed in the puddle.

"That's how you'll find the place Erland uses to cross over. For some reason he's decided to trust you with its location."

"Cross over?"

"Have you never been to our lands?" Abigayle asked.

"Faerie?"

"Yes, Faerie. What other lands could I possibly be referring to?"

And I'd thought Erland was direct. I shook my head. "No, I haven't."

"I understood that when you shook your head. Well, this is your chance to travel to our fair realm. Go there, speak to my brother and help him unravel whatever tedious mess he's gotten himself involved with now."

"Listen, I don't mean to be callous but I'm already up to my neck in trouble. If Erland's safe then he probably doesn't need me."

"He does need you, which is why I've gone to the trouble of coming here."

"Why can't you help him?" I asked, ignoring her bristling glare. The initial surprise of meeting her had worn off, and I was getting tired of her snark. "He's your brother after all."

"I have far more pressing issues to deal with right now. Erland understands this, which is why he's sent for you. He has an urgent task he cannot contend with on his own, one that will help you with the shade."

"Stroud?"

"Are you currently entangled with more than one shade?" Abigayle asked, arching her eyebrows.

"No."

She gave a thin smile. "Then I believe you know the answer to your question, Mr. Rook." Slowly, her face softened. "I apologize."

"For what?"

"My impatience. My brother's injuries were bad. *Are* bad. I told him long ago to stay away from this damnable place." She wrinkled her nose. "If not for the stench alone, but he didn't listen. He has a peculiar sentimentality, which is why he's given his best to this world of yours. And in return he's received a cursed knife to the gut, for his troubles." Abigayle reached into her pocket and brought out a small round apple.

It glowed, one side ruby-red, the other bottle green. She held it out to me.

"What's this for?" I asked as the apple's sweet enticing scent wafted up to my nose and made my mouth water.

"It's the key that will get you in." Abigayle said. "You have the coordinates, the map. Stand under the arch of stone, eat the apple and you'll find yourself on a hill overlooking the village where my brother is waiting."

"Seems simple enough." I slipped the apple into my pocket, resigning myself to the fact that her instructions made about as much sense as anything else in my life.

Abigayle gazed at me for a moment as if deciding something. "I came, Mr. Rook, because my brother asked for you. He trusts you, but I am of the opinion that his judgment often leaves much to be desired, so I feel you should be made aware of the fact that we do not throw open the doors to our lands the way we once did. To put it bluntly, your kind are no longer welcomed in Faerie. My advice to you is to remain unseen, as much as possible, while you're there."

"Fine."

"Go alone, do not attempt to bring anyone with you and do not divulge your destination." Her eyes flitted over mine. "You're already thinking of your newly forged alliances, I can see it. Don't. If you cross me I will find out. I may be overwrought with burdensome obligations but vengeance takes precedence where I come from and I will come calling if I need to, and you wouldn't want that."

Anger surged through me. I didn't appreciate her threats, but it didn't seem like the best idea to point it out. "Fine, I'll go alone."

"Good. I wish you and my brother the best. Perhaps we'll meet again, Mr. Rook. In better days." She nodded to me and strode back down the alley. As I began to turn a flash of lilac light burst through the gloom. I shielded my eyes in the crook of my arm as a warm breeze wafted over me. It carried the scent of parched heather and the sound of cawing crows. Then it all vanished with the heavy slam of a door.

When I glanced back down the alley it was empty and Abigayle Underwood was gone.

19

The air sizzled as a bolt of lightning lashed the sky. I pulled out my flashlight to examine the map. The numbers I'd been given were latitude and longitude. I ran my finger down the lines to the point where they intersected; a forest in the middle of a state park. The place was at least an hour away.

Silver light flashed over the walls and puddles and another boom roared out. I stashed the map in my coat and hoped the cab driver had followed my instructions. A trip out of town was the very last thing I needed right now, but I had to go. I grabbed my phone and dialed the burner I'd given Astrid.

"Morgan," she said.

"Hi."

"Are you okay?"

"Yeah. But I'm going to need to make a quick detour. It shouldn't take long."

"Where?" Astrid asked. There was concern in her voice. We'd grown close over these last few days, even though neither of us had acknowledged it, not with everything else we'd been facing. But it was still there. A potential glint of light after the relentless darkness of the last few years. "I can't tell you, I'm sorry. But it might lead to a solution to Stroud."

"Are you coming home before you go?" A cat purred loudly besides Astrid's phone. It sounded like Storm, which was apt.

"No, I need to go straight there. Can you and Samuel hold the fort while I'm gone?"

"Of course. Samuel was accosted by Mrs. Fitz just after you left, now he's downstairs helping her hang drapes. I can hear them laughing through the floorboards. It's…eerie."

I smiled. "Well once he's finished that deadly assignment, please try to tear him from her clutches and get over to the magical quarter? See if there's been any sightings of Endersley."

"Of course."

"Great. I…I'll see you soon."

"Take care." She hesitated, and I waited to see if she was going to say something more, then the line went dead.

The cab was parked near the end of the street and the driver still possessed a vacuous look as he gazed at me through the rain. His eyes narrowed as I opened the rear passenger door, which meant his trance was weakening. "Hi, thanks for waiting," I said as I slammed the door against the rain and slipped a crystal out of my bag.

I reached into my wallet, got fifty bucks out and cast a quick spell. He took it without looking and I watched in the mirror as his eyes glazed over. "Where to?" he asked.

"I need to get to the state park." I checked the map again and gave him directions.

He started the car, made a u-turn and we set off, his awareness keen enough to drive safely, while his reasoning and memory remained soft and pliable enough for me to influence.

I sat back in the seat. My coat and shirt were soaked and I was glad to be out of the storm but I kept a watchful eye on things. I checked the mirrors as we drove through the heart of the city to see if anyone was tailing us. The cars on the highway were little more than dark blurs. One, a battered old Lincoln, seemed suspicious for a while but eventually it veered toward the off ramp. Slowly, the rattle and spatter of the rain, along with the warmth and obscured steamy windows, lulled me into a much needed sleep.

When I woke, everything was still and quiet. The driver had parked in the lot outside the forestry service's visitor center and surrounding us were straight towering trees that jutted up like a wall of giant green arrows. It was getting dark, the downpour had stopped and the sky was filled with ragged clouds and a scattering of shiny white stars.

I was about to climb out of the car when the driver woke from his stupor. "What the fuck am I doing here?" he asked.

"A good deed," I replied, though I was fairly sure his question was rhetorical.

"Get out of my cab!"

"My pleasure." I opened the door, then paused. "I don't suppose you'd be willing to wait 'til I get back?" I jumped out as the car roared to life, filling the cool air with a cloud of exhaust, then the wheels squealed angrily and he sped away.

As I watched him go, I noticed one of the cars on the far side of the lot, and caught sight of a large, round figure behind a misted window. They seemed to glance my way before driving off.

I chalked it up to paranoia and took out the crumpled map Abigayle had given me. It looked like I had a five or six mile hike and it was getting close to pitch darkness. "Great." I grabbed a flashlight from my bag, took a deep breath of the pine scented air, and headed down a well worn trail as I punched Erland's coordinates into the GPS app on my phone.

The forest wasn't as still and serene as it had seemed from the cab. Animals scurried and trampled through the brush. In the darkness they sounded as big as cougars even though they were probably nothing more than the odd rabbit or covey of quail. Owls screeched, coyotes yipped and screamed, and frogs joined in the chorus. I pushed on, planting each step firmly on the rough stony path.

I stopped at a crossroads marked by a mossy wooden signpost, checked my GPS and groaned when it pointed me toward a steep incline. Clumps of tall arching ferns brushed my coat as I climbed and the beam of my flashlight cast eerie shadows on the branches above. I had to wonder how Erland dressed when he came to this place and grinned as I pictured him in bespoke galoshes and a designer pith helmet. But my amusement faded as a branch creaked and snapped behind me.

I whirled around, the flashlight illuminating thick tree trunks, heavy brush, and a pair of gleaming eyes. A buck. It stared my way before skittering across the path into the undergrowth.

A strange, heaviness passed through the air, and I knew that that careless, clumsy sound hadn't been made by the deer. Someone was here, someone had followed me. I pulled the glasses from my bag and swept their charged crystals over the woods, looking for the telltale glow of a heart.

Nothing.

But the lack of evidence was not conclusive. My pursuer, and I was certain I had one, could have cloaked themselves. I switched the flashlight off and waited, my ears primed for the sound of movement or breath.

Still nothing. I waited, focused a moment longer and held

my breath for as long as I could, before finally releasing it. I turned the flashlight back on and swept it around in a thin white arc of light.

Doubt was beginning to creep through me like a thief, robbing me of my certainty. If anyone had been following me, they'd gone. Either that or they'd transformed themselves, which couldn't entirely be ruled out.

I continued up the trail, my ears straining for any hint of pursuit, but there was none. Soon, a distant churning roar began to rise up over the cries and nighttime calls of the forest's creatures. It was the waterfall, a landmark I'd spotted on the map. I was getting close to Erland's crossing. I pushed on toward the top of the hill and came to a stop at its crest.

A stream glimmered nearby in the moonlight, the sound of its churn oddly comforting. I shone the flashlight over the brush beyond the narrow strip of water until I found it; a mossy arch made of stone that wouldn't have looked out of place in a Pagan British woodland. I leaped across the stream and righted myself as I slipped on a rock and plunged into the icy water. "Goddamn it!" I cursed as I grabbed at the reeds and ferns rustling along the bank and pulled myself out.

My boots squelched with each step as I walked through the dense vegetation and paused under the archway. "Well, here we go," I said. "Next stop fairyland." I pulled the apple from my pocket and was about to take a bite when a splash echoed out behind me.

Another wallowing splosh followed, then a gruff yet whiny voice shouted, "Fucking fuckaton!" and a roar burst forth rustling the foliage of the trees around me.

20

I swept my flashlight toward the growl erupting in the brush and caught sight of two glowing, yellow eyes. The wolf-like beast glanced my way and bowed its head, as if nodding to me. Then it took off, charging through the brush toward the hulking silhouette emerging from the stream. I watched the creature as it leaped and struck the figure in the chest, taking them down before I could see who it was.

"Get the hell off me!"

The voice was Osbert's. They'd sent a fellow agent after me again, and this time it was their most vicious ogre.

He growled and there was a high, keening yelp, then I heard what sounded like a shovel being thrust into earth over and over. Moments later Osbert rose to his feet, rusty knife in hand, its blade dripping with blood. He was cloaked in his chosen persona, a fat, red-headed teenager with a gold ring gleaming in his upper lip. I'd seen the ogre out of his disguise on prior occasions, and he didn't look too dissimilar, with his tufts of coppery hair and that round, warty stomach.

"What the hell are you doing here, Osbert?"

"I guess, I'm, um, following you." He shrugged. "Sorry, Morgan. Orders are orders."

"What orders?" I pulled my gun and held it below my flashlight. "Who sent you?" I spoke fast in an attempt to wrong foot him.

"Um, orders to kill you." He shrugged again and gave a weak, half-smile. "I like you, man, you know that but needs must when the devil drives." As he began to tramp toward me, he let his cloak drop and I was face to face with the ogre. "I don't want to do this," he continued, "but sometimes you just gotta-"

The first shot hit him square in the chest. He stopped and clutched a meaty hand to his hide, and his face fell. "You shouldn't have done that, Morgan. I was going to make it quick, but now you've pissed me right off." He ducked down and charged me.

My second shot clipped him in the shoulder and the next on the side of his throat.

"Yaaaaaaaaaaaaa!" he growled as he ran, head low, a juggernaut of heaving flesh.

I aimed at his head but he was coming too fast. My gun roared, and the bullet went wide and exploded into the trunk behind him.

Before I could reload he struck me like a fat, soggy freight train. I was pulverized by the blow. The trees and stars spun round as I lost my flashlight and struggled to keep a grip on my gun.

I was about to fire into his boulder-like skull when the ground dropped from below us, the air turned black and white, and the waterfall roared as we fell alongside it.

We hit the pool below. My coat spared me the brunt of the fall but the impact forced the air from my lungs. Ice-cold water filled my mouth and bubbles rose around me like shoals of round glassy fish. We struck the rocky bottom, hard. Osbert had me in his fists, his gimlet eyes boring into mine. He'd drown both of us if it meant getting the job done.

I pulled a knife from my sopping wet shoulder bag and stabbed at him.

Osbert roared in a torrent of tiny air bubbles, grabbed my wrist and wrenched it, forcing the weapon from my hand. I lashed out, punching at the clouded bloody water.

I seized the opportunity, as Osbert clutched his side, to turn and swim away, booting him in the face as I scrambled toward the shore. I broke the surface and gasped for air before half wading, half crawling as my shoulder bag dragged along the rocks like a dead weight.

I was near the edge of the pool when I heard him burst from the water. "Rook!" he shouted and all traces of the awkward teenager he'd cloaked himself as were gone.

Before I could reach the trees, he grabbed the strap of my bag and yanked me back. The wet worn leather snapped and the bag and its contents splashed into the water and mud around me. A fist caught me under the chin, thrusting my head back. I tried to stumble away but Osbert's ham-like hand grasped my throat and hurled me down.

The water slapped my face as I went under. I reached for the ground to propel myself back up but he'd seized the scruff of my neck and held me firm. Bubbles surged from my mouth as I screamed in rage and panic. There was no hyperbole in his threat, he was going to kill me.

I reached up to pry his hand away, my nails seeking purchase in his flesh, but his warty hide was too taut and tough. I held what was left of my breath, tried to calm myself and concentrate, but my chest convulsed and his hand had become an unmovable object.

I'm going to die. The thought was eerily serene and matter of fact. A simple truth. A minnow darted past me and I watched it as it vanished into the murk, then I closed my eyes and sought to focus a final assault on his hand. I grabbed it and pulled with everything I had.

It wasn't enough.

Darkness crept across my vision and the final scrap of air I'd held left my lips.

Move.

My dark other had spoken. His first words since we'd fought Wyght.

Part of me wanted to deny him, to keep him locked away; dead and buried. But my will to survive overrode all else and shoved my consciousness aside.

He seized Osbert's hand and focused hard, drawing the magic thrumming through the ogre's veins, into our own. He absorbed every scrap he could then punched the ogre in his wounded side. Osbert gasped and released us for a moment, but grabbed hold again.

A heavy pounding rang through my head like the tolling bell of a condemned man. Images flashed past my eyes. Willow laughing. Tom on a park bench feeding pigeons. The portal, the asylum. Mountains in another world…

A gift for you! My other clamped both hands on Osbert's warty wrist. His bones snapped, and the ogre released me and staggered back. I broke the water, gasping for air. My lungs burned and a heavy ache stole through my chest as I watched my other turn back to Osbert.

The ogre was gripping his wrist, his face filled with agony. As he snarled, I caught a glimpse of the scorched and blackened flesh on his arm.

My other tore open my sodden coat and reached for my sword. *No!* I put everything I had in trying to wrestle his consciousness back from the forefront.

Finish him! he growled, his words laced with fury.

There was no time to finish Osbert off. I had to get out of there fast. If the ogre had found me, other agents could be close behind. I stumbled into the woods, my coat sopping wet as I reached for a crystal that wasn't there. All I had was my sword and the apple in my coat pocket.

Another roar of fury echoed off the trees. "I'll find you, Rook!" Osbert cried. "I always find what I'm looking for. Always! And when I get my hands on you, I'll choke you with your own guts. You hurt me, you fucking prick!" He sounded as upset and distressed as he was angry. As if I'd betrayed him and irrevocably damaged our *friendship.* Not that his tracking me down and trying to kill me wouldn't have done that already.

I ran, my clothes weighty and sodden as I tore through the ferns and brambles with Osbert crashing through the brush behind me. He was a good tracker, one of our best but he was wounded and he seemed as disoriented as I was as he stumbled and veered off into the forest.

A flash of light glowed in the trees ahead.

Someone else was here.

Ebomee? Rhymes? Humble?

I had to get out, and fast. I pulled the apple from my pocket and it lit up the gloom as I took a bite.

It was like no other fruit I'd ever tasted. My teeth pierced through the skin, sank into the apple's flesh and its heady flavors instantly overwhelmed me. Sweet, sour and crisp. Its juice ran down my chin and the world seemed to glow as every leaf and twig appeared in startling detail and absolute clarity.

I spotted Osbert thundering through the ferns, keeping pace a few feet to one side. Then a suited figure appeared to my left, its flashlight arcing through the night like the tail of a comet.

I took one more bite of the apple, knowing it was enough to push me over the edge and into the other realm. With that mouthful, a heavy lethargy stole over me and my eyelids turned leaden as I thrust the remains of the apple into my pocket. I had to sleep, the lights were going out and fast. I stopped and slid down a tree trunk, and my eyes fell shut of their own volition.

The world seemed to tremble and shake, and amid the tumult I felt myself shift from one reality to another, and I knew without a shadow of a doubt I'd left the blinkered realm behind.

21

I slept in-between odd, restless dreams. Dreams that seemed to know they were being dreamt in another world. Dreams of a stranger in an even stranger place. Dreams that were being shared by others. I heard conscious cold whispers, as if hidden observers were privy to my most naive vulnerabilities and discussed them from the shadows. From time to time there were sharp fits of laughter as well as deadening silences.

When I woke my back was still against a tree, but the forest was gone and in its place was a meadow of blindingly green grass. Ahead the land dropped off under an expanse of sky as deep blue as a sapphire. I squinted against the glare of the sun, which was as huge and as golden as honey. But it was an unfamiliar light, one that had never guided me or shone upon on the place I'd left behind. Or indeed any place I'd ever been.

I forced myself to my feet amid the carpet of crunchy acorns at the base of an ancient oak tree.

"On your way!" A small irritable voice blurted out.

I turned left then right. There was no one around... then I glanced up into the lush leafy boughs to find a long fuzzy face spying from the foliage. Its two nut-brown eyes blinked rapidly and then with an angry whisper, followed by a rustle, the watcher vanished into the canopy.

The meadow that stood behind the tree stretched for miles and I could see hills in the distance and a colossal stone tower. But I turned back toward the fallow field that I'd faced when I woke and headed for the wide pebbled path of chalky stone and flint that ran along its far side. The track wound by the edge of a sheer cliff that overlooked a vast sparkling azure sea. Its intense vibrancy was stunning, almost hypnotic and I watched as immense grey and black dolphin-like creatures broke through the surface and frolicked in the waves. The spray tossed up by their enormous tails fell like thousands of silver coins.

"What are you mooning at?" asked a dry, raspy voice.

I turned to find an old man standing on the track behind me. And then I realized it was actually a painfully thin old woman in faded brown rags. She had a long white beard and her eyes were outlined in heavy smudged black makeup. Her clothes appeared to be stitched together from offcuts and the pieces all came together in a crazy mishmash of shapes, textures and weaves. Then a piebald horse with an ancient leather pack wandered up behind her and peered over her shoulder. The animal looked about ready to stagger into a glue factory and give itself up and it eyed me suspiciously before letting out a low, mocking snort.

"Care to buy some beans?" the old lady asked as she opened her palm and nodded for me to approach. Ten tiny orange beans glowed like wet jewels as they wriggled and danced in her grimy withered hand. "They're special."

"You telling me they're magic beans?"

"Oh, it does talk, Gerald," she said to the horse. "I told you it would."

"Doesn't he just," the horse said, his voice as weary as his eyes.

"Well, young fellow, would you consider them magic if they stopped a fool traveling through these parts from starving. Some might consider that a miracle. Others might consider it a curse." Her voice was laced with the sharp cruelty I often found in the lonely and friendless.

"Thanks, I think I'll pass," I said.

The woman stroked her beard and looked me up and down. "You're new to this place, aren't you?"

"I woke up here. Just now. Below that…" I was about to say tree, when I glanced back and spotted it shuffling off into the distance.

"Tricked were you?" the woman asked. "Did they promise you a hill of gold? Swap your child for a changeling? Or did they tempt you with the most perfectly marvelous fruit?"

"Yeah, an apple. But I knew what it was meant to do." My words seemed to take the wind out of her sails and she looked almost disappointed.

"I came from your world, not that I remember it much. T'was long long ago, centuries I expect." Her eyes flitted over me, sizing me up once more. She licked her lips, a fast, habitual gesture. "They tricked me, trapped me here, and then they cursed me with this." She pointed to her beard. "Watch yourself with the folk 'round here, they can be cruel. Crueler than our kind."

"I'll be on my guard." *Starting with you.* I glanced below my coat. My holster was empty and my bag of tricks was long gone, but I still had my sword. If it came to it. "I'm looking for someone-"

"Robble Heatherby?" she asked, her eyes eager. "He needs putting down, so he does. Or is it Catty Mopsnide? Dried up sniveling bitch. You lookin' to exact some revenge, are you?

You have the air of an assassin. There's murder and vengeance in those eyes of yours. That's what I see, and so I'm telling you."

"I'm looking for Erland Underwood. Do you know him?"

Her shoulders sank then she sighed and nodded. "I know him. He was rushed to the village a few days back. Bleeding like a stuck pig he was. Caught the attention of some very dark folk, he did." Her gaze danced over me. Whatever she was planning wasn't going to be good.

"Can you tell me where I can find him?"

"Stick to the path. After eight or ten furlongs it'll take a dip. Woooossshhh!" Her eyes twinkled as she made a sweeping motion with her hand. "Keep on going, 'cause you ain't there yet. You'll have to take a short jaunt through the woods but you'll come out the other side as fresh as a summer daisy. Then you'll see Kebbermadoo."

"That's the village, Kebbermadoo?" I asked. I guessed anything was possible in this place.

"Well, that's what we'll be having to call it. You couldn't expect me to give a stranger its true name! Ha, that'd be far too valuable a commodity. Names have-"

"Power, I know. I wasn't born yesterday." I snapped. I hadn't meant to be so direct, but I didn't like the way she was looking at me, it was unsettling, as if I was a goose on its way to market. She held her hand out, palm up and the beans were gone. "What?" I asked.

"I gave you something, now you give me something."

"What did you give me?"

"The way." She sneered. "Knowledge don't come free."

I sighed and rooted through my pocket. My wallet was still there, and it was only as I pulled it out that I realized that both it and my clothes were somehow bone dry. I grabbed a few crumpled dollar bills and handed them to her. She held them before the sun and peered through them. "These pictures aren't very pretty," she said, "and I don't like this starey eye pyramid." She wrinkled her nose and threw the money down. "Nope, not one bit. It's looking at me, and I don't like being watched."

I stooped down, picked the money up and put it back into my wallet. "Well it's all I've got, and frankly I don't know that your directions are worth a single cent."

"If you ain't got no gold, how's about a drop of blood." She licked her lips again. "I'll take anything I can get." She moved in closer. Too close.

"Back off."

She held her hand up and nodded. "No need to get all hot and bothered. I'll be on my way and you can get back to your mooning, right?"

"Right," I said as she grabbed the horse's reins and began to tug it back along the path in the direction she'd come from. She turned and glanced over her shoulder, her eyes darting over me one final time before she continued on her way.

I proceeded along the dusty chalk path. The distant splashes from the ocean wafted up as the leviathans leaped from the waters, and the rolling waves hit the rocky shore below. This entire place or world, or whatever it was, was so oddly off kilter, and I had the sense there was much more going on around me than I could see.

Finally the path rounded over the hill, revealing a sweeping view of the forested valley below. The bulk of the trees were oak and ash, but there were many I had no names for. The strangest were tall, spindly things and I watched their branches twist and bow, despite the lack of breeze.

I followed the track to where it plunged down the hill. It was steep, and I had to steady myself through a skid or two, but it wasn't quite the rollercoaster I'd been expecting from the old woman's description. Then again, she'd obviously been dwelling beyond the boundaries of sanity.

The foliage on the spindly trees rustled and whispered as I entered the valley, and the sun vanished behind the canopy. Then a strange, unsettling feeling crept through me and I gripped the pommel of my sword. There was something wrong, something I didn't like. I glanced back to check the path behind, it was empty and yet I felt eyes on me.

Lots and lots of eyes.

"Oh for fuck's sake!" I leaped as a fat brown spider the size of a rat scuttled from the brush, stood on the side of the trail and regarded me with beady black eyes. Then it opened its mouth and howled like a wolf.

Six more raced from the tree line and joined their leader, each regarding me closely, with their fat furry legs tensing to pounce.

I hurried on, abandoning the path and giving the spiders wide a berth, never once taking my eyes off them as I passed.

Snap

I looked down as something snagged my ankle, but before I could focus, I found myself thrown onto my back then, with a jerk of my foot I was yanked into the air.

A twisted hemp-like rope tethered me to the thick, heavy bough above. I tried to pull myself up but the branch was too high. I let myself fall back and watched as the seven spiders formed a circle below and howled at me like I was the harvest moon.

Then they turned back as the bushes behind them rustled violently and moments later the old woman emerged, her piebald horse beside her. She glanced up. "Fancy seeing you there!" she said, her voice smug and gloating. She curtsied and lifted the hem of her dress. "Come home my darlings," she said. The spiders yipped as they scampered across the grass and vanished under the folds of her skirt.

I shuddered, despite my rising fury. "Get me down. Now!"

"I only asked for something sparkly or a drop or two of blood, but the tide seems to have turned so I'll think I'll have to settle for more now. A lot more." She patted the horse's manky head. "His shiny eyes are earmarked for you, Gerald. They'll taste like chocolate and lice. I saw that when I first looked into them."

"You're rarely wrong when it comes to their eyes," the horse said, and ran his tongue across his long crooked teeth in imitation of his owner.

"Let me down," I said, "or I'll hurt you." Blood pounded in my head and I began to feel nauseous. I swung myself up, grabbed the rough hemp and peered back down. "Do it now."

"No, no, no," the woman said. "Does a poacher chase away the rabbit he's snared? Does the fisherman throw his wriggly fishes back into the treacherous sea? Does a-"

"I get the picture," I said. "But if you don't turn me loose, this fishy is going to snap through the line and hurt you just as I promised."

"I heard your threats, silly man." She began to root through the packs strapped to her weary horse. "Now where did I put it? Ouch!" she withdrew her hand and put a finger in her mouth, before giggling. "Well I only went and found it, so I did!" Slowly, she reached back into the pouch and withdrew an impossibly long silver pike, its tip caked in old, dried blood. "Now, din dins!"

22

The fall to the ground was at least ten feet. It was going to hurt. But so was the pike the crazy old bitch was jabbing into the air as she licked her lips and sang to herself, her words gibberish as far as I could tell.

I swung up, grabbed the rope with one hand, and unclasped the sword of intention with the other. And then I took a swing. The sword bit into the rope, but not enough.

"No!' the woman yelled, "that's not fair. I thought you were unarmed!"

"Seems you were wrong." I swung the sword a second time. It thudded into the rope and frayed it slightly before glancing off.

"Stop!" the woman cried. "That's my property!"

I glanced down to find her leaping into the air trying to skewer me with her pike as she cried, "That rope cost me three back teeth!"

"Cut!" I commanded. The sword blazed and bit through the rope as I swung. I dropped the sword and threw my hands up to grab the end of the severed hemp and hung there for a moment.

"Well, this is pretty!" the old lady said as she approached the sword. The tip had planted into the soil but its blade still glowed with fire as it stood proudly in the swaying grass.

I let go of the rope, fell, and landed hard. Pain shot through my ankles and white light flashed before my eyes. "Damn it!" I hobbled toward the lunatic woman. She turned my way and drew her lips back over her teeth, baring the few she had left.

And then she came at me, the tip of her pike gleaming as she thrust it at my chest. I dove aside, watched her sail past and forced myself to my feet, gritting my teeth against the pain, as I limped across the grass. Plucking the sword from the soft soil I whirled round just in time to parry her next attack. I stepped in past her and delivered an almighty slap to the side of her bearded face. She dropped her pike and began to cry.

"Stop that," I said. It was a horrible, pathetic sound, and I'd had enough of her madness.

"I... I... jus... just wanted a bite to eat. I... I... I'm so hungry!"

"Then catch something easier. Like a rabbit. They don't tend to be armed."

"The ones round here are. Vicious bastard creatures!"

"Put your pike away."

She nodded like a chastised child and slipped it back into her horse's pack. It vanished, into the short saddle bag as if she'd been dropping it down a well.

"You've got magic," I said, "why don't you use it to catch game?"

"Magic ain't no advantage here, this whole place is riddled with it," she said sullenly. "And everyone and everything's got a lot more of it than I do. I'm an interloper. Even though I've been in this wretched place for almost as long as I can remember."

"What about nuts and berries?"

"I'm sick of pissing berries!"

"And I'm sick of people trying to skewer me," I said, as I cut the snare from my ankle.

"Can I go now?" the woman asked. "Not to be rude, but if I can't eat you, or quench my thirst with a drop of blood then it's time to move on."

"Yeah, you're free to go." I aimed the tip of my sword at her scrawny chest. "But first you're going to take me to the village."

"I imagine there's no swaying you?"

"Your imagination's correct. Now lead on."

She sighed and nodded to her horse. "Come on, Gerald."

"Very well," Gerald said, his weary sigh even louder than hers. "On we trot. Why, I couldn't say."

I followed as the old woman led the way through the trees that continued to whisper and conspire around us.

We passed bizarre creatures along the path. A young girl with feathered wings and a perfectly blank face skipped by and flashed the diamond colored eyes embedded in her knees. And as we neared a crossroads we saw a huge hairless sphinx-like cat with warty flesh and a wide-brimmed hat. It winked at me before slinking off into the trees, singing a mournful refrain as it went.

"Stop gawking and dawdling!" the old woman hissed and shook her head. "You're aiming to get to the village and I'm anxious to be rid of you. Faster we walk, the sooner we both get our heart's desires."

Finally the trees thinned and gave way to a field of lush green grass and trembling bluebells. Beyond it was an old stone-walled village with tall, higgedly-piggedly stone houses and squat thatched cottages.

"Kebbermadoo!" the old lady said, and gave me an elaborate, sarcastic curtsy. I glanced up as two women appeared on horseback. They were beautiful, their eyes as vivid and deep as the flowers woven through their hair, but they seemed as cruel as they were beguiling.

"Good afternoon, Moonmade Sal!" one said to the old woman.

"Still dragging vermin into town, are we?" the other said as her eyes glinted from Sal to me.

"Don't call me that," she cried. "I'm not moonmade. I'm just Sal."

"Okay then, *just Sal*. We'll leave you and your... *man* to whatever grim pursuits you've arranged." The faerie gave the reins an irritable flick, and they cantered off toward the large wooden gate leading to the village.

"Bitchy bitchy foul old faes!" Sal growled.

"Yeah, they weren't very friendly" I agreed. "Are most faeries like that?"

"No, just the ones in these parts." Sal sighed, and when she looked at me again it was like she'd swallowed a fly. "Anyway, there's the pissing village. Go find your master and leave me in peace so I can find a way to fill my belly."

"Which house?" I asked. The village wasn't big but there must have been at least a fifty or sixty buildings.

"The one without windows," Sal said. "Dead or alive, that's where you'll find him. And by now it could be either."

23

I passed through the village gates, feeling more out of place than I could remember. And that was saying something.

For the most part the fae ignored me. They went about their business mending houses or gossiping by the well just like their blinkered counterparts at office water coolers, and I noticed others trading goats, cows and all manner of exotic beasts. But occasionally one would meet my gaze and give me the same withering looks as the faes we'd encountered near the field. As I continued my search I hurried past a shop selling roasted meat and golden brown pies. They filled the air with succulent promise and I considered *procuring* a couple for poor Moonmade Sal, but she'd long gone.

Finally, I stumbled upon a quiet lane of houses and shops that hawked all manner of unearthly items. It was there that a tall wide building with a low sloping gabled roof and an utter absence of windows drew me like a magnet to its threshold. The wooden door was painted an ominous shade of green and gilded with silver leaf glyphs and symbols that glimmered like stardust.

I reached for the knocker but hesitated as I felt energy thrumming before it. It was almost like it was aware and listening. The glyphs on the door began to merge, forming fearsome shapes; basilisks, manticores, dragons. Each of them hissed and growled until I stepped away.

"And what exactly are you supposed to be?" a voice demanded. "And what does a something like you want inside my temple?"

I turned to find a tall, severe looking faerie standing beside me. He wore simple brown robes and his orange eyes narrowed below his curled white hair. "Well?" he demanded, his tiny pinprick pupils dancing furiously.

"I'm looking for Erland Underwood."

"I'm sure you are," the faerie said. "But is he looking for you?"

"Yes. He sent for me."

The fae scrutinized me for a moment before giving a slight nod. "Come," he said. He strode to the door and held his hand up. The glyph creatures began to relax, their silver edges slowly morphing back into shiny symbols. "It's fortunate you didn't touch the door," he said, "for your hand would have liquefied into a stump if you had." He nodded to the ground where there were a number of fat, pale yellowed stains. "So you must own a sliver of sense within that brutish skull."

"I do own sense," I said, "but I'm better known for my incredible lack of patience. Especially when it comes to strangers patronizing me."

He gave a curdled smile. "I know all about your kind and their apish pride. But if you ever threaten me within the shadow of these walls again, you'll learn all about the sharp pride of a fae. It runs deep, and when unleashed, it brings all before it to their knees. So let us agree to be civil."

I nodded. It seemed like the best idea.

"Very good." He opened the door, and ushered me inside.

The shadowy chamber was lit with a few flickering candles and my hand strayed to my sword as a long, low agonizing scream issued from the gloom.

"If you touch that weapon I'll remove it from your person and melt it down for the rag and miscellany collectors," the fae said as he closed the door. Then a row of fresh candles burst to life on a plinth behind him, dowsing him in eerie light. "The screams you heard are from a man who came to be healed. It's what we do here, we heal." His gaze flitted over mine. "We draw out pain. And demons. You're a man who knows all about demons, are you not?"

I remained silent.

"As you please."

"Where's Erland?" I asked.

"This way."

I followed him along a corridor and, as we walked, the screams grew louder. I glanced through an open door to find a huge man lying naked upon a stone slab. Three tiny robed and hooded figures surrounded him. They were small, like children, but the hands that reached out from their robes were bony, withered things. One turned my way, but I hurried on, keen to remain ignorant to whatever lurked below its cowl-like hood.

"Down you go," the fae said, sweeping his hand toward an open door and a flight of stairs. I nodded to him and descended into smoke-scented air. The wide chamber below was filled with shadows so deep I couldn't see any surrounding walls. In fact, I couldn't see much at all. The place seemed empty but for a burgundy velvet wingback chair and the crackling fireplace with an ornate mantelpiece carved entirely from bone.

Erland sat in the chair, his strawberry blonde hair draped

over the shoulders of the simple muslin robe he wore. He leaned forward and tossed a handful of blue flowers into the fire. As they fell, the fire crackled and spat and the flames burned a deep shade of midnight blue. "Thank you for coming, Morgan."

"It's been my pleasure," I said, regretting the sarcasm. He looked terrible. His skin was the color of rancid milk, the veins on the side of his face as blue and livid as his eyes were bloody red. "What happened?"

He waved a hand, and a chair moved in from the shadows, pushed by one of the tiny, hooded creatures I'd spotted upstairs. Whatever the thing was, it wasn't fae. As it came forward its shiny snakelike flesh shimmered in the glow of the flames and I caught sight of a pair of slitted eyes. I waited until it returned to the shadows before taking my seat.

"Tell me your news," Erland said. "And then I'll share mine." There was still a touch of lilac in his eyes as they flitted over mine, but mostly they looked waxen.

As I gazed into the fire, a clamor of thoughts and emotions flooded through me. I'd always trusted Erland, for the most part, and yet I'd held things back. But now...

"I'm aware of far more than you think, Morgan. This is not the time for holding your cards close to your chest." He folded back his robe, revealing a long, garish red scar. "Things have gotten about as deadly as they can get."

"What about the..." I nodded to the wall of darkness beyond the fire.

"She won't hear us. We're of little interest to them, outside of our agonies, which are what nourishes them." He gave a pained smile. "But we have a purely symbiotic relationship, these days. Now, tell me the whole story, everything from the first moment you encountered Stroud to now."

I watched as he tossed a flower from the bowl at his side

into the fire, and as the crackle of vivid blue flames erupted I considered my options. What to tell. What to hold back.

And then I felt his gaze as he observed me like a scientist analyzing some new, unexpected strain of insect. "The truth, Morgan. The whole truth, and nothing but the truth."

24

I nodded. I couldn't see any benefit in holding back, not at this point. Either we were on the same side or we weren't. He was offering help and our resources were running thin. If Erland turned out to be an enemy, then he'd be dealt with as one, even though the idea of fulfilling that obligation was almost impossible for me to contemplate.

So I started at the beginning, from the hexling's first victim to our confrontation with Kitty Frostup.

"Franklin Lampton?" Erland steepled his fingers as he gazed into the flames. "Why am I not surprised? I take it the knight who betrayed his order…"

"Prentice Sykes," I said, recalling Hellwyn and Tom's old partner.

"Yes, Sykes. He was the one who persuaded Lampton to open a portal between the asylum and Penrythe."

"I believe so."

"And then you destroyed it." He glanced my way. "Or should I say, your other destroyed it."

"He's me, and I'm him." I could see the calculations going

through Erland's mind. Two assets for the price of one. "We might be different, but we're inseparable."

"Maybe. Maybe not. Just ask our friend in the shadows." His red-rimmed eyes flitted to the gloom. "But that's for another time. Right now, we need to find a way to prevent Endersley from accomplishing his master's goal. Hmm, the wholesale annihilation of both the blinkered and magical communities, no small feat then."

"Do you have any contacts that could lead us to Endersley?"

Erland shook his head. "No. But your instinct to go after Franklin Lampton is right on point. Most likely he's involved in Stroud's plans. Or is at least privy to them, seeings as he's the man that made Stroud's manifestation here possible in the first place."

"Okay," I said. "But even if I locate Stroud I can't do anything to stop him. He's a shade. A ghost…"

"That's why I brought you here."

"I thought you were dying and needed my help."

"I don't need your help in that department, Dr. Morgan." Erland smiled. "But I appreciate the offer." He glanced to his chest, and the scar hidden below the robe.

"What happened?"

"Someone tried to kill me. Actually, no, not a someone. *Someones*. First, they poisoned my wine, but thankfully I know a bad vintage when I smell one. Then they tried to shoot me and came very close to succeeding. When that failed a third assassin ambushed me and stuck me with a cursed blade." He winced at the memory. "It hurt like hell, but it could have been so much worse."

"Did you see the assailants?"

"No. Fortunately, or unfortunately depending how you look at it. Anyway my…instincts kicked in pretty fast and there wasn't much left of the third assailant, just blood and shredded flesh. But they're just pawns and therefore irrelevant, what matters is who sent them. And I'll be damned if it wasn't Franklin Lampton's pompous grandson. Damned even more than I already am."

"We need to take the Lamptons down."

"Yes. But we can't operate like that, Morgan, we need proof first, and allies. Lampton's well protected, which means we'll have to strip away his support. I'm working on that. The fae you just met, Aberfellow Hax, is a powerful healer but he's also a warrior and not someone to be trifled with by any measure. Aberfellow's very graciously granted me a week's stay in his sanctuary and the favor of his humble servants to draw out the last of the curse. It's enough time for me to heal and once I'm well enough, we'll travel across these lands, gather allies, and cross back to the blinkered realm to challenge their affronts. When we arrive, there will be blood." Fury seethed in his voice as he leaned forward in his chair. "Those who have colluded with Stroud, each and every last one of them, will pay dearly."

"And Stroud?" I asked. "How can we slay him?"

"There is always a way."

"Well, not to put a damper on things but my grasp on magic is beyond limited," I said. "As you probably intended."

"Exactly as I intended," Erland held my gaze. "I've been privy to your other since the moment you and I first met. I sensed his capacity for destruction, though he was little more than a lurking phantom back then, an unpleasant gleam in your eyes. It would have been wholly irresponsible for me to teach you how to wield magic in the blinkered realm. Him having access to that kind of power, unimaginable. And he… or you… were already well versed in magic, but it was a skill learned in another world, its methods and ways didn't fully translate within the blinkered one. Which, I believe, might have some bearing on why he was subdued for so long. In the meantime, we helped you develop the skills you needed in the sterling work you've done, but we drew a line. You've always been a good asset, Morgan, but I knew the day would come when you'd prove to be so much more. And here it is."

"And here I am, my magic hobbled while Stroud's mastered his. And as a shade, he's invulnerable."

"That's his power," Erland said. "Or so he thinks. But even a shade has weaknesses." He leaned in close. "There's a species in this realm with a claw capable of cutting through almost anything. We call them the mhudambe. The skintakers, for they walk amongst the living wearing the skins of the dead."

"Yeah," A memory returned to me. The poltergeist raging in Mrs. Fitz's cellar, and the creature tormenting him in the afterlife. Its claw had ripped through the poltergeist, mortally wounding his very soul. "I've seen one."

"Really?" Erland's brow furrowed. "I don't recall any reports of them in the blinkered world. I'm sure I'd remember..." he looked at me closely and then nodded. "Right. One of your private jobs."

"You..."

"Yes, I know about the moonlighting." He gave me a pained smile. "But I had no idea you'd tangled with a mhudambe. Interesting. I wouldn't have given them the credit for moving between realms, although it's possible someone brought it to the blinkered world. They make excellent bodyguards. They're vicious but compliant, as long as they're given the opportunity to be clothed in fresh skin."

"Nice," I said. "So, we capture a mhudambe and use its claw to kill Stroud?"

Erland's laugh became a wracking cough. "You could try,

but I don't think it would turn out so well. They only respect sadism and brutality, and while you've doled out more than your fair share of killings, you're no sadist." Erland tossed another flower onto the fire and inhaled the incense-like aroma. When he turned back to me, there was a little more color in his cheeks. "But funnily enough there's such an individual close by; Talamos Gin, a merchant of sorts. He lives not six miles from this town, close enough for the villagers to feel his shadow."

"Do you want me to knock on his door and see if I can borrow one of these creatures?"

"No. I want you to kill him and steal his dagger."

"Dagger?"

"The mhudambe shed their claws once every seven years. Gin collects them and uses a unique form of dark magic to render them down and make weapons. Weapons he then sells for exorbitant sums of gold."

"Why can't I just take the dagger? Why do you want me to kill him?"

"Because he defiled a young fae from this village, and when her father went to reckon with him, Gin and his creatures slaughtered him. One appeared outside the village gates wearing the fae father's skin and performed a sick sort of a victory lap, before returning to whatever stone it crawled out from." Erland scowled. "And that's why I want you to kill him."

"And here was I thinking Faerie was a place of-"

"Whimsy?" Erland asked. "Magic? There are wonders here to be sure, but there's also just as much evil and conniving as there is in the blinkered realm. More perhaps, this world is so much older, after all. But I digress." He stood, reached into the pocket of his robe and handed me a long curved fang suspended from a heavy silver chain.

"What's that?"

"A charm. A powerful one. It's been helping me to heal, but I can get another. Take it and use the magic within it to do what you must."

A mission in Faerie. It wasn't what I'd been expecting but if it meant finding a means to defeat Stroud then anything was worth considering.

"Here." Erland passed me a small black pill.

"What's this?"

"A one way ticket to an untimely death. Swallow that and you'll be dead within moments."

"And why would I want to do that?"

"Your death will be drawn out and agonizing if you're captured," Erland said. "Gin's known for making his enemies talk, and by the most brutal means. This action you're about to take cannot be traced back to me or the village. Because if it is, Gin will raze the place to the ground."

"Right." I slipped the pill into my pocket and suppressed a shiver.

"Now, you said you've already encountered a mhudambe. Did you vanquish it?"

"Kind of. A speeding SUV sort of stole the glory."

Erland gave me a wan smile. "They're as vicious as their claws are deadly, but they're vulnerable if hit hard enough." He pointed to his solar plexus. "That's their weak spot. Hit them with enough force and they'll be reduced to smoke and dust. But it's easier said than done. Fire will work just as well, if you have it at hand."

"Good to know, thanks." I stood and as my finger brushed the fang on the chain, my entire hand bristled with energy.

"I trust you Morgan," Erland said. "You always get the job done, but stay alert. And don't let your other cloud you. You won't be the first assassin to creep into Gin's dwelling this past week."

"What happened to the first one?" I asked, even though I was pretty sure I knew the answer.

"She didn't make it," Erland said. "She died. Horribly."

25

I sat with Erland before I headed out. We spoke about the past and the future, and we waited for twilight, which seemed to be more in line with the right time for someone setting out to rob and murder.

We had no windows or clock to mark the hours but Erland said the moment would be apparent enough and that he'd smell the rising moon. I had no reason to doubt him.

I sipped a strange soothing herbal tea that dulled my aches and pains, and when that was gone he rang a little silver bell. The servant lurking in the shadows shuffled out of the chamber and soon returned with a tray of roasted meats and succulent cheeses that were as tempting as the faerie feasts of legend. Erland assured me it was safe for me to eat, and when the time came he leaned back in his chair, stared into the flames and wished me well as I left.

Most of the villagers had settled along with the fading evening sun, but a few fae folk still meandered in the lamplight, their faces just as disapproving as the ones that had first set eyes on me. But now, I understood their concern. Their village was under threat. They had no idea if their neighbors were the same people they'd known all their lives, or a marauding mhudambe skulking in a stolen skin, so they were not about to befriend some odd stranger.

I followed Erland's instructions and took the chalky trail that wound past the village and cut through the golden fields of wheat.

The further I went, the darker it grew. Soon the birds stopped singing but I could still see their watchful moonlit eyes peering down from the branches. Then they all vanished at once, as dozens of cawing magpies and ravens took to the air and a trio of riders cantered by on fine horses. They stared down at me with a disdain that verged on outright hostility but I just smiled and nodded to them, eager for them to pass without incident.

The landscape began to change, the scrub-like trees grew smaller and thornier, and somber clouds gathered on the horizon, blotting out the moon and the scattered stars surrounding it.

Soon I found myself nearing a low marsh with bent, withered oak trees sprouting from the shoreline of its sinister waters. In the distance, beyond the reeds and mudflats was a tall house. It almost looked like a church with its high, broad steeple-like chimney and sharp, gabled roofline, but red and orange light filled its windows, and it flickered like hellfire.

I took the narrow twisting path across the marsh. It was still too early for what I had planned, so I hunkered down on a mossy rock and watched and waited. Thoughts of Astrid and Samuel crept into my mind. I wondered what they might be doing while I was stuck in this strange, haunting place. I'd heard so often that time in Faerie passed differently than time in the blinkered world, and now I wished I'd paid more attention to the discrepancies. I could be hours, minute or moments ahead, or behind them. Or maybe the gulf was already stretching out into weeks but hopefully it was nothing so drastic.

"Methinks I smell a man indulging in hope," a voice said.

I glanced around but there was no one there.

"Down here!"

"Right, it's a toad," I said as I saw the creature sitting in the dirt between my feet. "Makes sense. I already met a talking horse."

"Who do you think you are, calling me a toad?" it sputtered.

"You've got all the features of a toad, as far as I'm aware."

"Which probably isn't very far," it mumbled and gave a long depressed sigh.

I actually couldn't blame it for wanting to be something else. As toads went, it was one ugly-

"How's about a wish?" it asked, interrupting my thoughts.

"A wish?"

"That's what I said. Give me something to eat, a wee fly or spider would do, and in return I'll grant you a wish."

"I don't have any flies on me. Although I know a man who does." I replied as I peered out over the reeds.

"How's about a little toe then?" The toad asked as it knocked on my boot. "If you haven't got one to spare I'd take a scrap of gristle. Doesn't have to be from anywhere valuable."

"I'm sorry, it's a tempting offer, but right now I can't even think of what I'd wish for," I said as I eyed the glowing red reflection of the windows in the marsh. "And it's almost time for me to go."

26

I dismissed the toad with a curt farewell and trudged through the shadows of the twisted trees that stretched across the foul sodden ground. As the path neared the rushes, it narrowed and I was forced to walk through a patch of marsh to rejoin it on the other side. The water was shockingly cold, then the sensation of fingers wrapping around my ankle sent a panicked charge through me. They tugged and pulled; trying to drag me down and I grabbed the sword of intention and plunged it into the water. The blade hissed as it struck something soft and malleable. Moments later a scream rose up from the swamp and bubbles broke upon its surface, bringing a god awful stench. I pulled my foot out, wrenched the sword free, and caught my breath. I knew exactly what I'd have said if that toad was to ask me about wishes again. but it was long gone.

The structure of the house became clearer to me the closer I got. It was more like a broad stone tower, and it had more arched windows than I'd first spotted. Firelight, from the bonfire burning in the yard, flickered in the leaded glass panes.

I took cover, crouching behind trees as I drew nearer, and cursed, not for the first time, that I had lost my bag and gun.

I was almost at the edge of the yard when I felt it. Contact. The proximity of someone, or *something*. The air fizzled and I slowly glanced up as a creature appeared on the small rise above me. I caught a glimpse of its dark green, mantis-like shape, and thick heavy thorax.

The mhudambe.

It was long and lean and its eyes blazed as it spat out a series of strange, clipped sounds. Then, quick as a flash, it lashed a hand toward me and a single silver, pearlescent claw sliced the air before my face. I leapt back and pulled my sword as the creature twitched forward with a dry rustle of limbs and snapping mandibles.

I blocked the next swipe with my sword and threw a punch that landed squarely on its hard angular face. The creature's enormous eyes blinked as it thrust its head forward and tried to take a bite out of me. I drew back, mindful of its deadly claw as it swept toward me, slashing the air perilously close to my throat.

The mhudambe spat alien words as it prowled, its eyes unblinking and fixed on me.

I took a step back, steadied myself against the tree behind me, and waited for it to strike.

The mhudambe hacked up a rattling din from its throat and leaped. I watched its silver claw plunge toward me and dodged, turning to watch it sink into the hard woody trunk like a diver slipping through the surface of a pool.

Before the creature could yank its claw free I swung the sword. The blade found more resistance than usual and I had to pour my intention into it in order to lop off the creature's arm. Smoke gushed from the wound and its eyes narrowed to fiery points. As it pounced I thrust the sword into its thorax. "End!" I cried.

I watched the creature totter and twist before vanishing into wisps and curls of smoke that carried a heavy reek of sulfur.

It took a moment for me to catch my breath and slow my hammering pulse. I searched for the mhudambe's gleaming claw but it had dissipated along with the rest of the creature so I turned and headed across the yard.

As I neared the house I spotted a figure standing beside a tree.

A fae?

Its silhouette was tall and I could see the side of its face as it stared up at the sky, its lips quietly moving. Then I saw the stitches along its jawline and down the side of its neck. Another mhudambe, this one wearing a fae's flesh. The back of one of its hands had a tear and I could see its slick chitin and the gleam of a single shiny claw. I grabbed the fang charm Erland had given me and gasped as its magic flooded through me. I moved in a slow circle so I could get behind the mhudambe. I was nearing my position, and about to strike when it snapped its head my way and its eyes blazed through its fleshy mask.

Before I could act it leaped and hit me full on, shoving me down to the dirt.

It raised its fist to impale me with its claw. I rolled to the side. It struck the ground and sank in deep. The mhudambe wrenched it free and as it raised it again I grabbed its wrist and twisted, enjoying the savage snapping sound it produced.

The mhudambe roared and seized my throat with its other hand and squeezed hard. I clutched at it with both hands and tried to pry it away but it bore down on me, its eyes blazing through the slits in its fae mask.

You seem to need help, my other chided. Again

I struggled, trying to wrench off the mhudambe's hand but I was locked in its grip. The creature expelled a dry, harsh sound and held me tighter.

Move aside.

I had no idea how his powers might manifest in this otherworld. Or if I could wrestle back control when all was said and done.

My heaving chest felt as if it were on fire as the creature continued to squeeze, and my lungs were riddled with tingling pain. I was on the verge of blacking out when I let my consciousness drift aside so my other could step in.

Finally

I watched as he forced my head further back against the ground, soaking up the magic fizzling through the marshy soil. It flooded through us like a wave.

How could you not use this? It's everywhere. The split second the energy reached my fingertips he seized the creature's hand, squeezing hard, using the dark magic to sear clean through the fae's skin to the mhudambe below. The reek of charred flesh was nauseating. The creature's head twitched as it leaped off, clenching its smoldering hand under its arm.

I haven't finished, my other announced as my fist slammed into the creature's borrowed face, sending it stumbling back into the marsh. Then he raised my sword and plunged it through the mhudambe's skull, driving it into the ground. A terrible death rattle issued from the creature's mouth as it flailed in the mud, pinned down by the blade.

He laughed as he brought my boot down on its throat, crushing its neck with a single blow, and slowly it came apart as smoke.

There. His voice was loud, commanding. And this is not the first time I've ensured our survival. Maybe it's time for you to concede.

The fact he hadn't simply taken control over our mind implied that he couldn't. "Get back in your box," I said as I shoved him aside.

There's gratitude. I wonder what'll happen next time you need me. He vanished, and only then did I take a deep breath.

I continued on, hugging the tree line as I approached the house again. Bitter smoke filled the air and the crackle of the unfamiliar magic toyed with my senses.

To my horror seven more mhudambe had emerged. They were prowling toward the fire where three lifeless bodies had been laid out in the flickering light like offerings. Two were fae and one human; a scrawny, bearded man. The mhudambe hunkered around him and began prodding his flesh. Then one sniffed him, its actions almost innocent until it began to knead the cadaver like it was tenderizing a cut of beef.

I grabbed the fang charm from my pocket and clutched it. Its power thrummed through my fingers and into my veins, then to my very cells. *Make me unseen,* I commanded, *hide me from the mhudambe.* I glanced down, half expecting to see the results, but my mud caked jeans were still there as plain as day. I had no idea if my spell was flawed or if my own eyes had simply remained unaffected.

"There's only one way to find out." I whispered then took a deep breath, clasped the pommel of my sword and broke from the trees, walking softly past the mhudambe as they began to feast.

27

The mhudambe were distracted with their gory meal as I slipped past. I did my best to ignore the snapping and tearing as I fixed my gaze on the house and the long wooden spikes jutting out along its wall. Several of them had been topped with a severed fae's head and I was certain that at least some of them in this gruesome display were the assassins Erland had mentioned that had failed to dispatch Gin. Which meant I had to stay sharp or I might just be joining them.

I looked myself over. I still seemed perfectly visible in my filthy jeans, caked boots and muddy coat. Then I glanced at the mhudambe as they shifted from the first corpse, now little more than a pile of bloody bones, to the next. None of them looked my way as I backed toward the tower's threshold. I counted it as evidence that Erland's charm had worked.

Holding out one hand, I waved my palm over the stout oak planks and banded metal that made up Gin's front door, searching for curses or traps. It wasn't rigged and seemed oddly safe but given his reputation as well as the monsters surrounding the place, I could see reason in why he hadn't gone to the trouble of hexing it.

As I stepped inside the medieval scent of damask roses wafted through the air, a welcome mask to the sulfurous stench of the mhudambe. The clean, warm hall was not what I'd been expecting. It was painted wine red with one wall covered in garish paintings in gilded frames and the other lined with glass curio cabinets. Many of the shelves were lined with skulls, featured prominently as if they were trophies. Most must have been fae, or possibly human, but there were others that were clearly neither.

I searched the rooms one by one, but there was no sign of Gin or the dagger, just more spoils, artifacts, and an abundance of bound leather books.

I stole back to the stairs and crept up them like a thief, testing each before putting my full weight down. My heart raced and adrenaline coursed through me, taking the edge off of the magical buzz I'd gotten from the fang charm.

There was only one large chamber to search on the second floor. The tables lining the hallway that led to its entrance held large bowls of rose petals. They glowed soft and pink in the flickering candlelight but their scent wasn't strong enough to disguise the sulfurous odor that lingered there.

I reached out, opened the door and peered into the fetid room. The space beyond was festooned from floor to ceiling with large silken cocoons. Some were as much as half my height, some slightly smaller and their yellowed webbing glistened like candy floss in the flickering light of the stout tallow candles.

As I made my way into the room to search for the dagger, my boots became entangled in thick fibrous strands. I yanked them free, almost losing my footing in the process. The webs were everywhere; they stretched across the floor and up the walls. The twisted filaments even hung down from the rafters enveloping the chandelier.

I held the sleeve of my coat over my nose and mouth as the sulfur grew stronger and jolted as I saw a form swaddled within the gauzy fabric watching me. No, not watching. Staring sightlessly. She looked like a woman carved from wood, a woman petrified. In the center of her swollen stomach was a gaping hole, the place the larval mhudambe had spilled from before spinning their pods and awaiting their metamorphosis.

The far side of the room yielded nothing of interest, no cabinets, no gleaming magical dagger, just more webs and a pungent reek that made my eyes water.

Something shifted beside me as I headed back across the room. I froze and glanced down to find two shining eyes peering through sheer strands of webbing. Its mandibles snapped open then a pair of small hands pressed against the cocoon and a long silver claw slipped through the strands and began tearing away the casing. I winced as I grabbed the sticky top of the creature's head with one hand and drew my sword across its throat with the other.

There was a brief, plaintive gurgling cry and then silence as the remains of the creature turned to wisps of nicotine brown smoke. Another creature mewled, and another. I rushed toward the hall as the pods began to tremble and shudder and dozens of tiny hands prodded and struggled against the webbing.

Leaping out of the nightmarish room, I slammed the door on their muffled cries, and prayed to whatever deity that might be watching over this world that the mhudambe out by the bonfire hadn't heard their younglings stir. So far I'd managed to slay them but that had been one on one and I was under no delusions as to what would happen if a mob of them attacked.

I climbed the stairs toward the top floor and glanced out the window on the short landing as I rounded the bend. The bright moonlight glimmered over the boggy marsh and the crooked trees that seemed to fidget and twitch.

The short hall at the top led to three doors. I glanced through the first to find a room with a large bed. Its thick wooden frame was stout and fitted in tethers. Whips, coshes and nightmarish implements hung on the walls and blood had stained the floorboards. *Lots* of blood.

A stab of cold hard fury shook me as Erland's tale of the village girl leaped through my mind. I had to close the door on the gruesome sight and calmly still my rage. It wouldn't do any good. I couldn't afford to lose control. Not here, not now.

I headed to the next chamber. A plush four poster bed, a pair of wardrobes and a long dresser furnished the space. I assumed this was where the sadist slept, a mere stone's throw away from where he tortured and raped. I pulled my sword as I crept to the final door. It was closed. I pulled the fang from my pocket and squeezed it, taking in everything it had to give. My hands trembled and the magic raced through me with such force that the fang cracked.

Shit.

I slipped it back into my pocket and leaned in close as I inspected the threshold for traps. There were none, and I gasped as I opened the door onto a room brimming with a vibrant colorful light.

Jewels and gleaming crystals that I couldn't begin to name shimmered in the tall glass cases that lined the chamber. In the midst of their glittering beauty lay a long translucent skull that twinkled and pulsed. I had no idea what species it belonged to, but whatever it was, slaying it must have proved a formidable challenge. Coins were displayed on several of the lower shelves, carefully laid out in the light of the gems, like a prized collection. Some were gold, some were silver, and many were made from metals unlike anything I'd seen before.

In the center of this treasure hoard was the cabinet that held the dagger. It was back-lit by an unseen source and its blade had a pearlescent glow, like frosted platinum. The handle was carved from bone, its surface covered with tiny, intricate, morbid iconography. I crouched to check the cabinet for traps. No wires, alarms or telltale signs of magic. Nothing.

"It's not protected." The quiet, silken voice came from behind me. "There was only one trap. And you triggered it the moment you entered my house."

28

Talamos Gin stood in the doorway. The fae was smaller than I'd expected, and scrawny, with papery blue tinted complexion. His eyes were narrow, golden, and I saw a cruel, wily strength in them. A predator's strength. The kind that knows only to strike when the odds are tipped in its favor. And it seemed, by the half smile dancing on his lips, that the odds were favoring him right now. "Why are you here?" He made the question sound almost reasonable.

"I've come to kill you and take the dagger."

"That's refreshingly honest, but why would you do such a thing? As far as I'm aware we've never met, and I'm certain from the stench hanging like a haze around you that I've never visited whatever hope-forsaken world you crawled here from. So, who sent you? And why take my dagger?"

"I need it to kill a shade."

Gin nodded. "It could do that. And more."

I pulled my sword and stepped toward him. He didn't move and his smile didn't falter. "You can tell me who sent you now, or you can wait until later. Depending on how much pain you'd like to endure."

I raised my sword. "Give me the dagger."

"You can take it yourself."

I shook my head. "No, you're going to open the cabinet."

Gin stared at me and I saw a flicker of... desire? Not sexual. Desire for sadism and torture. Slowly he clapped his hands and for a moment I thought he was mocking me until I realized it was a summons.

I ran at him. "End!" I shouted, thrusting the sword at his chest. It struck the invisible barrier shielding him and glanced off amid a blaze of bright blue sparks.

Somewhere, on one of the floors below, a door burst open and I heard the clatter of feet on the stairs.

"They're coming. For you," Gin said, "I'll have them swaddle you in one of their cocoons, then the fun will begin and I'll make it last. Unless you tell me who sent you. If you do, I might even forbid my servants to wear your skin. "

I turned away from him and brought the sword of intention down on the cabinet. It struck another invisible barrier. I reached into my pocket for Erland's charm but it was cracked, broken.

Help me, I called to my other. He ignored me. I glanced at the walls and cabinets. My other had absorbed magic from the yard and used it against the mhudambe. This place must be teeming with it. The quandary was it would be Gin's magic, dark and malevolent... but there was no time to be choosey. "Fuck you." I said it to Gin as well as my other, then I closed my eyes and focused on the magic seeping through the walls. This was going to be like the asylum all over again.

The mhudambe were on the landing now, I could hear their twitching limbs and clacking mandibles.

I pressed my hand to the wall. A deep harsh energy leaped into me, my body buckled as it entered my system and the surge forced my eyes open.

Gin watched from the doorway as his creatures gathered behind him, his steady gaze piqued with curiosity as I commandeered his magic. It was as if he'd never seen someone do such a thing before. I smiled as my mind began to sort through the numerous ways I could hurt him. Yeah, why not? There was no rush…

It wasn't my voice. Wasn't me. It was the sadistic tone of the magic. I smashed my fist through the cabinet and grabbed the dagger along with the sheath it rested upon. The blade felt substantial yet curiously light in my grip.

Gin looked shocked and surprised as I turned and threw it. It slipped through his invisible shield and embedded itself in his chest. Blood seeped from the corners of his lips. "Wh…"

I crossed the room, yanked the dagger free and kicked him back into the horde of mhudambe lurking behind him. They froze, their heads cocked as they gazed down at their dying master. I slammed the door before they could react, cast a sealing spell and shoved a nearby cabinet in front of it. Neither of these flimsy measures would last, which meant I had to get out, and fast.

I crossed the room, snatched back the heavy velvet drapes and looked out across the marshlands. The bonfire still blazed in the yard, and three pools of blood soaked the soil where the corpses had been. I'd become the fourth one if I didn't move quickly.

The rattling alien cries of the mhudambe filled the hall, and the door began to buckle. I turned back to the window and pulled it open. The drop was at least thirty feet…

I glanced at the window ledge just below mine, and the one beyond that. My other stirred, roused by the arrival of the cruel furious power surging through our veins. I laughed as I climbed out the window; if he showed his face now I'd smother him.

The wind was icy on the back of my neck as I gripped the sill, turned and slipped over the side where I hung for a moment before letting go.

I fell. Stone wall and glass panes flew past me, and then I grabbed the next sill.

Agony tore through my arms. It was all I could do to keep my grip.

I considered smashing the window before me and climbing through, until I caught a glimpse of the cocoons clinging to the ceiling inside. I glanced down to the next sill, focusing the magic thrumming through me. And then dropped.

A blur of stone, a whistle of air... I snatched the sill, jerked to a halt and screamed as a deep violent pain shot through my limbs. I gritted my teeth, took a sharp breath and before I could think about it, dropped again.

The ground rushed toward me. I hit it hard. A stinging ache cracked like a whip through my ankles and up my spine.

I hobbled away from the house and glanced up through the bonfire's drifting smoke as a mhudambe thrust its head through the open window. Glowing light shimmered around it as it glared down at me and rattled off a cry to the others.

I looked to the marsh, then up to the creature's cold glinting eyes and I backed away as a fresh wave of pain surged through me. There was no way I'd ever make it.

A haunting chorus of cries echoed through the stone tower and the mhudambe withdrew its head from the window.

They were coming.

29

I staggered past the bonfire, to the door of Talamos Gin's house and thrust my hands against the thick planks. My fingers singed the wood as I soaked up the last dregs of his magic and I shuddered as the ominous power rushed into me. The depths of its malevolence was almost irrepressible. Images of Gin's wicked deeds came with it. Stark horrible visions of cowering, bloody faces, many of them young, all of them screaming. I fell back and puked on the dusty ground.

The mhudambe were coming. I could hear them clattering down the stairs.

I leaped back toward the door, sealed it and reinforced the spell a second time. And as I staggered back toward the bonfire, I got an idea.

Summon your fire, I commanded my other.

I sensed his presence, sulking amid the torrents of my newly acquired power but he did not reply.

Summon your own. The voice wasn't his; it was Talamos Gin, his essence infusing the magic I'd leeched from his dark dwelling. *Do it. Burn it all.*

An ironclad hatred engulfed my senses as I glanced back to

the house. The door buckled in its frame and a mhudambe burst through a window and prepared to leap.

Cruel notions flooded through me along with a torrent of memories featuring Gin's most prized assaults and retaliations. Bile scorched my throat and my stomach flipped as I clasped my hands together to consolidate the dark power within me. When I drew them apart, black flames danced in my palms. I rubbed them together, coaxing them to burn brighter.

"More!" I demanded. The swirling flames flickered, twisted and rose, forming orbs of black fire. I hurled one at the door as it flew open. It smashed into the emerging mhudambe, consuming the creature in an instant. It roared and its body turned to smoke. With a wave of my hand the door slammed shut and violent flames leaped across the oak trapping the creatures inside.

I conjured another burning black sphere and a savage thrill filled me as I cast it through the broken window. Within moments an inferno raged and the mhudambe screamed as it disintegrated

"You want more?" Another fireball leaped up from my palm and my ire shifted to the mhudambe's young. A slow, cruel smile tugged my lips as I hurled the orb through their nursery window, and pictured their foul cocoons blazing.

I stood back and watched as the tower was engulfed by a raging black inferno.

Mhudambe leapt from windows, and I relished the crack of their limbs as they hit the ground and twitched in crumpled heaps. I strode toward them, my own pain vanquished by the dark magic, and grabbed one. It glanced up at me and its eyes narrowed in agony as I pried open its mandibles, stuffed black fire into its mouth and clamped its jaw shut.

The creature convulsed as it writhed in…

What the hell am I doing? It was the first true thought, of my own, that I'd had since Gin's magic had tainted my mind. I looked down as the mhudambe vanished to smoke, and the others tried to crawl away.

I pulled my sword and put an end to their suffering. Then, thrusting the blade into the tangled grass, I staggered to the marsh and plunged my palms into the murky water, dowsing the flames. I doubled over and puked again as my system tried to purge itself of the dark fae's tainted magic.

30

I made my way back through the marsh hoping I was going in the right direction. Everything seemed turned around, backward, out of order. Even the moon. I was dogged by a dark, foreboding mood as I passed the bent little trees and leaped across the boggy trails. It was the same darkness that had plagued me after the slaughter in Galloway Asylum and in Copperwood Falls after I'd used the black crystals to follow that lowlife dealer into the underworld to save his sorry soul.

I'd been warned about using other people's magic and the consequences were becoming clear as the last vestiges of Talamos Gin's malign energy crawled through my blood. I was certain it was his essence that had inspired the sickening pleasure I'd felt slaughtering the mhudambe. Gin's magic, like most, left its own imprint.

I pulled his dagger from its sheath and held it in the moonlight. It glistened with an iridescent sheen. I turned to sever a branch from a tree and there was almost no friction, the blade just slipped through the heavy limb and it fell away, splashing into the water.

But would it work on Stroud? I was itching to be the one to cut his wretched throat a second time and send him to whatever special hell awaited men like him. I'd never fought a shade before, my dealings with spirits and ghosts had been limited, but if Erland was right about this blade, it would destroy Stroud. If he was wrong, the world as I knew it was about to end. No more blinkereds. No more Mrs. Fitz. No more drunken antics with my friends in the Rocket Bar. Just restless devastation. And watching over it all, Stroud. The ender of worlds...

Splosh.

"Great!" I'd taken a bad step and was up to my knees in icy water.

"Oh dear," said a low, sullen voice. It was the toad. He sat on a log watching me closely with his twinkling golden eyes.

"Oh dear what?"

"You smell awful. Just... horrible."

"Thanks" I called as I slogged away through the marsh. The last thing I needed was insults from a maudlin amphibian.

"Are you sure you don't want that wish?" he called. "You really look like you could use it."

"I'm sure," I said.

"Don't worry, things can get better, you know!" the toad cried. "It happens. Sometimes."

I bit my tongue and waved over my shoulder as I walked.

Dawn tinged the sky with a deep marmalade hue and eventually I found the path leading back to the village. My journey to the temple was pretty quiet save for a singing caravan full of strange, hairy folk I had no name for, and a group of fae that shot a few insults my way as they trotted by. Perhaps, once word spread of the fall of Talamos Gin, my name might garner some respect from the fae. But I wasn't banking on it.

I stood outside the temple and waited as the glyphs morphed into fearsome beasts. Then the door opened, Aberfellow Hax appeared and with a courteous nod he ushered me inside. "Is the deed done?" he asked.

"Yes. There won't be any more trouble"

"Good man." He smiled briefly. "Please accept my apologies for my initial curtness. In this realm our memories are long. But you're not responsible for that…sordid history, and neither am I. So please know you're welcome in my house, Mr. Rook, whenever you have need of it."

"Thank you."

"Now," Aberfellow said, "I'll leave you to your business with Erland." He gave me a slight bow and vanished into a side room as the short, agonized moan of his patient rang out.

I made my way downstairs and found Erland asleep in his chair by the fire. I stood for a moment watching. He looked different asleep, almost childlike. It was a strange, unsettling sight that was compounded as his eyes opened and found me with laser-like precision. "How did it go?"

"Gin's dead." I replied as I handed him the dagger. He slid the blade from its sheath and gazed at it, his expression both fascinated and repulsed.

"Be very careful with this weapon, Morgan. It's sharper than any sword but it's fragile." His eyes flitted over mine. "I suggest you keep it well hidden until it's time to confront Stroud."

"I will."

"Now, I expect you must be ready to venture back to reality?" Erland said, with a rare smile. "Or what passes for reality in the blinkered world."

"Yeah, I'm especially anxious to pay Grandfather Lampton a visit. And Endersley too, hopefully. Before he manages to unleash his pestilence."

"I can't think of a better man for the job, Morgan." He fell to silence for a moment, before adding, "I wish I'd trusted you more than I did. And that I'd taught you how to wield your own magic. But I will one day, once things have settled."

"I'm not sure there'll be an Organization left by the end of all this. After my run-ins with Osbert and Ebomee, and the way Rhymes was on my tail when I went after Wyght, it seems the Organization aren't the good guys anymore."

"It's complicated. Avoid them for now. But if you come up against those agents again, and they mean to harm you, execute them. I'll deal with the partners myself. At least one of them's working with Lampton, and the Council appears to be against our interests. As soon as I'm healed I'll be back, and when I am there will be a day of reckoning. I swear it. But in the meantime you must find Endersley and Stroud. Definitely start with Franklin Lampton. He could very well be the weak link that brings them all down."

"I will."

"Here," Erland reached into his pocket and pulled out a small, golden skinned apple. "For your journey back."

"Where should I eat it?"

"Climb the hill opposite to the one you arrived on. There's an arch of marble at its crest. Eat the apple there and you'll be transported back to a safe room within the heart of the city. Of course, you'll be sound sleep the moment you cross but frankly you look like you need it. And don't worry, you'll be alright there, the place is secure." Erland held his hand out and I shook it. "I'll be back soon, Morgan. And once I am…" he smiled, "I can get out of this drab robe and into some decent clothes."

"Yeah, I'm not sure beige is your color."

We said goodbye and I left the temple, tucking the dagger into my waistband and the apple into my pocket as I went. The fae villagers snubbed me as I headed out toward the vast swath of bluebells.

I followed the chalk path and took the fork that led to the hill across from the one where I'd awoken. As I climbed, the orange sky was almost too striking to behold.

After a mile or so I found the marble arch and pulled the apple from my pocket, gave Faery one last glance for posterity, and took a bite.

31

I woke to find myself... in a comfortable leather office chair overlooking a pristine walnut desk. Tidy stacks of papers rested under a green reading lamp and a small plate of cookies sat next to a glass of water tagged with a yellow sticky note that read;

'Help yourself.'

Bookcases crammed with stuffy-looking books lined the walls. I glanced over the embossed gold titles, they appeared to be a collection of reference books whose subject matter was centered around laws and legislation. Scant light filtered in from the edges of the broad window behind me so I slipped the blinds apart. I was right in the heart of the city, just as Erland had said. It was early, but the streets were beginning to brim with a quiet business-like bustle beneath the same rainy slate-grey skies that were fast becoming routine. I turned back to check the time; it was seven thirty am.

I glanced down as I patted my pockets to make sure I had everything.

Sword, check. mhudambe dagger, check. Gun, no. And no phone or bag of tricks. They were still lying in the state park where any blinkered hiker could find them. It worried me for a moment but, while Osbert might be murderous, he was a professional. So I was pretty sure he'd have had my things whisked away and plunked back into the hands of the Organization by now. Thankfully I had a back-up phone at home and the rest of the stuff could be replaced, with the pull of a few strings.

I opened the office door and peered out into a short corridor. At the end, clutching a heavy book in his hand, was a small man in a waistcoat and pin-striped trousers. He glanced my way and gave a brief, friendly smile. "I hope you don't mind that I moved you," he said. "For some reason you *arrived* in our supply closet." He peered at the watch on his wrist. "Thankfully no one else is pathetic enough to be here at this time in the morning, so no one witnessed it."

"Thank you," I said. My head was still light from the faerie fruit, as well as the magic I'd *borrowed*. "I appreciate it."

"Is Erland okay?"

"Yes, he's on the mend. You know him?"

"Oh yes, we're old friends. We share a tailor." The man smiled again. "Not to be pushy, but some of the others will be arriving soon. So if you don't mind…"

"Consider me gone. And thank you."

"Anytime." He nodded and returned to his book, tracing his finger across the page as he mumbled the words to himself.

I emerged on the street amid a squall of rain that seemed to find every hole and tear in my clothes. My boots were still caked with mud from the marshes, my sword clanked by my side and my coat was spattered with blood and who knew what else. To say I felt conspicuous would have been a huge understatement.

Cabs flew by and I tried to flag one down but the driver

glanced me over and sped off, so I dashed along in a half walk, half run through the half soaked city.

———

I raced up the stairs past Mrs. Fitz's tidy winter-readied garden, grabbed the spare key from under the mat and let myself in. The hallway was filled with quiet early morning gloom. I walked softly up the stairs, intending to creep past Mrs. Fitz's door, but it flew open before I'd even reached it, throwing warm light across the carpet.

"Good morning, Mr. Rook," Mrs. Fitz said, before throwing a towel to me. "I saw you scurrying across the street, like a drowning rat."

"You're up early," I said as I dabbed the rain from my face and neck.

"Yes." She held up the small notebook she was clutching in her hand. "I've been tracking them."

"Them?"

"The cats. I want to know where each and every one of the furry little bastards is coming from."

"You're still having problems?"

"Always, Mr. Rook. Always. And there seems to be even more of them this year. There's been at least five new ones over the last month alone. They try to hide, but I know they're there. Under cars, bushes and lampposts. Watching." She gave a tired smile and shook her head. "You must think I'm a mad old thing!"

"Not at all. Everyone has a fear of something."

"And what's your fear, Mr. Rook?"

In that moment my biggest fear was of Endersley and Stroud achieving their objectives. Not that I could say it. I shrugged. "I'm not so keen on spiders."

Mrs. Fitz gave me a long, searching look before grasping my wrist. "I know you have your secrets, dear. We all do. And I know you don't work in insurance, and those two young people staying with you are not in the real estate business. I haven't a clue what any of you are up to, and I couldn't care less. Because," her eyes twinkled, and she smiled, "I know you're a force of light." She patted her hand against her chest. "I feel it in here. You're good, but the world out there," she glanced downstairs, "is brimming with evil. And I don't just mean the cats." She looked up at me and sighed. "I saw him again, in my dream…"

"Saw who?"

"The man in the shadows. The man with the sadness and desolation in his eyes. I told you about him before. This time he was alone in an empty city. It was like a hurricane had torn through it and taken every living soul." Mrs. Fitz shook her head. "It was ghastly. Such bleakness, such wanton destruction and anger. But then you appeared… just you and him standing before one another. I knew you were stronger than him but you'd been betrayed, so you were weak and in pain. And then," her eyes glistened, and she wiped them quickly with the back of her hand, "and then he sent wolves after you. Horrible, grey beasts with snarling teeth and burning eyes. They chased you for miles and miles, they ran you ragged." A single tear fell from Mrs. Fitz's eye and she clasped my wrist with both hands. "I'm sorry, Mr. Rook. It's probably just my overactive imagination, but it was terrible. Just terrible."

"I appreciate your concern," I said, not knowing what else to say. "But I'll be fine. I have good people around me. Including the best landlady there ever was."

Mrs. Fitz smiled and the crows feet by her eyes danced. "I'm a cranky old lunatic, and we both know it. But yes, I suppose I am your landlady, although I'd let you live here for nothing, Mr. Rook. If it came to it. Because I hold you very dear. Now," she clutched her notebook, " I must get back to work; someone's got to keep track of those furry little buggers."

"Thank you." I said and handed her back her towel.

"Anytime," she said, before turning and softly closing her door.

I stood on the landing for a moment, my senses reeling. Her dreams had always left me feeling unsettled. Mostly because more than a few had come to pass. But this one... this one really had me rattled. And it wasn't the idea of facing down Stroud or dealing with a pack of feral wolves. No, it was the betrayal.

That was the part that had sunk its teeth right into me.

32

I continued up the stairs and stopped outside my apartment. The television was on, so someone was home. I knocked on the door and a moment later Samuel answered, his pipe clamped to his lips. "You came back then," he said, ushering me inside.

"How long have I been gone?"

"Since yesterday afternoon. Why?" Samuel went over to the coffeemaker and filled a cup, before pressing it into my hand.

"Because I took a trip to the lands of Faery, and I have no idea how long I was gone for."

"Faery?" Samuel smiled. "Sounds like an adventure, do tell."

"I will. Where's Astrid?"

"Out. She's following up on a possible sighting of Endersley. We're not expecting it will amount to much. We left our number with a few of the people we talked to in the magical quarter, mostly keepers at inns and taverns. Astrid said the caller sounded odd, possibly drunk, hence our pessimism. But anyway, you were about to fill me in on that hugely important thing. The one that made you tear yourself away from our company and scuttle off to Faery."

"Indeed." I sat back in my chair, took a sip of coffee, and began my tale.

"Interesting," Samuel said, as I finished my story. "You have the blade with you now?"

I felt a strange sense of resistance as I pulled it out from under my coat and handed it to him. He slipped it from its sheath and held it to the light. "Nasty," he said. "Can you feel it?"

"Feel what?"

"The darkness. This is a wicked implement, Morgan." He handed it back to me. "Be careful with it."

"You're the second person that's said that to me." I laid it on the armrest, planning to quietly hide it away as soon as I got the chance.

"So now what?"

"I've got to check in with Haskins, see if there's been any more incidents."

"There's been nothing on the television," Samuel said.

"The television's about the last place to go for news," I said. "Anyway, after I've talked to Haskins we should find Astrid and stock up on weapons and crystals. I need a new bag of tricks too." I checked the time. "The Electric Video Club opens at ten. If we get there on the dot, I should be able to get in and out before any agents turn up. In theory at least."

"So we're visiting the famous armory. Exciting stuff."

"Yup, and you'll get to meet a good friend of mine. I think you'll like him. You two have a lot in common, and not just the beard. Just give me a moment to freshen up and we'll go."

"*Freshen up?* Come on, Morgie, we're only going out to find good old Astrid." Samuel winked at me.

I shook my head, which suddenly felt like it was twice its normal size and full of radiators. "I..."

"Relax," Samuel said. "She likes you, you like her...."

"And you're okay...."

"Me?" Samuel asked. "I see Astrid the way I see you. We're allies. Companions. Soldiers. You're like my brother and sister. You're the sister and she's the brother, in case you wondered." He grinned as he began to stack his pipe once more. "I'd be pleased to see the pair of you happy. The gods know it's been an age since Astrid's had much to smile about. Hence the frosty demeanor. But maybe it's right to hold back, for now. You know, until..." he tailed off awkwardly.

"Until the job's done. Stroud and Endersley," I said. Clearly Samuel felt a little awkward saying so, but I got it, and I had the sense Astrid did too. "No distractions until we're finished."

"Exactly," Samuel said. "Now go *freshen up* tough guy." He lit his pipe, slid the window open, and stuck his head out. "Morning ladies," he said as two petite Siamese cats slipped past him. I petted them and dished out some tuna, and then I went for the shower I'd been looking forward to for what felt like days.

We met Astrid outside Rathbones; a shop that specialized in rare and unusual magical artifacts. She was sitting on a bench, a coffee in her hand and a sour expression on her face.

"Everything okay?" I asked as we walked up.

"He never showed. It was a waste of time." Her features softened as she glanced my way. "Everything okay with you?"

I gave her the highlights of my time in Faery and was about to suggest a visit to the armory when something shoved past my leg. I looked down as an imp, swaddled in two coats and a porkpie hat, grabbed the edge of the bench, tried to pull himself up and failed, falling back on his ass.

"Don't you fucking dare!" he snarled as Samuel stooped to help him.

"Otto?" Astrid asked, as the imp gripped the bench once more and clambered up.

"I am he. And time is money. So let'sss talk, sugar tits."

"What did you call me?" Astrid gasped in surprise.

"Watch it, *Otto*" I said. "Have a little respect. And get to the point. You've kept her waiting long enough." My last encounter with pickled imps had been riddled with similar frustration and insults and we didn't have time for any crap. Plus, brokering in half truths was a well known pastime for these habitual drunkards.

"Right," Otto glared my way. "I'll not be hearing another word from you, or your bearded boyfriend. I'm talking to the lady, and if ssshe deigns to tolerate your company while we trade words and coin, that'sss on her." Otto turned to Astrid. "First up, money."

"Tell me about Endersley, you'll be paid afterwards. That's how I do business." Astrid held his gaze until finally he glanced away.

"Right. You're looking for Endersssley," the imp said. "I've seen him. Standing there as brazen as a pair of bright red buttocks." He held his hands up and shook them, like he was doing jazz hands. "He had claws as long as kitchen knives, and eyes that could burn you in half. And then half again!"

"Quarters?" Samuel asked.

"Don't you go lording it up with me, fella," Otto growled, "I'm telling you what I saw." He half smiled at Astrid, who looked about ready to break his nose. "And he had a cane. Or it could have been a rowdy black serpent!"

Astrid stood, threw her cup into the trash, and turned back to Otto. "You wasted my time."

"Didn't. Maybe I might have overstated a few details, but I can tell you where he is this very moment. But first the bacon."

"Bacon?" Samuel seemed genuinely baffled.

"Beans, bones, blue buggering cheese. Moolah, chits, clams!" Otto screamed. "I didn't come out here for charity you fucks!"

I handed him a five to shut him up. "Get yourself a hot drink. Preferably something that isn't laced with whiskey."

We began to walk away as Otto screamed out, "Oh you can go if you want. But if you do, I won't tell you where his castle is. Horrible place. Black as petrified dung and twice as high as a buttered…"

"Sorry about that," I said to Astrid. "I would have warned you if I'd known the so-called informant was an imp."

She shrugged and then chuckled deeply, and I realized I'd never heard her laugh so hard before. "Sugar tits," she said. "It was pretty funny."

Astrid and Samuel cloaked themselves as we left the magical quarter and I wished I could do the same with as much ease. Being out in the city was making me feel jittery and I was half expecting to find agents around every corner. Ebomee on a rooftop, Osbert in an alley, and Rhymes… anywhere and everywhere. I shivered as I thought of him. If push came to shove, and I was certain it probably would, I was going to enjoy putting a bullet right between his burning eyes.

We were about a block from the Electric Video Club when a car horn blared in the street beside me. I turned to find a beat up old BMW cutting off another vehicle. Its windows were tinted but the passenger door was ajar and I caught a glimpse of wild ash-grey hair and crazed eyes. The magician from the bank.

The car swerved out onto the other side of the road and cut back in again as it screeched to a stop outside the video shop.

I froze as the doors flew open and three men in suits and shades got out. All of them were huge and bald, which was an irony because I caught a glimpse below their cloaks and saw that they were werewolves. Werewolves just on the verge of shifting.

The passenger door swung open and the magician jumped out, his staff in hand. He stood on the sidewalk and stared down the blinkereds streaming toward him and they broke like a parting sea and streamed around him.

I fastened my coat up as I considered my last confrontation with him, and the torrents of fire he'd unleashed.

"Problem?" Samuel asked, jarring me from my thoughts.

"Yeah," I said. "Big time."

33

I ran to the Electric Video Club's grimy storefront and peered through the window. All I could see was gloom, which meant Madhav hadn't even had a chance to switch the lights on before the magician and his thugs had stormed in. I glanced back at their getaway car. "You up for slashing some tires?" I asked Astrid.

She nodded, walked to the car, pulled her dagger and there was a hiss as the BMW slumped to the ground. Somehow she'd managed to make her actions look entirely reasonable and the passing blinkereds hurried by without a second glance.

Samuel raised his eyebrows and nodded for us to join him as he slipped the shop door open, without disturbing the bells above the door. Analogue security for an analogue store.

His movements were swift and fluid as he flitted inside. I crept in behind him with Astrid at my back.

The counter that sat dead ahead was obscured by the three werewolves. They were huge, slabs of fur and muscle and I could smell their fetid breath from where I stood. The magician was at their side, with the tip of his staff poised under Madhav's chin. "Open the door, boy. Now," he said.

Madhav's eyes flashed toward me and back to the magician. "There's no door to open. Other than the one you just came through."

"That's not what my intelligence told me," the magician replied.

Madhav's smiled but his glare was withering. "Which one of your dogs did you name Intelligence, 'cause all three of them look pretty thick to me?"

The magician ignored the barb. "I know the armory's here, and that you're the fool assigned as its sentry. Now tell me where the fuck it is before I pry your mind open and pluck the answer out by force."

"I expect you'd have done that already if it were so simple." Madhav replied, glancing my way as I slowly drew my blade and Samuel raised his short sword.

Red-orange light enveloped Madhav's jaw line as the tip of the staff burst into flames. He yelped and tried to flinch away. A strange shimmer passed through the air before him as he whispered, and slowly the scorched red wound on his chin began to fade.

"That was just a taste of what's to come, boy, you won't be able to heal the next injury," the magician said, "now where's the fucking door?"

"You shouldn't have done that." Madhav's eyes flashed like burnished gold as he stared at the magician.

"No, you really shouldn't have," I agreed.

The werewolves and magician turned our way. Samuel stabbed the nearest beast in the chest with his short sword. It pulled the weapon out as if it were no more than a toothpick, and head butted Samuel to the floor.

Astrid slashed at one as it stalked toward her and the other one ran at me. I thrust my sword at its midriff, but it growled and shoved it away. I sidestepped and wheeled around for another attack, giving the swing everything I had in me. Which wasn't much…

The werewolf parried the swipe but the flames that had engulfed my blade set its fur ablaze.

I leaped forward as it swiped its great paw trying to douse the fire, and kneed it hard in the nuts. It yelped and took a step back before charging at me like a runaway train filled with claws and teeth. I ducked down an aisle as it hurtled by.

The magician thrust his staff into the air, summoning a fresh arc of fire. Madhav stood before him, his hands outstretched. Long golden claws sprang from his fingers and his eyes brimmed with light. He'd summoned a shield with the strange magic he was wielding. It absorbed the magician's blast, before reflecting it back at him. The magician ducked and the fire shot over his head, roared past my face and exploded behind me.

I turned back as the floor shook. The werewolf was coming at me hard and the wall behind me was on fire. I tried to sidestep again, but it grabbed my coat and whirled me round as it skidded to a stop. I punched it hard in the stomach and winced at the pain shooting through my knuckles. It felt like I'd just hit a rock. Then the entire shop seemed to topple and whirl as the werewolf hurled me down the aisle into the burning wall.

My coat spared me from the brunt of the searing heat, but I had to roll across the floor and slap the stray flames out before they could spread.

I glanced up in time to see the beast charging toward me, its eyes wide, its grin a steely trap of yellowed teeth. I stumbled to my right but ducked left at the last moment and let it career into the burning wall.

The supernatural flames caught in its fur and raged fast as its meaty paw swiped and swatted them out. I pressed forward to take advantage of its distraction but it struck my hand, sending the sword of intention skittering into the gloom.

I kicked my heels and tried to push myself out of the way as the werewolf thundered over me like a wave of dark animalistic fury. It fell on me, slamming me into the ground, its breath vile, its eyes boring into mine with savage malicious intention.

34

I could only watch as the werewolf raised its paw above my face, its claws long and black as they descended toward me like a hand of knives. I closed my eyes instinctively and braced myself.

And then a hollow thump rang out above me and the beast slammed into me. I looked past its drooling maw to find Bastion Stout standing above me. His eyes twinkled as he yanked a large silver ax from the beast's back. "Morgan," he said, as if I'd just strolled into the armory.

"Bastion," I returned, my entire torso aching, my chest winded.

He pulled at the werewolf and I pushed until finally we rolled the dead beast off to my side. A glow of golden red light lit the shop as I ran to the counter with Bastion behind me, ax in hand. The magician stood before Madhav his staff ablaze as he uttered a spell.

Bastion threw his ax, but the magician whirled around to face him and it struck whatever invisible aura shielded him and clattered to the ground. And then the magician summoned a stream of fire from his staff and sent it blazing at Madhav.

Madhav held his hands out, his fingertips flickering with light as he absorbed the fire into his palms. Flames burned in his mouth and in his eyes and he grinned as he threw it back, striking the magician with his own spell and smashing his invisible shield.

"I told you you should leave," Madhav said.

The magician roared his anger and flew past me, shoving me aside as he went.

I was about to go after him when I spotted Samuel wheeling around another werewolf, while Astrid battled the other, her daggers whirling and spraying the air with blood. It was pushing her back, and I was torn between helping her or Samuel until Bastion ran to Astrid's aid and swung his ax into the werewolf's torso. It howled with agony and then fury as I seized the other around the throat and wrestled it from Samuel.

The werewolf turned and batted me away. I flew into a display case, sending video cassettes raining down around me. I just had time to note the irony as An American Werewolf in London smacked onto my knuckles, when the beast came again.

I scrambled to my feet and led the werewolf away from the others, freeing them up to deal with the monster attacking Astrid, before realizing I was out of space to run.

"Here!" Samuel called. He threw the sword of intention. It blazed with fire as I caught it.

I put my right foot forward and waited for the creature to come, my eyes locked onto its bestial glare. It slowed, revealing hesitation, no doubt as its human brain calculated the odds. Two against five.

"Yeah, not great," I said as I swung the sword, and lopped its head off.

The remaining werewolf was badly injured but his wounds seemed to only ignite his fury as he bounded toward Bastion, his paw poised to deliver a killing swipe.

Bright golden light shot through the air, hitting him squarely in the chest, sending him flying back. He struck the wall with a thud and fell to the ground, his eyes smoldering one last time before the life in them fizzled out.

I grabbed the edge of a display case and caught my breath. The air reeked of burned fur and flesh, and musty, animal sweat.

"Thank you," Madhav said, as he walked past me and quenched the fires with a stream of magic from his fingers. The golden fire had left his eyes and his spectral claws had receded. But I was still in awe of him as I watched him tidy up with fast, magical efficiency.

"You okay?" Bastion asked Astrid as he helped her up.

"I'll be fine," she said. But she didn't look fine, and I saw the way she clutched her side.

"I'm supposed to call the Organization the moment you come here," Madhav said as he returned to his place behind the counter.

"And I'm guessing you weren't supposed to tell me that," I said.

"Indeed, I wasn't. But we rarely do the things we're supposed to do, do we?" Madhav picked his phone up and began reading what looked like a comic. "I can give you thirty minutes," he added. "And then I'll have to call, Humble." He gave me a slight nod. "Good luck, Morgan. I hope you get the bastards. Each and every last one of them."

"Thanks," I said.

"I take it you came to stock up?" Bastion asked, wincing

slightly as looked up at me. For a moment I thought he'd been injured, but his black suit was unmarked. Which probably meant his injury was from the vengeful ghosts of whatever he'd drunk the night before.

"I did," I said. "I lost my gun, my bag and a bunch of potions and crystals."

"Indeed," Bastion said with a wry grin. "And Osbert recovered them and handed them in to me. Good ogre that he is."

"That was nice of him," I said, "especially after all the efforts he'd gone to to kill me."

"Bastion Stout," Bastion said, offering his hand to Astrid. "Pleased to meet you."

"Pleased to meet you too." Astrid's face softened as she shook his hand.

"And this is Samuel," I said.

Bastion shook Samuel's hand. "Excuse my trembling," Bastion said. "That was my first encounter with a werewolf, and it wasn't a pleasant one. Plus I have a hangover the size of a particularly tall mountain, which means I should probably slip a little restorative into the coffee I was brewing out back. Care to join me?"

"That sounds marvelous," Samuel said, and I could tell by the gleam in his eye that he'd taken an instant liking to Bastion, as had Astrid.

"Come this way then." Bastion led us down an aisle and through an illusion of a storeroom cluttered with buckets, stepladders and broken video players. We emerged into the armory and the bright light from the crystals glowing in their display cases.

"Well this is impressive," Samuel said as he took in the room. He stooped before a glass cabinet filled with deep blue crystals, while Astrid wandered to the wall with the blades, daggers, and long swords.

"Here!" Bastion shouted, throwing something toward me. My bag. "I could have given you a new one," he added, "but I think that one suits you best. It's tough, leathery and riddled with holes."

"Thanks." I strapped the bag around my shoulder. It felt good to have it back again, tattered though it was.

"Now why don't you fill it with whatever you need," Bastion offered as he strode toward his counter, "and I'll look the other way and pretend you were never here. Right?"

"What about Snarksmuth?" I asked. "Won't he notice things have gone missing?" Personally I couldn't have given a shit about the whiny old goblin, but I didn't want Bastion getting into trouble on my account.

Bastion gave a hearty laugh and vanished behind the counter. "I've been screwing with his stock takes from the first day that little bastard arrived. So no, he won't know anything missing, which is just the way we like it." Something sputtered and whirred and moments later Bastion's hand appeared and set a coffee mug upon the counter, followed by three more. He pulled himself up onto his customary stool and thumped an expensive-looking bottle of whiskey down. "Now," he said, raising his voice, "who's for Irish Coffee?"

"I could be interested in that," Samuel said as he appeared like a flash and inspected the bottle.

"Astrid?" Bastion called.

She shook her head. "I need to keep my mind clear, but I'll take a coffee if you're offering it."

"Me too," I said. In that moment there was nothing more that I would have liked than to join Bastion and Samuel for a dram or two, but I had to have my full wits about me. I began to fill my bag and by the time I'd finished I was fully stocked on an ammo, had a new gun in my holster, and enough crystals to take down half the city.

I caught Astrid's eye as I strode to the counter. She smiled and I returned it, even though I felt as ragged as the bag around my shoulder, and not just from the fight. Because Mrs. Fitz's words were still haunting me and I still didn't know what to make of them. *I knew you were stronger than him, but you'd been betrayed and so you were weak and in pain.*

"It's good stuff," Samuel said as Bastion slipped another measure into his coffee.

"It is that," Bastion said and turned my way. "Find everything you need?"

"I did. Thanks for your help."

"It's my pleasure, Morgan. Always." His eyes twinkled as he lifted his cup to me. "Cheers, old friend. Here's to the end of times. We'll have to have our pub crawl before they come. By hook or by crook. In this world, or the next if needs be."

We clinked cups.

"Pub crawl?" Samuel asked.

"He'll give you the details," Bastion said, nodding to me. "It was his idea. I think." He continued to smile but his thick brow knitted as he regarded me once more. "Be careful, Morgan. I'd like to get everything back in one piece if possible. Including you. Now," he glanced to the door behind him, "Snarksmuth's due any moment so you should leave before he pisses all over your day as well as mine." He slurped down the rest of his cup and raised his empty cup to me. I nodded to him. There was no need to say anything more.

35

As we left the video club I watched the blinkereds hurrying along the street on their way to work, their faces grave above their thick winter coats. I wondered if they'd somehow picked up on things, if they could see that the world around them was on the brink.

"Are we going to *borrow* another car?" Samuel asked. It sounded like he was relishing the prospect. "Not that one." He nodded to the magician's battered old BMW with its sagging tires and then his eyes gleamed as he pointed to a nearby Ferrari. "That might be good."

"It's too busy here. Come on," I said.

We ducked down a side street lined with upmarket boutiques and overpriced cafes, and glanced back as a low thump of bass rattled the air. A sleek black customized truck rolled into view, amid music so loud I could see the shop windows and car windshields rattle as it parked. I tried to spot the driver but the windows were tinted. Finally he emerged, resplendent in wraparound shades, despite the rolling grey November sky. All in all the perfect mark.

I cut him off before he could reach the ritzy electronics

store, peddling premium phones at exorbitant prices, and snatched his shades off.

"What the-"

"Keys," I said. I held his angry, then panicked gaze. I had one hand on the crystal in my pocket, and the other on his wrist. He tried to pull away, but I held him firm and continued to stare into his eyes until his expression turned from outrage to simple terror.

"I don't... I don't understand," he said.

"There's nothing to understand. We just need to borrow your vehicle for a while and you want to lend us it. You're not worried and won't give it a further thought until tomorrow morning."

"Right." He handed me the keys, glanced from me to Samuel, then his eyes lingered on Astrid and he winked. She stared back at him until he strode away, glancing around like he'd forgotten something but had no idea what.

The first thing I did after starting it up, was switch the music off. Then I opened the windows to get rid of the stench of weed and we headed for the highway and the distant, darkening clouds.

Albany turned out to be a small town with two main streets that amounted to nothing much at all. I stopped outside a rundown grocers and asked if they knew of a man called Lampton, or a sprawling estate with a lodge, but they'd never heard of either. Finally, after an hour of driving in what felt like circle after circle, I pulled into a gas station to fill up.

The man behind the counter was a scrawny suspicious old goat who eyed me as if I was about to rob the place. Like that was his only plausible explanation for an out of towner stopping by. I handed him money for the gas and asked him if he'd heard of a place people called The Lodge.

"Nope." He shook his head to emphasize the point.

"It's a big house on several acres of land. The owner's a bit...reclusive."

His eyes wandered and I saw him give a slight shudder. "There could be somewhere, now I think about it... the property's mostly taken up with woods. It's out on Crescent Way, about two miles south of here." His eyes flashed over mine and he added, "creepy frigging place."

"In what way?"

He shrugged and looked a little sheepish. "I don't know. It just has that *stay the hell away from here* vibe about it. Know what I mean?"

"Yeah, I know exactly what you mean." I thanked him, climbed back in the truck and headed south.

"There," Astrid said. I glanced in the rear view mirror and reversed as I spotted the driveway I'd somehow missed. It looked like a narrow lane winding through the trees, nothing ostentatious. Not what I'd have expected from a Lampton. I put it back in drive, made a u-turn and pulled over on a residential road. The truck with its overblown customizations and tinted windows stood out like the proverbial sore thumb, but thankfully the street was empty as I pulled my bag and checked my gun.

We crossed the highway and stood before the thick bank of trees. The place was posted with a sign that read:

'No Hunting. No Trespassing.'

"Ready?" I asked, as I glanced along the highway to make sure it was clear.

"Ready." Samuel stared into the woods and I saw a flicker of apprehension in his eyes. I got it. Even from where we stood

I could feel it. The low, heavy buzz in the air. There was evil here. No question.

We trudged into the trees and I took the lead, with Astrid bringing up the rear. The place was gloomy, the canopy above thick with evergreens and the ground carpeted with pine straw and moss. As I climbed over a log the side broke away and beetles rolled out like black coins from a slot machine.

All was quiet but for the occasional bird fluttering in the tangle above. I grabbed a fallen branch and used it to push away the long arching brambles as we climbed a steep rise. The woodsy smell of decomposition grew steadily stronger the further in we hiked.

"Wait," Samuel called in a hushed whisper. I turned back to find him stooped by a tree, examining the ground near its trunk.

"What is it?" Astrid asked, one hand straying beneath her cloak for a weapon.

"Tracks. Looks like hounds," Samuel said.

"So?" Astrid asked.

A hand full of dirt and leaf litter slipped through Samuel's fingers. "We need to be on guard. Something rotten's passed through here recently."

"Like what?"

"Like a dead body." Samuel said.

I took a deep sniff. All I could smell was earth and pine but there was definitely a trace of malice hanging in the air. And a feeling of hidden eyes watching.

"This entire place is rigged," Astrid said.

"With what?"

"Spells to deter trespassers. They're mostly aimed at warding blinkereds off, but I'm guessing they're going to get stronger and probably switch from magical to physical the closer in we get."

We continued up the slope and the ground leveled out and we passed through a clearing with a pond at its center. It was only a few yards long and wide, and yet I got the distinct feeling the waters ran deep. And that there were things within its depths that I'd sooner not encounter.

I glanced over as something moved on the far side of the pond. A squat, reddish-brown dog, its eyes glowing as it raised its head. It took a step toward us and I could see there was something very wrong with it. It lurched forward again, its gait almost a limp. As if it was injured.

Several others lingered behind it in the shadowy tree line. At least five or six; they were hounds, hunting dogs. They stared at me for a moment, and then to the leader as he raised his head and gave a half-strangled bark.

"Shit," Samuel said as he pulled his bow from his shoulder.

I reached for my gun but realized it would be too loud and the last thing we needed in this place was to draw attention to ourselves.

Daggers gleamed in Astrid's hands as the pack spread out and advanced.

"They're infected. Restless," Samuel said, and I knew by their strange bounding stride that he was right. Every single one of them was dead. Yet they ran toward us, their jaws wide, their eyes glowing, and their teeth like shards of flint.

36

As the dogs charged from the shadows, I saw the raw red holes along their bodies. They looked like gunshot wounds and their fur was matted with dried black blood.

The wet stench of their decomposition came at us in a wave. Samuel loosed an arrow and struck the pack leader in the throat but it didn't faze the beast. It still came at me, its unblinking milky-blue eyes locked onto mine, like there was no one else in the world, just me and him.

I planted my feet firmly, steadying myself as the sword of intention flashed in the gloom. The alpha growled and slowed as the rest of the pack fanned out around him and prepared to attack. Another arrow struck one of the hounds, but it didn't flinch. I kept my eyes on the leader as Astrid ran toward me, daggers in hand.

The lead dog lunged. I swung the sword to decapitate it, but another hound charged, intercepting the blow. The blade struck its flank and stuck, the momentum knocking us both off our feet.

I tried to pull the blade free but before I could, the pack

leader was on me. I grabbed the rank wet fur around his throat and thrust him back as his jaws snapped in my face. The stench was horrific.

He was strong. Stronger than me. It was only a matter of moments…

Astrid descended on him, her knife flashing above his dark silhouette. He yelped but there was no reaction or pain in his eyes. Just a killing intent. He turned on Astrid but I held it tight with one hand and grabbed the hilt of Talamos Gin's knife with my other, pulling it from its sheath. I brought it up to the beast's throat and it slipped through it like it was nothing more than wet newspaper. The blade kept going, arcing up through its skull and emerging stained with gore. I grimaced as I pushed him back and dozens of fat pale maggots tumbled from its carcass and wriggled upon my chest. The revulsion gave me a second wind and I hurled his twitching corpse off of me.

I was barely up before another hound lunged, knocking the dagger from my hand. I fell and grabbed its sopping wet snout, forcing it shut as I held it back. The thing was relentless, a killing machine. Its lifeless eyes bored into mine as it twisted its head and the slather around its lips frothed and foamed. As my fingers sunk into its fur, I caught a glimpse of the monster that had created it.

A burst of light hit my eyes. Like a flash bulb in a dark room then a snapshot of Endersley filled my mind's eye. I saw him standing over me… no, not me, the dog. A smile tugged his lips, like he was about to receive a much longed for reward. And then a man with a flat cap fired a shotgun. The dog collapsed and Endersley rushed over and slipped a long needle into the wound, his eyes wide with anticipation.

The connection burned the tips of my fingers as I shoved the dog away and leaped to my feet. It fell back, snarling as I seized the dagger from the ground and lopped its head off. I sheathed the blade and retrieved the sword of intention from the carcass of the dead dog near the pond. The mhudambe blade was too vital, and dangerous.

I turned as Samuel backed toward the woods, firing a volley of arrows. Astrid struggled under a hound that had pinned her down. "Come!" I called to the zombified dog snapping at Astrid. It looked my way, and I swung the sword, sending its head flying into the murky water. I yanked its corpse off Astrid and jumped back as another dog flew past me.

Two more followed, but their loping gait was impeded by the arrows lodged in their legs. I stepped toward them, swung hard and fast, and eliminated them one by one.

I felt sick. For the devastation, and the way these poor beasts had been mistreated. My sword sank into the ground as I leaned on its handle and tried to steady myself. Nausea passed through me and bile scorched my throat. I leant over and puked as white dots danced before my eyes.

"Here," Samuel said as he held out an expensive handkerchief. I took it, noting that the gold and scarlet monogram in the corner was not his.

"Thanks." I wiped my face and offered it back, half smiling as he flinched.

"Keep it. Or better yet, burn it."

"What about them?" Astrid glanced at the dead hounds. "We can't just leave this mess here. Someone's bound to come across it."

"Right," I agreed. I grabbed one of the dogs by its slack leg, dragged it to the pond and shoved it in. It wasn't exactly the most thorough or pleasant solution, but the clock was ticking. We worked together and cleared most of the carnage away before setting off under the steadily darkening sky.

The thin trail that led away from the meadow was buried under dead fern fronds and leaf litter, but we followed it as best we could. It took us to the edge of a clearing and there at the center was The Lodge; a sprawling stone walled mansion with a gabled roofline and dark arched windows. Snaking past the cold facade was a pebbled drive peppered with weeds. As it swept away from the house it transitioned into a long, potholed road that vanished into the forest. A stagnant fountain loomed over the unkempt lawn. Its centerpiece was a buxom woman clutching a trident, her once alabaster skin colored green by the algae flourishing in the thick putrid water.

"Nice place," Samuel said.

"It was once," I said. "Too bad old man Lampton's let it go to seed." I turned to Astrid. "Have you spotted any traps?"

"There's one by the fountain, but we should be fine if we keep our distance."

"He probably figures no one's crazy enough to come near this place," Samuel said. "And he has a good-" He stopped as something clicked behind us.

The unmistakable snap of a shotgun barrel locking into place.

37

The man wore a flat tweed cap that left most of his face in shadows, but his white glowing eyes stood out well enough. So did the shotgun pointed our way. It took a moment to register the true cadaverousness of his appearance; the bloodless gash in his cheek that was so deep it exposed muscle and bone. As well as the mauling claw marks that could only have been a result of tangling with the undead hounds.

"He's one of them. He's infected." Astrid whispered.

The zombie glanced at the shotgun. His face lined with concentration as his eyes flitted over the weapon. It seemed he was struggling to work out what to do next.

"Be quick," Astrid said as she darted into the gloom. He followed her movement, and I was about to disarm him when he jerked the barrel back my way.

"Now hold up there." Samuel said easily, like the matter was of no serious consequence. As if the zombie had merely caught its coat upon a nail. "I don't think you're supposed to be pointing that thing *at us*."

The zombie gurgled and turned its weapon toward Samuel.

"Did you know that over five hundred Wednesdays have gone missing since the day was named?" Samuel asked, and somewhere, hidden within his nonsense was a spell of confounding. "Or that the flies that land around cows' eyes are collecting tears to top up the seas. Yes, cow tears are highly sought after and often-" Samuel took the gun from the zombie and stepped back. "Something or other."

The zombie growled and lumbered toward him. I pulled my sword and swung, decapitating it just as Astrid emerged from the shadows, to presumably do the same thing.

"Another one of Endersley's hideous experiments," I said.

"Yeah," Samuel agreed, "it's looking like Lampton merrily handed over his groundskeeper and those hounds to the sicko."

"This place is insane," I said, before glancing back to the house. "And there's the heart of it. How are we going to get in?"

"Leave that to me." Samuel pointed to a window on the ground floor. "Wait over there." Then he turned with his trademark flourish and jogged into the trees.

We made our way around, hugging the shadowy tree line until we reached the closest point between the woods and the house, then we ran low, leaping over the graveled drive and landing in the tall brown grass near the window.

I glanced back toward the squalid fountain and the shadowy unkept garden, glad for Astrid's company. The place reeked of evil and neglect, and I tried not to think about the innumerable dark deeds that must have taken place here over the decades.

"Morgan," Astrid whispered, just before the window behind us slid open and Samuel appeared. He smiled but there was tension in his eyes. Astrid slipped through first and I passed my sword up to them before following her.

The hall was like a haunting memorial to faded grandeur. The once elegant maroon damask wallpaper was mostly faded, washed out to a sickly pinkish brown, and great swaths of it were torn or peeling. Everything was dusty and unkempt, from the oak tables dotted with expensive looking trinkets, to the framed portraits hanging along the wall. One was of a man in his early twenties and if I hadn't known better I might have confused Lampton for his grandson. They had the same severely parted black hair and cold beady eyes but his attire was from a lost era. And below it, on a stand, was a framed photograph of Lampton with his grandson standing in what looked like a penthouse overlooking the city. Their body language was stern and domineering, as was the hard look in their eyes and the image seemed to suggest the city was theirs and theirs alone.

I glanced up as music began to play upstairs. *Bach, Cello Suite No.1.* Thanks to Mrs. Fitz I knew it like the back of my hand. I listened intently. Below the quieter refrains came the sound of footsteps on creaking boards.

"Come on," I whispered as I led Astrid and Samuel along the sparsely furnished hallway and past the bust of a soulless looking man with hard, cruel eyes that overlooked the foot of the stairs.

We were about halfway up the first flight when a strange flickering lightning-like flash filled the hallway, but no rumble of thunder followed.

38

Astrid and Samuel shrugged as I glanced back at them. The strange flash was clearly as much a mystery to them as it was to me. I nodded for us to continue, cautiously expecting someone to appear on the landing above.

At the top of the stairs was a short corridor that led to a room with candlelight flickering over a dusty floor. We moved toward it, each of us tensed for whatever lay ahead.

The room beyond was spacious but sparsely decorated with paintings and a few dreary objets d'art displayed on tables and stands. In the corner, sitting by an old-fashioned record player, was Lampton. He wore a crumpled blazer over wrinkled satin pajamas and was too absorbed with pouring himself a glass of brandy or whiskey from a decanter to notice us.

He didn't look well. His hair was still severely parted though it had thinned considerably, and what little of it that was left was the color of ash and snow. Liver spots marred most of his gaunt wrinkled face and his hand shook as he took a desperate gulp from his glass and stared out through the drape-less window.

I drew my sword and scanned the room for undead servants, as Astrid slipped into the shadows. The music dipped and as it did, Lampton raised his glass and toasted his reflection. "To your good health, sir," he said, his voice little more than a rasp.

"Cheers!" I said.

He turned my way and his startled eyes grew wide with fear then fury. He reached down beside his chair and raised a handgun. "Who the fucking hell are you?" he demanded.

"Charmed, I'm sure," I said. "I suggest you put the gun down."

"So do I." Samuel stepped into the flickering light, his bow tensed as Astrid appeared before Lampton, dagger in hand.

Lampton scowled, and it took him a moment, but eventually he set his gun down on the armrest. Astrid snatched it away and it disappeared into the folds of her cloak.

"If you came here to rob me, then you'll leave as paupers," Lampton said, with a short, bitter laugh. I watched him closely, as if I was dealing with a cobra. There was no question the man had access to magic. Summoning and enslaving a succubus had been no small feat, but it seemed his skills had atrophied along with his physique and the splendor of his home. He looked tired and feeble as I crossed the room and plucked the needle from the record.

"Philistine," Lampton spat, still attempting to convey control.

"I came to talk about your grandson and the plans he's been hatching with Stroud and Endersley."

"I don't have the slightest idea what-"

"We know about it all," I said. "The portals, the Silver Spiral. The restless disease."

"Restless disease?"

"The contagion that reanimated your hounds and their master."

"Oh, those things." Lampton nodded. "What of 'em?"

"Your dogs and your groundskeeper, or whatever the poor bastard was, aren't of any consequence to you?" I asked, even though I was pretty sure I already knew the answer.

"Dogs?" Lampton shrugged. "They're just dogs, and as for Baxter, he was a miserable, drunken blinkered. Nothing to be missed or mourned, as I often say. Is that why you're here? All this trouble's over blinkered old Baxter and a pack of bloody hounds?" His words were slurred but I could see the booze hadn't entirely impaired his concern over his own mortality.

"No. I'm here about Endersley, Stroud and their connection to your grandson." I fixed his gaze to mine, snatched his whiskey away and slammed it down on the record.

Lampton stared me in the eye, and for an instance I caught a glimpse of the man he'd once been. Then I took another step toward him and he shrank back in his chair. "I've never had any encounters with Stroud," he said, "but I know of him. Through Prentice Sykes."

"How did you meet Sykes?"

Lampton shrugged, as if the information were of no consequence. "He sought me out." Lampton sat up in his seat and added, "My family has achieved a great many things in this dreary little world you know."

"What did Sykes want?"

"To open a portal. In exchange for treasures."

"A portal to Penrythe?"

"Yes, that's what he called it. *Penrythe.* That was where he said he was from, and that he'd found his way to our world after hearing about it in a place called The Hinterlands. Said he'd had to pay a fortune to be brought here, but he'd gotten himself stuck, somehow or other."

"Hence wanting help to open a portal," I said.

"Indeed. And in exchange he promised to return with lots of priceless trinkets for me." Lampton smiled. "Naturally I agreed to it, more for the promise of knowledge than treasure. After that it was a simple matter of opening the damned thing. I won't deny it was a little beyond the bounds of my abilities, formidable though they were." He paused and gave a hacking cough.

I glanced around for some water but there was none, so I handed him the whiskey and he took a greedy swallow, before thrusting the glass back at me. "Continue," I said, ignoring his clumsy stab at dominance.

"I asked Sykes what the simplest way to open a portal would be and he explained that one approach he'd heard of was the focus of many, many minds. He also said there was an inherent risk, because attempting to do this could cause them to break." A thin smile passed over Lampton's lips. "So I considered his warning carefully, because openly propagating madness wouldn't go unnoticed. But what difference would it make if the minds we used were already broken? And I just so happened to know a place where we could find such folk."

"Galloway."

"Someone give the lug a prize," Lampton responded. "Yes, Galloway Asylum. The only problem was the owner was a putrid little God botherer, a real boy scout. So I sent my she-devil to work her wiles on him. It didn't take long for her to get him wrapped around her little finger. Then it was just a matter of waiting for a particularly fortuitous phase of the moon and drugging the patients to get the bloody portal open. It was a roaring success actually, we only lost a few of the wall gazers in the process, not enough to register on the authorities' radar."

"And then what?" I asked as Lampton drifted into nostalgic reverie.

His eyes flashed my way. "I made a *shit ton* of money which bought me a shit ton more influence. And Sykes went back and forth between worlds and brought me treasures in return for keeping the portal open and my mouth shut."

"Treasures like this?" Samuel asked as he picked up a small silver figurine from the mantelpiece. A soldier, with a helmet shaped like a wolf's head. The sight of it jarred me. I'd seen armor like that before, in a foggy distant memory. "This looks like it was a part of the royal collection."

"Yes," Lampton agreed, "I believe Sykes said he stole it from a princess. What of it?"

"So that's why you destroyed countless lives?" I asked as my patience finally began to wear thin. "Money?" I swept my hand around the room. "Seems like your family probably had more than enough already. Or at least they did once upon a time."

"We *still* have money," Lampton barked. "And it was never about that anyway. It was a fuck you to the Organization and their ilk. Those who tell us what we can and cannot do, enforcing ham-fisted laws dreamed up by tedious little men. Plus having a way out of this tiresome place, should I need it, was more than appealing. But yeah, I took the money."

"It looks to me like it's long gone," I said, gesturing to the faded glamor surrounding him.

"Well, the grandson needed it more than me." He gave me a slow, impish smile. "Destroying civilizations is a costly business, I'll have you know. I let Hugo take whatever he needed and kept just enough to eat and be merry." His eyes fell upon the whiskey once more. I moved it away.

Hugo. That was the little prick's name? I could still picture his beady eyes as he'd lectured me at the Council meeting below Eveningside Station. "Who else came through the portal?" I asked.

"A few of his fellow knights. A dreary drunk of a man named Tom." His eyes flitted to Astrid. "And there was a woman. Looked like her. A nasty, stuck-up bitch. Thought she was too good for me."

Astrid took a step toward him but I held up my hand.

"I sent people back the other way too," Lampton continued. "Mercenaries, idiots, moon gazers."

"Why?"

"To see what treasures and knowledge they could find. I had suspicions that Sykes was holding out on me."

"And did any of them return?"

Lampton shook his head. "None. Not that anyone would have noticed they were missing."

"Why?" I asked. "Why risk opening a door to another world? You had no idea what could come through."

Lampton laughed. "I was perfectly aware my salad days were over at that point. But I could see the potential for my heirs to keep the Lampton torch burning, and for Hugo to rise even higher than I had. At least once his damnable mother had passed on. I can tell you, sacrificing my son to that marriage was quite the cross to bear, but it was worth it. Once we had her in our nest, we could siphon off information from the Council. Then she went and left the door open for Hugo to replace her, so it all worked out in the end."

"What about Endersley?"

"What about him?"

"What was he doing here? Clearly the undead dogs and their master was his handiwork."

"I gave him shelter for a while. That was all."

"So what's he got planned?" I demanded.

"You think he told me his plans? Think he'd trust them to a frail old man like me?"

"I think you know more than you're telling." I seized his dry wrinkled jaw in my fingers and stared hard into his eyes.

Lampton tried to pull away but finally he nodded, and another slow, malevolent smile crept over his lips. "I suppose I can tell you one thing at least." He leaned forward as if delivering a particularly salacious piece of gossip. "The city's about to catch quite a cold."

"What does that mean?"

Lampton folded his arms. "Just what I said. And that's all I'm giving you."

I slapped him hard enough for his head to jerk back. "Tell me what it means, because if you don't my friend will use her knives on you. We'll take your fingers and your toes, one by one." I glanced to Astrid, and she gave a solemn nod as she pulled a dagger from her belt.

Lampton gazed from Astrid to me and I could see him sizing things up. Slowly he slumped back in his chair. "I don't know what Endersley's planning, just that it's imminent. Have you ever encountered the man?" he asked as he twirled a finger at the side of his head. "He's utterly unhinged, but he has bags of talent, and he's proud of his work. It was his idea to turn Baxter and the hounds from living to dead and then to something in-between. Personally I think he did it to show off, but fair play, he did a good job."

"So he can turn blinkereds to restless now," I said to Astrid. She glanced from me to Lampton as he continued.

"By restless I take it you mean zombies?" Lampton asked. "If so, then the answer's a resounding yes. But not all of them. He tried it on the kitchen maid, but she ran around like a headless chicken for nearly an hour, smashing into walls and all sorts." He laughed. "It was quite amusing, actually."

"Sounds hilarious," I said. "Maybe we can get a dose of Endersley's virus and try it on you. See if you find that funny."

Lampton's smile faded. "My point was, he can make it work on some people to full effect, but not others and the means he has of spreading it is still primitive. Which is why he wants to try his latest strain on a crowd. Hence me telling you the city's about to catch a cold."

"Yes, I get it." I grabbed his face and forced his rheumy old eyes to meet mine. "What crowd? Where?"

"He didn't give details. But," Lampton raised his arm and glanced at the chunky watch on his withered wrist. "He should be conducting another test right about now. After that he'll cast his net a lot wider."

I let go of him and watched as he made a big deal about fastening his blazer and smoothing his hair. I was tempted to punch the smug prick, but I might as well have punched a baby. I turned to Samuel. "Wipe his mind, once this shit's over and order is restored, we'll have him sent to Stardim."

Lampton shot me a feral glare. "Fuck you!"

"You should be grateful, Stardim will be an improvement on this festering old pile of rubble," I said.

Before I could move, Lampton clambered from his chair and ran across the room with surprising dexterity. I raced after him as he emerged onto the upper landing and made for the stairs.

"Stop struggling-" I paused as a blinding flash filled the room. "What is that?" I demanded.

"Damned if I know," Lampton said. "Probably something to do with the boy."

"Boy?"

"Hugo. He loves all the latest spells, gadgets and whatnots.

You can ask him maybe. Just before he has you eviscerated like the pathetic peasant you are." As he spoke, his eyes drifted slightly and the air between us fizzled. He was summoning magic. Something wicked.

I back handed him to break the spell and slapped him across the top of his head, before dragging him back down the corridor and shoving him into the room. "Wipe the old bastard's mind. Leave him with nothing, no memories of his *salad days*, nothing to be proud of or to gloat over. Make him what he is, a sick old ghost haunting a sick old house."

"It will by my pleasure," Samuel said as he leaned on his haunches and began to tell Lampton one of his nonsensical stories.

It seemed Lampton's psychic defenses had been weakened by the booze because within moments a slow grin passed over his face and he began to nod along as Samuel slowly drew out his memories and replaced them with a long doddering string of nagging nonsense.

39

When we emerged from the woods surrounding the Lampton estate, and stepped back onto the main road, it felt like we'd just returned from another world entirely. I switched my phone on and it flashed, rumbled and chirped as message after message appeared.

Missed Call: Haskins

Over and over…

I called him. He answered immediately. "Where the hell have you been, Rook?"

"Good evening, Detective," I said. Clearly something was up, but after what I'd been through tonight I wasn't in the mood to bite.

"There's been another *incident*. Just like the one at the library, only this time there's more of *them*. A lot more."

"Where?"

"Downtown, outside a theater called The Playhouse, just look for the flashing lights. It's like a disco nightmare out here, you can't miss it."

"I'm on my way."

Our drive back to the city took the best part of an hour, and we saw the lights of the emergency vehicles long before we reached the scene There were ambulances everywhere and a line of police cars had cordoned off the street.

"Time to make ourselves look respectable," I said as I climbed out of the truck. Samuel cast an illusion spell as we walked, making us look like cops and I tried not to let my eyes linger on the tight folds of Astrid's snug blue uniform.

We crossed the barrier and nodded to any cops who looked our way. They nodded back, but a few did double-takes, as if they were trying to figure out who the hell we were. The red lights shot across the theater's old brick walls, washing out the round white bulbs on the old marquee that spelled out its name:

The Playhouse.

The scene was chaos. Blood spattered the sidewalk, the box office and the front doors. There was a sickening amount of it. People staggered by, many of them helped along by medics they didn't seem to notice.

I stepped back as an old man snapped his head my way and growled, gritting his dentures like a particularly pissed off Rottweiler. His eyes were wild, reasonless things with one goal only; to feed. The woman beside him licked her lips and ran a bloody finger over her gums like it had been slathered with cocaine. She barely glanced up as the police manhandled them both into a van and slammed the doors.

Yellow tape fluttered through the air near the theater's front entrance. As we took in the scene I caught sight of one of the victims. A young girl, she couldn't have been more than thirteen. Her head was at an oddly bent angle, her eyes glassy and the side of her throat was open and red. Then I saw the wounds on her shoulder and thigh as the pool of blood curdling around her reflected the theater's name like a dark mirror.

"They were chewing on her like she was drumstick," Haskins said, as he appeared at my side. His eyes glinted, and he wiped them quickly with the back of his hand. "Twelve years old. Her whole life ahead of her," he said, his voice breaking, "and then this shit happens."

"I'm sorry," I said.

"You're sorry?" Haskins voice was choked with anger. His hands curled into fists and a deep flush passed through his cheeks.

"I'm trying to stop this, Haskins," I said, "it's why we're here."

He glanced past me to Astrid and Samuel and shot them a venomous look. "So they're part of your freak show?" he asked.

"You can see us?" Samuel asked. He'd cast his illusion spell to deceive, but also to prod any curious or suspicious onlookers to turn away and take little notice of us.

"Of course I can see you," Haskins said. "And I know you ain't real cops. So what the fuck are you doing at my crime scene?" He rounded on me. "Well?"

"They're helping."

"Really?" Haskins asked, "cause I ain't seeing a lot of progress. It's been days since that librarian…"

"I know, and we're working on it." I felt for Haskins. He was right. The pointless deaths, the blood, the slow burning destruction was coming from our side of the city. But I was trying to stop it, I was doing everything I could.

"Those people," Haskins nodded to the theatergoers as they were led away, some on foot, many on stretchers, "they're headed for a hospital. They'll run tests and it's only a matter of time before the federal authorities are notified. And when they are there's going to be big questions. And consequences. Mark my words."

"They won't know what it is. It's not of this world," I said.

"I beg your pardon?" Haskins said. "Did you just say it's not of this world?"

"I did. Which means they're going to hit a dead end. But hopefully we'll have eliminated the man responsible before he can cause any more devastation. "

"*Hopefully?*" Haskins barked, causing more than a few cops to glance our way.

"Like I said, we're working on it." I looked down as my phone began to ring:

Dauple

"One second, Haskins" I said as I answered "I'll have to call you back, Dauple. There's been a-"

"No. You have to come and see me. Right away. You know where I live." He sounded exhausted, scared. I was about to tell him to give me some time but he hung up. I turned back to Haskins. "I's sorry, I've got to go."

Haskins grabbed the pocket on my *uniform*, which in reality was the lapel of my coat. "Get this fixed, Rook, because it's really starting to become a tale of two cities and I know which one's going to be burned down to the ground if this shit carries on. Here's a clue, it ain't going to be ours."

"I understand." I firmly removed his hands from my clothes. "Keep me posted and I'll do the same."

Haskins continued to glare at me, but finally he gave a sharp nod and strode away.

"We need to find a cab," I said as we walked back down the block. Police cars had boxed in our stolen truck, and I wasn't confident the spell I'd placed on its owner was going to hold out for much longer.

"Where are we going?" Astrid asked.

"To see a friend. An unusual friend."

Finally we flagged down a cab, Samuel called shotgun and I climbed into the back with Astrid. Half way down the block he started regaling the driver with one of his stories and soon the guy was laughing like they were the oldest of buddies.

I glanced out the window as a streak of silver lightning split the sky and a rumble shook the city. The storm was raging again, and rain pelted the windshield in wave-like torrents. It seemed apt. The car slowed near a bar at the intersection and its soft pink and blue lights twinkled in stark contrast to the men fighting outside. Five or six drunk morons trading blows, their heads snapping back, blood and teeth flying.

The city was on edge.

Everything was on edge. And about to crumble away.

40

We pulled up outside the building that housed Dauple's squalid basement apartment.

"That place doesn't look like it's going to be standing for too much longer," Samuel remarked as I paid the cab driver.

"Yeah, but it'll be okay for the next fifteen or twenty minutes. Now, I should warn you...expect the kind of squalor you'd find in a thirteen year old boy's bedroom. In other words, try not to be shocked, don't touch anything, and whatever you do, don't accept anything to eat or drink. And there will be flies. Don't swat 'em. There's a chance they're Dauple's friends."

"Friends?" Astrid arched an eyebrow.

"Yup."

"Great," Samuel clapped his hands. "Lead on."

We navigated the crooked concrete steps leading to the subterranean lair, dodging the pile of splitting garbage bags as we went. There were notably fewer flies this time round and it seemed by the tiny winged corpses scattered around the stairs that the changing of the season had claimed a fair few of Dauple's buddies. I knocked on the faded blue door. Within moments it opened a crack and Dauple's startled eye peered out at me. "Morgan," he said. "Oh, I am so glad to see you" He sounded drunk and looked relieved. Until he noticed Astrid and Samuel. "Who are they?"

"Friends," I said. "Can we come in?"

"Sorry." Dauple fiddled with the chain and opened the door, before waving us inside with a jerky sweep of his hand.

The smell wasn't as bad as I'd expected and it looked like he'd cleaned the place up, a little. His old sofa still rested lopsidedly against the spotted peeling wall, although someone had thoughtfully covered the scorched hole in the cushion with a throw. Tinny music played from the vintage radio on his wonky three-legged table, bringing to mind a vintage Hollywood film score being played in a wind tunnel.

Astrid and Samuel waited awkwardly in the middle of the room. She looked around with both horror and pity, while Samuel seemed to take it all in his stride.

With a loud clap of his hands Dauple scuttled off to the kitchen and returned with his good old dented platter. He'd loaded it up with a bottle of chocolate liqueur, a styrofoam cup, a wine glass and a pair of personalized mugs; one with a picture of himself in his top hat, the other a snapshot of his homely ex-girlfriend, the *drenched chipmunk*.

He set it down on his coffee table and gestured for us to gather around and help ourselves. Then he slopped a large measure into his mug, gulped it down, topped it back up, and bolted that one down too. "Whew!" he cried, then smiled at Astrid and gave her an awkward bow, before offering his hand to Samuel, who shook it firmly and gave one of his winning smiles. I introduced everyone, then poured myself a little of the liqueur and pretended to drink it, so as to not hurt his feelings. "So, what's all this about, Dauple?" I asked.

He cleared his throat. "This is not an easy thing to say."

"You can speak freely in front of us."

Dauple gave me a quick, furtive glance before continuing. "I was in the Cadaver Club earlier, and-"

"The what?"

"It's an underground bar that caters to people of my profession, as well as a limited number of *corpse enthusiasts*. It's a cracking place actually, everything's black; the decor, the drinks, the lights. And the music's a treat." He gave a brief smile. "We should go there, make a night of it."

"Sounds great," I said, hoping it sounded convincing.

"Yes," Dauple's smile faded as he continued, "I went there tonight because, frankly, today's been a total and utter shit of a day and I needed to be around friends." He poured another drink, before continuing. "And of course it wasn't long before Scaly Jackson turned up." He looked at me like I should know who that was.

"Scaly Jackson? Doesn't ring a bell."

"Sure he does, he works in the morgue, and fronts a band called The Doomed Years of Peregrine Golightly The Third." Dauple glanced at me, hoping for recognition. I shook my head. "Well anyway, Scaly came in, bought us all a round of Black Russians and started bragging that he had gossip that was juicier than a fresh corpse, and…"

"And what?"

Dauple glanced up at me then his gaze sank to the floor. "He said one of our agents screwed up big time and was due for the chopping block, literally. He was talking about you, Morgan."

"Really? What are they pinning on me now?" I did my best

to ignore the low sinking feeling that was reaching through me with cold, lingering fingers.

Dauple poured another shot, gulped it down and blurted the words out so fast I almost missed them. "The murder of Franklin Lampton."

41

"Look, I'll show you." Dauple pulled a phone with a sleek black case out of his pocket, tapped the screen and brought up a site with a flaming nine-pointed star enclosed in a circle. The official logo of The Hidden Times; a scurrilous tabloid that was big in the magical quarter. Its headline read:

'Slain In His Own Home By The Bloodied Hand Of The Law!'

I recognized the accompanying image immediately; Franklin Lampton's house. It must have been taken in better days because its lawn was clipped, its fountain gushed crystal clear water, and there, in the foreground stood Lampton impeccably dressed in a smart grey suit.

Dauple played the accompanying video, which consisted of hastily shot footage of an attractive, yet vacuous reporter standing outside Franklin's estate. I glanced at my watch. We'd been in the exact same place no less than two hours ago, which meant whoever had murdered him must have called the press before they'd even committed the crime.

"… slaughtered in his home, surrounded by portraits and pictures of his loved ones." The reporter paused to look solemn and then the video cut to an image of Franklin Lampton lying on the floor of his drawing room with his ashen face encircled by a heavy pool of blood.

"It's too early to say exactly what occurred at the Lampton Estate," the reporter continued, raising her painted eyebrow, "but the authorities have named a person of interest who is wanted for questioning in relation to the crime; Morgan Rook, a rogue agent formerly with the Organization."

The video made a jump-cut to grainy footage of me on the landing above Lampton's staircase as he tried to run from me. They'd got me shouting in his face and back handing him before slapping him over the top of the head. Another cut, and they had me dragging him back down the corridor and shoving him into the drawing room. And then a somber, fade to black.

My head was reeling; this had to be Hugo Lampton's doing. My thoughts jumped to the flash of light we'd seen when we'd first entered the house. Presumably some sort of device had notified Hugo Lampton of our arrival. I pictured him scrambling from the city, his plan already cooked. Perhaps he'd been looking to off his grandfather for a while. I couldn't imagine the old man would have served much use to Hugo once he'd handed over the family fortune, and Hugo didn't exactly strike me as a sentimental kind of guy.

Dauple looked at me like he desperately needed some reassurance, and I couldn't blame him. "It looks really bad," I said, "but I didn't do it. You know that, right?"

Dauple nodded. "Of course."

"It was a set up. Plain and simple. And-" I glanced up as a loud boom echoed outside and the lights flickered.

"What the heck was that?" Dauple asked.

"I don't know," I said as I walked over to the window. "But it didn't sound good."

42

I pulled back the damp curtain and looked outside. All I could see was rain, gloom and the grey, chipped stairs leading up to the driveway. Another distant boom rang out. "I think it's time to go," I said, "We need to find out what in the hell's going on."

"You want to take my car?" Dauple offered. He pulled his keys from his pocket and held them out to me.

"Sure," I said, "but you better stay here. Keep out of it. I'll text you, to let you know where I've left the car."

"Rightio," Dauple said. "I think I'll go and have a little nightcap and lie down." His smile was watery and wretched as I shook his hand. Like he'd had enough of the darkness and chaos raging through the city and I knew exactly how he felt.

"Thanks, Dauple" I called as I followed Astrid and Samuel out.

The hearse was parked on the street, wedged between two sleek cars that made it look even more like a long dark metallic beetle. I opened the back door for Astrid and Samuel before climbing into the driver's seat and fastening the clammy seatbelt into place.

"This car…" Samuel began, his voice trailing off.

"It's used for transporting the dearly departed."

"Delightful. I thought it smelt a bit dead. Now I know why."

I had my phone in hand and was about to call Haskins, but he beat me to it. "What's the situation?" I asked.

"There's *several* situations," Haskins shouted as sirens whined and blared around him.

"What was the boom? It sounded big."

"A car blew up on Sixth, then another one went off on the same block. The bomb squad's on the way, but right now I've got another problem. As in a really frigging urgent problem. Meet me at that burger joint on Fourth Street. Fast."

"What's going on?"

"The place is full of kids that went there for a birthday party. And now there's a bunch of fucking zombies outside looking to make a meal of 'em. I got backup on the way but I don't how long they're going to take, not with all the other shit that's happening right now."

"I'm on it." I gunned the engine. The car rattled, a cloud of bitter blue smoke drifted past the windows, and we were off speeding down the dark, empty streets. Now and then I caught sight of a few blinkereds milling around, looking dazed, as if the world was falling down around them. It seemed like it was.

As we approached the heart of the city, cop cars and ambulances tore past us, each of them heading in the same direction.

"This is chaos," Astrid said.

"It sure is," I agreed. "And it reeks of orchestrated chaos." I pulled up on Fourth Street beside a burst hydrant and took a soaking as I ran to the median. The burger place was across the street and a huge crowd had gathered around it. Their hospital gowns fluttered in the breeze as they lumbered toward the window, their snarls and moans filling the air.

"Get ready." I turned to Astrid and Samuel. They were already armed.

As we crossed the street I spotted Haskins' car. He was crouched behind it, his gun aimed at the horde. I nodded to him and as we got closer, I saw the tags around their ankles. They'd all come from the morgue. The living dead. It seemed Endersley had perfected at least one aspect of his virus.

The restaurant windows were shot through with web-like cracks and spotted with blood. Kids stood huddled behind them, their faces wracked with horror as they watched one of the restless run into the window and began to hammer his fists upon the shattered glass.

"Hey!" I called, drawing the attention of a few of the restless from the restaurant. They shuffled toward us, gurgling and growling as they approached.

"What are we supposed to do?" Samuel asked. "They're blinkereds."

"They're reanimated blinkereds," I said. "This is Enderley's handiwork and we have to do whatever it takes to stop them or we're going to have a massacre on our hands." I grabbed a crystal, soaked up its magic and pushed through the shuffling throng.

The kids stared wide eyed as I laid my palm on the window, turning the glass as black as ebony to shield them from the imminent melee. Then I pulled my sword and we set to work, moving as one.

I swung my blade, striking heads from zombies as Astrid threw daggers in flashing, deliberate arcs. Above the moans and screams was the roar of Haskins' gun as he took out the creepers closest to the restaurant while Samuel covered us all with his bow, eliminating the restless shambling up behind us, his piercing arrows bringing them down with ruthless efficiency.

I glanced up as two more of the wretches came toward me. My sword blazed as I shouted, "End!" Their heads struck the ground with a thud, like flat basketballs and their eyes twitched and blinked. It was a sickening sight. These *monsters* were mothers, fathers, aunts and uncles, grandparents, and kids whose lives had been snatched away, only to find themselves subjected to this final, grotesque humiliation. Anger flared through me and I swore to visit this very same torment on Endersley.

We continued to fight until we were down to the last few restless and that was when I felt him, my other, stirring in the depths of my soul like a piranha drawn to the scent of blood. *Look what you've done,* he said. A tinge of gallows humor laced his words. *Corpses everywhere and you, as ever, right there in the middle of it.*

I forced him away from my consciousness. He went without a fight, but still the encounter had unsettled me. We'd fought together to destroy Elsbeth Wyght, but ever since that had been accomplished, we'd been more divided than ever.

"Done," Astrid said, as she downed the last shuffling zombie.

"Interesting choice of weapons," Haskins said. He looked Astrid and Samuel up and down as he walked over and barely suppressed his scowl as he turned to me. "I might say good going, if I was ignorant to the reason why all this shit's going down."

"Give it a rest," I said. "I'm trying to get this fixed."

"My guys have been out here all night risking their lives, and this," he swept a hand toward the bodies in the road, 'this mess is on you." A line of police cars sped by us, lighting up the scene as Haskins' phone rang. He answered and placed a finger in his other ear. Slowly his face grew paler and paler. "Perfect," he said as he hung up.

"What?" I asked.

"Now there's a hostage situation."

"Where?"

"Meadow Street. At some swanky fundraiser."

"Who's there?"

"Oh," Haskins shrugged, "just the city's big shots. You know, the cream of the fucking crop."

"Looks like they were the primary target tonight, and all of this out here was just bread and circuses," I said. "Come on, let's go."

Haskins called in ambulances and police officers to secure the area while I went inside and reassured the families, telling them to sit tight and that help was on the way. As soon as they seemed reasonably under control, we all headed to Haskins' car.

The city was little more than a neon blur as we sped toward the scene.

"This is it," Haskins barked as he abruptly pulled over in the middle of a block lined with old brick buildings. Black limos and expensive cars filled the street and prestigious law offices and private clinics were scattered amid the upmarket galleries and design studios that surrounded the auction house. Any paparazzi that might have been there were long gone but the red carpet and rope cordons were still set up outside the mirrored glass entrance.

I glanced up as a window in the auction house shattered and glass rained down. A figure appeared, staff in hand. He gazed at us for a moment, before casting a fireball that streamed across the night sky, lighting us in its wake.

"God, I hate this freaky shit," Haskins said. "Is that the prick from the bank?" He gave me another accusatory glare and ran low toward the limos. I was about to follow when Samuel cocked his head like a hound on the trail of bloody and succulent prey, then he leaped forward and shoved me hard.

A violent whine whizzed through the air and shattered the car window behind me. "Run!" Samuel grabbed my arm and yanked me up.

We raced across the street, zigzagging as another round hit the pavement with a loud ping.

I knew the sound well.

Sniper fire.

43

Ebomee? The magician had used a blinkered sniper in the bank. But this shot had had a quality that was beyond deadly accurate, and I'd have been lying in the road with half my skull missing if it hadn't have been for Samuel.

I ran low, past Haskins' car, using it for cover as another bullet zinged off the asphalt, and I met Astrid's gaze as she took cover in a doorway and pointed up and left.

"Where's it coming from?" Samuel shouted as he crouched beside me, carefully pulling his bow from his shoulder and setting it down.

"Astrid reckons up there." I nodded to the end of the street. "The top of that multilevel parking garage. I'll see if I can get a better look." I pulled a telescope from my bag and swept it toward the upper floors. Its magical lens revealed a steady red heart beating slow and calm through a heavy wall. Right on the level she'd pointed out. I snatched my head down as a bullet split the air and pinged off the brick doorway beside me.

Another upper window of the auction house shattered and a body fell to the ground. A man in a tuxedo, his silent descent indicating he'd been killed before he'd been tossed from the building. I looked back up to find the magician. He raised his staff to the sky and released a stream of fire that coiled, spiraled and bloomed with red and yellow embers as it formed into a wyvern. Only it wasn't an illusion this time, but a sentient creature of fire. The beast pulled back its wings and soared, dipping its head as it spotted us, and swept down.

Whumph!

It shot over the street, passing within a few feet of us, and then roared back up into the air, circling as it kept us within its blazing, watchful gaze.

"Great." I turned back to the auction house where Haskins was hidden behind one of the limos, gun in hand. He glanced my way and I pointed to myself and then to the end of the street. Haskins nodded. I turned to Samuel, "We need to eliminate the sniper. Fast. You ready?"

"Always."

"Cover me as I move in. Haskins is going to do the same."

Samuel nodded as he notched an arrow.

"Go!" I shouted. Haskins leaped up and fired at the garage as Samuel aimed and loosed an arrow. I ran down the street. Astrid's footfalls rang out behind me and I ducked into a doorway. She squeezed in behind me as Haskins' gunfire ceased and all of a sudden we were stuck there, up close and locked tightly together.

I peered round the wall, but it was hard to see the top floors of the garage in the darkness, then the wyvern soared by lighting the street up like a Christmas tree.

I pulled Astrid in as a bullet whistled into the wall beside the doorway and tore off a chunk of concrete. "Shit!" I peered out but could only see Haskins. I held up my hand, five fingers, four, three. "Get ready" I said to Astrid. Two fingers, one. "Go!"

ENDER OF WORLDS

We ran as Haskins' gun cracked and whined. Then a long arrow pierced cleanly through the fiery wyvern and its shaft burst with light as it continued on its trajectory towards the garage. A chime rang out as it hit a large metal sign and illuminated the silhouette of a small, powerful-looking figure poised with a rifle.

I fired at the garage as Haskins' shots rang out behind us and the wyvern roared at our backs. "Take cover!" I cried as I leaped over a car. I turned back as Astrid tumbled over its hood and landed beside me.

We dived into the garage before the sniper could get off another shot and scuttled aside as a huge, feral roar boomed behind us and the ground lit up. The wyvern flashed by, the intensity of its heat scorching the side of my face. And then it blazed through the lot and began to wheel back toward us.

"This way!" I ran for the stairwell. Astrid passed me before I could reach it. She shoved the door open with her shoulder and held it for me as the bright orange beast snapped at my shoulders and its incandescent flames glowed vivid red in the polished finish on the cars.

I burst through the opening and Astrid slammed the heavy door shut behind me. Fire leapt through the cracks as the wyvern crashed into the steel with a roar. I heard the beat of its wings as it soared away.

We headed up the stairwell, slowly, carefully, checking for signs of the sniper in the darkness. Gunfire rang out from the street. Presumably Haskins was keeping the sniper busy. If I was right and it was Ebomee it meant two things. First, I'd better be at the top of my game. Second, this was a set up and we'd been expected here, so there was a fair chance there could be other agents around.

"I'll scout ahead," Astrid whispered, and before I could say a word she ran up the stairs.

Finally I cleared the top step and reached for the door when it opened of its own accord, admitting a faint wash of moonlight. Astrid appeared and nodded for me to follow. We ducked behind an SUV and she whispered in my ear, her breath warm and sweet. "At the end of the next row."

I glanced round the car to see Ebomee leaning casually against the wall at the end of the lot. She wore one of her trademark suits and she might have looked approachable if it wasn't for the sniper rifle leaning on the wall beside her. She picked it up and peered over the parapet to take aim when she suddenly cried out and doubled over, clutching her arm. It took a moment to spot the arrow embedded near her elbow. She gritted her teeth as she wrenched it out.

"Can you get close to her?" I whispered to Astrid.

She nodded. "Do you want me to eliminate her?"

"No. Move in and wait for me."

Astrid slipped into the darkness. Ebomee winced as she seized the rifle back up. I waited for her to lean over the wall, before moving in, treading as lightly as I could, my gun trained on her.

She fired and before I could call out to her to drop the rifle an arrow whistled past her head and thudded into the darkness. As Ebomee turned toward it she met my gaze and swept her rifle toward me. She looked me in the eye, and I knew she was committed to pulling the trigger. Until Astrid emerged from the shadows and placed a knife against her throat. "Drop it," Astrid demanded.

Ebomee smiled. "I'm losing my touch."

"It was four against one," I said as I kept my gun on her. "Although you did have the advantage, initially. Now like the lady said, drop it."

"She a friend?" Ebomee asked.

Roooaaaaarrrrrr!

The wyvern spiraled over the wall, its blinding fire flooding the entire level with light. It hovered for a moment, distracting me as Ebomee dropped her rifle, shoved Astrid back and pulled a pistol from her jacket. Before I could fire it was held tight against the side of Astrid's head.

"Put the gun down, Morgan," Ebomee said.

"You know I won't."

"Shoot the bitch," Astrid cried, her voice furious.

Ebomee smiled. "Seems we're at an impasse."

The wyvern crackled, its heat intensifying as it began to swoop in toward the garage. I kept my sights on Ebomee and ducked behind a car as I waited for the fiery beast to soar past. "We're not at an impasse," I called. "I'll shoot. You might get one round off, or maybe you won't. You've been careless once more. You forgot about my friends in the street."

Ebomee hooked her arm around Astrid and began to inch away from the wall. I took my shot. It clipped her shoulder, and her gun fell to the ground. Astrid sprang free and seized it.

"Fuck!" Ebomee clapped a hand to her shoulder, her face creased with pain.

"I'll call this in and get you some help once I've dealt with the wyvern and its creator," I said.

"And why are you sparing me?"

"You saved my hide once, don't you remember?" I said. It had happened on one of my very first jobs with the Organization, and I'd never forgotten it.

"I only did that because I'd have been down a gun if you'd died."

"I don't believe that," I said. "You're about the only agent I ever had any respect for."

"Why?" Ebomee asked, and looked genuinely puzzled.

"Because I knew you had respect for me."

"You're delusional, I was willing and fully prepared to blow out your brains not five minutes ago. And I'd still do it, given the chance."

"Sound like you're trying to convince me to shoot?" I asked.

"Maybe I am."

"Why?"

She sighed. She looked tired. Finished. "Because I'd prefer a quick end to a slow one. It was made crystal clear to me that if I didn't bag you tonight, I'd suffer. And so would my husband."

"Who put you up to it? Who threatened you? Humble? Lampton?"

"Give it up, Morgan," Ebomee said. "It's over."

"What's over?"

"Everything. The die is cast. There's going to be countless of us passing into the night. Things won't ever be the way they were, not now. Not for us." She gave a tired, bittersweet smile.

"I'm not giving in," I said. "Never."

"And that's where you and I differ." Ebomee reached into her jacket.

I fired. The round hit her in the chest and her hand fell from her coat as she collapsed. It was empty.

44

"Ladies, gentlemen," Samuel said as he appeared on the top floor of the garage. He glanced from Astrid to me, and then to Ebomee, before adjusting his tone. "You okay?"

"I guess." I wasn't okay. Not by a long shot. Ebomee and I hadn't exactly been buddies, but I'd never felt an enmity between us either. And I was pretty sure she hadn't been very happy with being assigned to take me out, not like Rhymes would have been. I glanced into the sky as the wyvern circled above us. "That thing's got to go."

"Yeah," Samuel said, "it's giving me a headache."

"Then let's do this." I picked up Ebomee's rifle, adjusted the scope and peered over the wall. Haskins was still taking cover behind the limo and as he spotted me he raised his gun my way. I lowered the rifle, waved and watched as his diminutive figure gave a single wave in return. I peered back through the scope and swept it over the auction house roof.

"So what's the plan?" Samuel asked.

I nodded to the auction house roof across the way. "If we

can reach that, we might have the element of surprise. Do you have any means of getting up there?"

"Yes," Samuel said. "Climbing and hoping for the best."

"Without that thing spotting us," Astrid nodded to the wyvern. "Maybe you can go to the street and draw it away from us."

"Good plan," Samuel said, "leave us to climb in darkness. That way no one will see our embarrassment as we plunge to our certain deaths."

"Try not to die," I said. "Once you're up there, there should be access to the building below, a door or a hatch. Haskins and I can work our way up from the ground floor. Between us we should be able to take them out and meet up with you somewhere in the middle."

"And what's our endgame exactly?" Samuel asked. "Aside from killing the baddies?"

"The magician, we need to find out what he knows about Endersley. But be careful, he has hostages, we'll have to move in 1-"

"Like shadows. Or mice. Or shadow mice," Samuel said. "We'll disguise ourselves. It probably won't work on the magician but it should fool his thugs. Just as long as they're blinkered."

"Good," I said.

"How do you want to appear?" Astrid asked.

"Black clothes, boots, shaven head, feral and then just hit me with the ugly stick a few times and I should blend right in with the hired muscle."

"Your wish is my command." Samuel whispered as he placed his hands on my shoulders.

The air shifted, and a static like sensation swept over my clothes and hair. I peered down and caught a glimpse of the illusion. "Great," I said, "I'll see you on the inside."

"Not if we see you first, dog face." Samuel strode away across the rooftop.

"Take care," Astrid called as she followed him.

I headed back down the stairwell and out to the street. The wyvern wheeled above me and began to hover, as if it were trying to read me or see past my disguise. I strolled along the sidewalk like I owned it, gun in hand, an exaggerated swagger in my step. The wyvern flew down and flapped its fiery wings above me and its blazing ember-eyes bore into mine. I glanced up like it was of no concern and continued on my way. The wyvern watched for a moment, and then a warm breeze from its wings brushed my face as it turned and flew back into the sky. It appeared it wasn't just the blinkereds that could be taken in by Samuel's illusion, but the magician too. For now at least.

"Freeze," Haskins called. He had his gun trained on me as he peered over the hood of the limo. "Oh, it's you, Rook" he said, before lowering his weapon.

"You saw past the illusion," I said.

"I've spent most my life trying to see through people's bullshit, so don't look so surprised. Where are your buddies?"

"On the roof, they'll be making their way down through the auction house while I work my way up. You in?"

"I guess. I sent for backup but my team's already up to their necks in it. This is the day from hell."

"Then it's time to send the devil packing," I said. "You hold back a minute or two." I strode to the main doors. They were locked. I cupped my hand against the tinted glass and peered inside.

Two thugs stood at a receptionist's desk with a bottle of champagne poking out of an ice bucket beside them, no doubt from the soiree upstairs. Both looked soused as they glanced my way. One strode toward me, his gun raised. I looked back at him like he was nothing and gestured for him to open the door. He did but blocked my path. "Who the fuck are you?" he asked, his breath sour with booze.

"Let me in you prick. I've done my circuit, the targets are down."

"Down? You sure?"

"Yeah, the sniper capped 'em. Now are you going to let me in or am I going to have to knock your fucking teeth down your throat?" I stared as he opened the door wider, muttered, and wandered back to the counter. One brief introduction to the butt of my gun was enough to knock him out cold and he fell before the other could reach for his weapon.

Gunfire thundered above us, distracting me. When I glanced back to the thug at the desk he'd armed himself.

"Put it down-" Haskins' warning was cut short as the thug's gun roared. His bullet whizzed past my head and took out the glass pane behind me. Haskins and I returned fire. I wasn't sure which of our rounds hit first, but the thug's face exploded into red mush and what was left of him slumped over the counter.

"Not quite the stealthy entrance I was planning," I said, as I made my way through the foyer. There was a bank of three elevators next to a stairway. I grabbed a handful of crystals from my pocket and soaked up their magic. Haskins watched with a scowl, but he left it there.

"Ready?" I asked, as the power jolted through me. He nodded, and we began to climb, until a series of heavy footsteps clattered on the stairs above us.

Three armed thugs rounded the landing, semi automatics raised. I forced a steady, focused calm over myself and fired. I took one down and then the other, while Haskins' gun blazed beside me, felling the third. We stepped over the corpses and spent cartridges and bounded up the next flight as the door burst open on the upper landing. A blinkered with a cruel face and bored, languid eyes appeared. He had a gun clamped to the side of a young woman's head and the dark streaks of mascara that ran down her cheeks matched her dress.

"Drop the guns," the man said with an almost listless drawl. I faced him down as the crystal's magic ripped through my system, and tried to hold him in my unsteady sights.

My dark other's power had guided bullets in the past. *Want to do it again?* I asked. He ignored me, but I let it go. I focused the crystal's magic and tried to draw on my own untapped powers. They'd been hidden deep within me but they were there alright; I'd felt them stirring since my clash with Talamos Gin.

The man shot at me. I ignored the flash and report of his weapon and returned fire, clipping him in the shoulder and punching him back into the wall behind him. Before he could recover, I strode up the stairs and shot point blank. I could have spared him but I'd seen the inherent cruelty in his eyes and had decided the world would be safer without him.

"Please," the woman began to sob, "my husband's in there. They have them…"

"How many gunmen?"

"Ten, mmm…maybe more."

"Don't worry, we've got this." I turned to Haskins. "Can you get her to safety?"

"What about the other goons?" he asked.

"We can handle it. Cover the street in case any more show up."

Haskins nodded, reached for the trembling woman and led her down the stairs. It sounded, from the low chatter of voices and occasional cries and yelps, like the auction room was on the next floor. The ultra keen sense of purpose and focus was still with me, at least until red light flared as the wyvern struck the tinted glass window outside. Its flaming claws sank into the side of the building and its smoldering eyes found mine.

I'd been discovered. The magician had seen through my illusion.

I ran, taking two steps at a time and hurtled up to the next landing. It ended in an antique wooden door with an ornate brass plaque to one side. I shoved it open and entered a long banquet room with round tables covered with white tablecloths and candles that threw an eerie light over the faces of the people gathered around them.

The men wore tuxes and had the imperious look of old and new money while the women wore little black numbers. The lady closest to me looked sick and I noticed her pearls were flecked with blood. Beside each table the magician's men loomed, their guns pointed at the hostages' heads, their eyes locked onto mine.

"Morgan Rook!" A voice called. I followed it to the stage where the magician stood behind a podium with his glowing staff, as if he was the emcee. An orb shimmered in his hand and I guessed it was the scrying glass he'd been using to track me through his fiery familiar's eyes. Slowly, he aimed the long scepter-like rod my way and before I could move, he cried out a word of power.

45

I gathered my coat around me as a bolt of fire flew from the magician's wand and hit me dead on. Screams from the guests filled the air. I crouched, waiting for the flames to subside, and once they had I stood, untouched.

"Those are some powerful rags you got there," the magician said.

"Release the hostages." I stared into his wild eyes as they gleamed by the candlelight. "Now."

He laughed. I didn't blame him. It wasn't like I had an edge on the situation. I glanced past him as something moved in the shadows. Astrid? Samuel? I hoped so. "I'm serious. If you want to live then let these people go."

"You got lucky at the armory" the magician said. "We weren't expecting anyone else to be there."

"Yeah, a dwarf and a shopkeeper against three werewolves and a fire magician," I said, "sounds like a lame joke."

"You've had your fun, Mr. Rook." The magician gazed behind me. "But now you'll see what happens when you fuck with me."

"That was your last chance to live," I said.

"Your friends helped before." The magician raised his staff. "But now you're alone."

"Oh, I'm never alone," I said. "Believe me." I watched as Astrid slipped from the darkness backstage and before his men could react or warn him, she had a knife at his jugular. "See," I said, as the magician's eyes widened. I turned to the thugs at the tables. "Release the hostages and throw your guns down. Now."

They stared in silence, some scowled, but none disarmed or made a move. It seemed they had no loyalty to the magician, only to themselves. One raised a gun and fired. The round was stopped by my coat, but I fought to catch my breath as I returned fire, taking the side of his head off.

I glanced back as another thug jolted in his seat and slumped dead to the floor. Samuel stepped from the shadows in the back of the room, just long enough for me to see him notching another arrow.

"Take that fucking coat off," a goon at a nearby table yelled. The back of his hand looked like a twitching mosaic of tattoos as it gripped a young woman's slender throat. In his other hand was a hunting knife, its tip poised under her eye. "Do it!"

I stared him down, willing my dark other to meet his gaze and scramble his resolve with a dose of fear.

Nothing.

I was about to take a shot, when the lady in his grip screamed, shoved his arm away and tried to run. He threw the knife. It struck her in the back with a sickening thump. The thug grinned as he leaned over to retrieve his weapon and as he rose an arrow head passed through his trachea, stealing his breath. His eyes widened, as he scrambled to pull it from his neck, then he toppled over.

There were only five of the thugs left, but they were panicking, big league. "Back off or I'll fucking shoot him!" one yelled as he jumped up from his table, his gun clamped against an old man's head. The others rose around him and made similar threats, but I saw them scanning the darkness in the corners of the room, nervously.

That's right. Beware of the shadows. Always.

I took one down with a single shot and was about to eliminate another when I saw him glance to the stage behind me. Astrid still had the magician in her grip, but his lips were moving. He was casting a spell but she hadn't noticed. "Astrid!" I cried.

The doors blew open and dazzling bright red light drenched the room as the wyvern stormed in. It turned and shot toward the stage, illuminating Samuel as he aimed his bow at the magician. Gunfire roared as the thugs took pot shots at him but Samuel ran low, vanishing into what was left of the gloom. The wyvern wheeled and soared toward me and I dropped to my knees as it shot overhead.

Astrid released the magician and rolled away before the wyvern could strike and it became tangled in the long curtains that framed the stage, igniting them as it flailed. It seemed to be independent of its master's control, making it more dangerous than ever.

I fired at the magician as he stooped amid the smoke to recover his staff but the round went wide and he scampered backstage. I ducked as the wyvern flew across the room, its fiery claws raking at a hostage as she tried to flee for the door. Flames engulfed her dress and she howled in pain and terror. I ran to her, wrenched my coat off and used it to smother the flames then I scanned the crowd for the remaining criminals as the hostages began to flee.

The thugs were all down, some by arrow others by dagger but there was no sign of the magician. Donning my coat, I ran toward the stage. On the wall beside it were two fire extinguishers. I grabbed one, doused the flames as best I could and spun around as the wyvern hurtled my way.

I stood my ground and gave it a blast from the canister, snuffing out one of its wings. It roared as it lost control and crashed to the floor, and then it rose straight up and began to hobble toward me. I pulled the mhudambe blade from its sheath and slashed at the wyvern's head. It tore through its fiery skull and the flames that formed it withered away around the wound as the beast reared up.

Before it could spring I lunged at its flaming throat. It gave a strange, eerie cry and collapsed to the floor in a smoldering heap. I blasted it with the extinguisher, before tossing it over to Samuel. "Put the fires out," I called as I sheathed the knife and ran across the stage in the direction the magician had fled. At the back of the smoky prop room, amid easels and stands, I found a door. I kicked it open onto a stairwell and a trail of sooty footprints led up. I followed them floor after floor, until they vanished at a barred emergency exit. My intuition told me opening the door would be a bad idea. But I had no choice.

I slammed the bar down, stepped out and ducked as a bolt of fire hurtled toward me. It struck the wall as I pulled my gun, fired into the darkness and stumbled out onto the rooftop.

Another bolt roared from the gloom, hitting me square in the chest, knocking me down. I rolled, quenching the flames, and glanced up to see the magician looming over me. I tried to stand as his staff rose and eldritch blue light glowed at its tip. He struck me in the face with the blunt end and the stony asphalt bit into my palms as I fell back on the rooftop.

"Morgan fucking Rook!" He stood over me. The light

radiating from his staff lit his wild eyes and gaunt features. It seemed he was high on his own madness. I tried to retrieve my fallen gun but he pinned my hand under his foot and swung the staff around, aiming it at my heart. "This is going to hurt," he said. "I promise."

46

deadly charge crackled and fizzled from the magician's staff. I had nowhere to go. My other shifted, as if rising to the selfish call of his own preservation, but he was too late. My only hope was that the agony would be brief and the kill, fast.

Shoooooooph.

I threw my arms up to cover my face as blood and gore exploded from the magician's chest. His staff clattered to the ground, and he fell to his knees, his fingers slick with blood. I glanced across the roof, expecting to find Samuel or Astrid, but there was no one.

Then I spotted a figure moving along the roof of the parking garage. Haskins, holding Ebomee's sniper rifle in his hand.

I signaled that the threat was neutralized and for him to return to the street, then I hunkered down beside the magician. He was still alive, but barely. His eyes flickered over mine and he whispered words I couldn't understand. "Where's Endersley?" I asked, calmly.

He laughed, the sound little more than a hacking gurgle. "Go to hell!"

I drew away as he spat out blood and glared up at Astrid and Samuel as they appeared behind me.

"I thought we weren't going to shoot him," Samuel said.

"Haskins got him. He saved my life," I said.

Astrid leaned down and gazed into the magician's eyes. "He doesn't have long. Minutes maybe."

"That's far too much time to spend in the company of filth like you," the magician coughed. "Traitorous bitch."

"Traitor?" Astrid's eyes flashed dangerously as she traced a finger around the wound in his chest, causing him to howl in agony.

"Attacking your own, siding with blinkered filth." The magician spat again, over estimating his own strength, as it oozed down the side of his face. Astrid shot him a look of revulsion and stepped back.

"Is there any way to keep him alive a little longer?" I asked.

"Yes," Astrid said.

"Good, I'll make sure every second of it is spent in abject pain. Unless he gives us the information we need." I pulled a small bottle of Rawblynde from my bag, and shook it in front of the magician's face. "We're given this to sear off old or abandoned magical binds. It's quick and reliable but you have to use it very, very carefully because even the smallest speck on your skin burns like you can't believe." I smiled as I unscrewed the cap. "You look skeptical, but you'll see what I mean."

His glare turned from fury to fear and then contempt. He forced a sneer. "Go on. Get it done."

"Fine." I took the pipette from the bottle and let a single drop fall upon his throat.

He gave a terrible, hoarse cry and furiously wiped his neck

with trembling fingers, and then he panicked and twitched as his hands began to blister. I grabbed a cloth from my bag and wiped the Rawblynde off as best I could. "Imagine it sinking into an open wound. By the time it wears off, you'll feel like you've suffered a thousand lifetimes in hell."

"I don't know where Endersley is," the magician coughed, "he left."

I believed him. "But you do know where his base of operations is."

"He has hidey-holes all over the damned place and we're all in the dark; he's refused to see anyone until after the event, including me. So no one knows where he is."

Event. I made a mental note to return to the topic. "What was all this about? And don't tell me it was just a robbery. I know part of it was a trap for me. What else happened tonight?"

"Nothing. It was just a robbery, I swear it."

I dipped the pipette into the Rawblynde and held it over him.

He snarled, but finally spoke. "Some of Endersley's people were bringing their devices into the city. The robbery was a ruse, to distract the authorities."

"Devices?"

He managed a strangled laugh. "Bombs. A means to spread the restless virus far and wide."

"Where?"

"I don't know. Most things with Endersley are on a need to know basis. Just enough knowledge to get our jobs done. Mine was to extract cash from these pampered fools and draw you to the assassin."

"Why does Endersley need money?"

"The blinkereds need the money. Endersley's paying them to work on the bombs and the cull…"

"The cull?" A slow, nauseating feeling passed through me.

As he looked at me his face turned ashen and then his eyes flitted to the heavens. He didn't have long. I grabbed his wrist but his magical defenses were still strong enough to keep me from entering his mind. I closed my eyes and concentrated, absorbing a little of his power, just enough to use against him.

"What are you doing?" Astrid asked.

"What needs to be done," I replied. The magician's power flowed toward mine.

Flashes of the magician's life passed through me. Of his wife, strung up from the mossy branch of an oak tree by his very own hands. Of his children trying to flee the horrific scene, and him bringing each of them to their knees with fire, magic and rage. Of how he'd wandered lost through the dark, haunted byways until Stroud appeared in a place choked with death, shining like a beacon and whispering promises of power. The magician gladly rose to his call and crossed the gulf between worlds, only to land in this filthy primitive city. A place infested with a people he felt were little more than cattle ripe for the slaughter.

The scene shifted, and he was with Endersley in some kind of a mill or foundry. It was full of rusting machinery and old wooden workbenches stacked with homemade bombs. Endersley stood near a table laden with glowing beakers and jars as he gently removed pouches and vials from his leather bag. There were people there with him; three young, nervous blinkereds, each of them seduced by Enderley's money and his promise of better days. Days in which they'd want for nothing, days when they'd rise like royalty, if they only did this one job...

I clutched the magician's wrist firmly as it twitched in my grip. He was dying, and I was hastening his demise as I drained his memories and magic. I browsed faster through his recollections, seeking the most recent.

There.

This morning. The magician and his crew waiting along a potholed road near a cluster of industrial buildings. A courier truck stopped, its doors swung open and a tall, powerful looking man stood on the edge of the corrugated truck bed. He was blinkered and his eyes seemed... dead. No, not dead, one eye was real and as cold as winter, the other was made of glass. His hair was slicked back, his face lean and marred with a shiny scar below his missing eye. Beside him were four thuggish looking men.

The magician handed the man a canvas bag filled with cash then watched expectantly as the guy flexed his arm, judging the weight of it before tossing it into the clutches of a scrawny guy with spiky red hair and a lewd grin. The man with the glass eye stared back at the magician, as if making a decision. A *big* decision. One that didn't come easy, even to a man as remorseless as him. Finally he nodded. "We'll do it."

"Do what?" I demanded, as the magician's memories began to evaporate and the last of the power flowing through his veins ebbed. I pulled my hand away and gazed down at him. His face was pale, his eyes full of blood.

He stared up, sightlessly. "Kill me. Just... kill me."

I glanced at Astrid and Samuel. Neither met my gaze. The magician cried out, the sound high and keening. I placed my gun to his head. "I'll end your misery. But I need to know what the cull is and where it's taking place."

"It's the great slaughter that will set the blinkereds against the magical community... and the magical community against the blinkereds. The aftershocks will spread around the world." There was no pleasure in his voice now, only anguish.

"Where?" I asked, my voice little more than a growl.

"The…Winter Festival. Tomorrow." The magician gurgled something else, and his body began to spasm.

"End it," Astrid said. I looked up to find her staring at me.

I turned away from the magician, pulled the trigger, and stood. "You said we had to get Endersley by any means. That's what we're doing."

"No, you were playing with fire," Astrid replied. "I warned you about stealing other people's magic. Especially dark magic. Sooner or later it will get its fangs in you, Morgan, and when it does, you won't be you anymore. You'll be a concern," She gestured to Samuel. "And we'll be forced to make a hard decision."

"I did what needed to be done. We don't have time on our side, we never did. And I'm not going to watch any more innocent people die. Not if I can prevent it." I glanced back as I heard footsteps on the rooftop.

Haskins appeared, Ebomee's sniper rifle slung over his shoulder. He glanced at the magician's corpse and his face furrowed with disgust. "Please tell me this is the sicko that's trying to infect the city."

"I wish I could," I said.

"Well you'd better tell me you have your sights on him, or I'm going to have to start getting honest with the top brass."

"Believe me, you don't want to do that," I said. "That's what they want. A war between your lot and mine. It'll be a massacre, on both sides. Now we're real close to tracking down the man we're after, but we need your help. You know of any perps with a glass eye? Tall, powerful looking, definitely not someone you'd want to get into a dust up with."

"Sounds like Sean Slater. Lost an eye when another prison lowlife shanked him."

"What was he in for?"

"Gun running mostly but he'd had his fingers in all sorts of pies. He was serving a life sentence until him and some other scumbags escaped earlier this year. We caught all of them, except Slater."

I remembered the reports, they'd been all over the blinkered TV and the media had reported on it consistently, until the full tilt manhunt had been surreptitiously called off.

"Why do you want to know about Slater?" Haskins asked.

"I think he's involved. He had a man with him, red hair and-"

"Michael Adams. Grew up with Slater on the wrong side of town. I've arrested that piece of shit more times than I care to remember, but he's as sly as I'm tired, and I've never managed to pin anything on him that stuck. I had him under surveillance recently, to see if we could turn up anything on Slater, but the budget...we're not exactly flush with cash right now. Not with all the other crap going on."

"Where can I find him?" I asked.

"He's a joint owner of the Three Horses Tavern; it's out on the east side. Lives in the apartment above the bar. Not exactly a warm and fuzzy kind of place. I tried to get a search warrant, but like I said, shit doesn't stick to Adams."

"Well," I said, "we'll be operating under different terms of engagement. And he might just find his luck has run out."

"Do whatever you need to. I'll drop you off there and you can burn the fucking place to the ground, for all I care. Just as long as I'm not close enough to have it pinned on me. But if you have a lead on Slater-"

"I don't, just a very strong hunch he's involved. But, if we find him, I'll hand him over to you. Dead or alive."

"Good," Haskins said, "because I'm going to need to land a pretty big fish to make up for all the momentous fuckery over the last twenty four hours."

"We'll do our damnedest to get you one. In the meantime

you're going to want to keep a tight rein on the Winter Festival."

"Why?"

"That's their target, they've got something big planned. I don't know what exactly, but our aim is to finish it long before it even begins."

"And what if you can't?" Haskins demanded. "It's only a few hours away. There'll be thousands of people there. Families, kids…"

"We'll get it sorted," I said. "Look, this is our chance to bring them down fast. If they don't hit now, they'll hit later, and we won't know where or when. Like I said, we're going to do everything we can to take them out long before they can strike. All you need to do is stay vigilant. Tell the Chief you caught wind of a credible terrorist threat and be prepared to evacuate people fast."

"You better not let me down Rook!" Haskins growled.

"I don't intend to."

47

Haskins shuttled us across town and dropped us off a few blocks away from the Three Horses Tavern. It was early. Six am early. Aside from a few cars, buses and delivery trucks, the city was still.

"You think the tavern's open at this hour?" I asked Haskins, my breath frosting the air as I climbed from the car.

"It doesn't close. They have their overnight crowd of degenerates that turns into the breakfast crowd. If you count toast and beer as breakfast."

"Sounds good," Samuel said. He'd disguised himself as a street musician, and his bow as a guitar case. Then he made me and Astrid look like we were making our way home after a late night of clubbing.

Haskins gazed at me and I saw and understood the conflict playing behind his eyes. If we didn't eliminate Endersley and his thugs, there was going to be a massacre in the next few hours. It didn't exactly rest easy with me either. "We'll take them down," I said, "just make sure your people are on their toes."

Haskins nodded. "Don't fuck this up, Rook."

273

"I won't," I said, and hoped to hell I was right.

We walked down the gritty sidewalk and passed a few people shuffling off to work. "Here," I said as I stood at a bus stop across from the Tavern and waited there as we staked the place out. It was a wood-framed building, its facade was dark and the barred windows obscured by heavy drapes. But I could see light through the cracks in the curtains and a bare light bulb shining in the upstairs apartment. It seemed our target was awake. Not that I could imagine the piece of shit sleeping with what he had planned for today.

"We going in?" Samuel asked.

"No," I said, "I'll go in on my own, I need you to stay here and keep watch. If you see a shifty guy with red hair coming out, stop him. Astrid, can you look for an access road or alley and cover the back of the building?"

"Sure."

"Good. Right, let's do this," I crossed the street and shoved the tavern door open. It caught on the ratty carpet and needed an extra shove, which took me half stumbling into the room. Not the best entrance, but at least it fit the illusion Samuel had cast over me.

Six or seven regulars were perched around a table strewn with beer bottles and playing cards. They glanced up at me, great lumps of men with thick brows, poorly reset noses and missing teeth. And that was the better looking ones.

Another pair stood around a pool table, their faces sickly in the florescent light. They watched me with slow, cunning gazes as they paused their game. I ignored them and headed to the bar amid the middle-of-the-road rock music playing in the background. It did little to thaw the icy atmosphere. This place was for regulars, not strangers, and they didn't come much stranger than me.

The barman was a wiry red-haired man, but he wasn't

Adams. Maybe his brother. But at the end of the bar, nursing a cup of coffee, was the man I was after. He'd made an effort to smooth down his spiky hair, and he looked like he was getting ready to head out, judging by the tight suede jacket he wore over his sweater. He gave me a cursory glance and turned his gaze back to the phone resting on the bar.

"Help you?" the barman called as he stood under a 'no smoking sign' and lit his cigarette.

"Yeah, can I get a beer?" I asked as I gave him a warm, weary smile and watched Adams from the corner of my eye.

"Not at this hour. That would be against the law," the barman said.

I glanced toward the table as several of the meatheads eyed me, raised their bottles and took long hard swigs. Subtle. "Right. How about a cup of coffee and a bite to eat?" I asked. I glanced up at the menu on the wall and slowly edged toward Adams.

"We're out of coffee and food," the barman said. "There's a shop across the street. Sells frappalappadingdongs and whatnot. You should go there. Now." Low, heavy laughter broke around the table behind me.

"You know, I think I'd rather stay here," I said, taking another step toward Adams. "I like the cozy warmth and the winning atmosphere, you know?" I was planning on pulling my gun then frog marching Adams out of the bar, and was almost upon him when I heard the whistling sound of displaced air.

I ducked as a pool cue swished over my head and smashed into the counter. I grabbed it before the assailant could pull it back and snapped it over my knee, concealing the shot of pain as I threw it to the floor.

Adams began to reach into his jacket.

I turned and punched my attacker squarely in the nose as

he came at me. A green glow glinted in the dim room, and I dodged aside as a beer bottle sailed through the air and smashed into the bar behind me.

The thugs around the table were up and ready as the guy at the pool table pulled something from his waistband. Adams had his gun out and the barman was bringing his shotgun up from under the counter.

I fired at the barman first. The bullet struck just below his shoulder. He fell fast.

Then I turned on the guy by the pool table before he could get a shot off.

Within seconds the place was a riot of noise and hot flashes of light. Adams narrowly missed me and his round took down one of the bastards at the card table. I spun around and ran at Adams. He ducked behind the counter, stumbled over the barman, and dashed through a door leading to the back room.

Bullets roared around me and several whiskey bottles exploded along the bar as I dashed past them. I jumped over an overturned beer keg Adams had left in my path and tore through a small kitchen, my eyes on the swinging back door. Adams ran out across a yard and for a moment he seemed to fly through the air before crashing to the ground.

Astrid appeared, knife in hand. Adams turned from where he lay and fired. I shoved Astrid aside and took the impact of the bullet in my coat before returning fire. I aimed for his arm but my rounds went wide. He scrambled to his feet and leaped neatly over a fence.

"You okay?" I asked Astrid.

"Go!" She shouted as she ran over to the building behind us.

I clambered over the chain-link and fell hard on a stony, potholed path. Adams was running hard and fast down the alley, springing over icy puddles. He fired a few shots but his bullets whined past me and when his magazine was empty he threw his gun to the ground. I holstered my weapon as I ran. From the corner of my eye I saw Astrid following across the rooftops.

I snatched up Adam's gun and stashed it in my bag, and then a dog leaped out from behind a cluster of garbage cans. It really threw me, and I lost momentum as I drew back from its gnashing teeth. Slather hung in curtains from its scabby snout as it lunged again. The chain around its neck snapped taut, saving me from having half my leg torn off.

By the time I recovered my stride there was no sign of Adams. I ran on, crunching through the ice in the gutter as I tore out into the street beyond.

It was empty.

Adams was gone.

48

"Over there!" Astrid called from the roof at the end of the alley. I followed her finger to the subway entrance across the street and ran, my chest tight, my breath ragged.

I flew down the worn steps and weaved in and out of sleepy-faced commuters. There was no sign of Adams, but there were plenty of upset people looking back behind them. I leaped the turnstiles, ran through the knot of passengers and wound my way down the escalator.

There. At the bottom; Adams shoving and pushing his way toward the platform.

I raced down the shifting stairs as people watched agape. There was always tension on the subway these days as the specter of violence and terrorism hung over the city. Several commuters reached for their phones, which meant it was only a matter of time before security or the police would be on my case. I glanced back as I heard rapid footsteps behind me. Astrid.

We leaped off the escalator, raced across the concourse and

a sinking feeling passed through me as I heard the mechanical drone of a train pulling away.

I ran onto the platform to find Adams sprinting alongside one of the cars, hammering at the button to open its doors. He glanced back my way and ran harder, following the train as it vanished into the tunnel. I grabbed a crystal and cast a spell to illuminate his footsteps. They glowed red as they led us into the darkness. "Keep clear of the tracks," I whispered to Astrid as we walked alongside the rails.

The footprints ended a few yards in and I could just make out his form against the wall. I made like I was walking past him before turning and grabbing him around the throat. "Next time," I said, "try holding your breath. It reeks and you sound like a broken vacuum cleaner." I turned to Astrid. "You got a light? I need to look him in the eye or he's going to lie as soon as I start with the questions."

"Who..."

I clamped a hand over his mouth. "You only speak when spoken too, asshole." I waited until Astrid summoned a small orb of light into her hand, just enough to show Adams' wretched features. He gave me a hard stare, and I read its inherent threat. *Do you know who I am? Do you know the people I know?* Yeah, I did. I removed my hand from his mouth.

"Who the fuck are you? Feds?" he demanded.

"You ever see the feds summon a magical orb of light, jackass?" I asked. "No, I'm the man that's going to beat the living shit out of you if you don't cooperate. And if you piss me off, I'll kill you." I held his gaze. "You doubt me?"

The rails clattered and light flickered on the wall near the bend of the tunnel. I yanked Adams away from the wall, marched him to the tracks, and held him there as the train rumbled closer. "The driver won't even notice until he sees your head bouncing off the rails in the station." I shouted over the din. "You want that?"

Adams continued to stare at me, his eyes filled with defiance, but it faded as the train drew closer. He shook his head, and I pulled him back and shoved him against the wall. The tunnel lit up as the train went by, and as it slowed I saw Adams gazing up at the windows almost imploringly. "No one can see us," I said. "I took care of that, and I know you know what that means. You've seen Endersley's powers. We're worse." I glanced at my watch. "The next train will be by in three minutes. You'll be all over it if you don't tell me what I need to know."

"What do you want?" he shouted. His face was a greasy shade of white, his lips flecked with spit.

"I want to knock out each and every last one of your teeth from your sick, rotten skull. But instead I'll settle for details about what you and your gang of miscreant fucks have planned for the Winter Festival. And don't bother trying to lie. Seriously, don't."

He stared at me and I saw him weighing things up. What to tell, what not to tell… He screamed, the sound loud in my ears. I looked down to find Astrid jerking a blade back from wherever she'd stuck it. "Sorry," she said. "It's hard to see down here."

"Three bombs are set to go off at eleven. They're being carried by two men and a girl."

"Girl?"

"She's about twenty, I guess." He shook his head. "I didn't want anything to do with it. Seriously. I told him that. I grew up in this city. But…"

I gazed deeply into his eyes and could see he was telling the truth. He didn't like the plan and had genuinely considered backing out. And he might have done it if it hadn't been for the insane amount of cash Endersley had offered him. Which meant he was just as bad as they were, if not worse. "Don't give me that shit. You've had a long illustrious career preying off this city and using your muscle to extort. Don't give me that fake sentimental crap about caring. Don't go there. So three bombers... is that it?"

"No, there's shooters too. Five or more. They'll be there by ten thirty."

"When are they going to strike?" I demanded and shoved his head back further into the wall.

"When the bombs go off at eleven. The crowd'll be rushing past them as they try to escape the explosions." A tear ran down the side of his face. "I..."

"Why?" I asked. "What the fuck is this about?"

"I don't know, I don't." Adams cried. "Endersley only told me what I needed to know so I could work with Slater to coordinate things. He might have told Slater more but he made all of us go our own ways after we knew our part of the plan."

Which meant there was a possibility the shooters and bombs weren't the only attacks they had planned. "Where's Slater going to be?"

"Leading the gunners."

"And where are the bombers coming from?" I asked. "Or are they already in place?"

"I don't know, they might be" Adams said. "They said there's not going to be much in the way of security because..."

"Because the festival's been running peacefully for the last forty years with no problems at all," I said. "Which makes you and your friends real trailblazers." I had to stop myself from turning his face into a soft, wet pulp. Instead I grabbed his wrist and tore through his memories.

The first I found was of him at the tavern earlier, drinking coffee and trying to read a gambling site on his phone, his thoughts riddled with fear, anticipation and nervous excitement.

I went back further until I saw him leaving a steel mill in his car. The place had long been deserted and I could see the restless prowling around the fenced-in grounds like guard dogs. None of them approached Adams because Endersley had placed binds around him to make him untouchable. I rifled further through his memories until I found one from the day before when Endersley had summoned Adams.

He'd gone to the building that looked like a hangar where Endersley had set up the meeting. His system had been flooded with adrenaline. He didn't like Endersley, hated the weird spooky hocus-pocus that surrounded him. Like the huge black painting on the wall behind his benches. It had been painted so recently it still reeked of solvents and empty paint tubes had littered the metallic walkway. He'd seen the painters too, and none of them had been right in the head. Their screamed has filled the air just before the guns went off. After that he'd been coerced into helping dump their bodies into the furnace.

Then three new people had shown up to speak with Endersley. The bombers. One was a tall teenager in tight-fitting pants and a padded green jacket. His hair was bright blue and his face was filled with piercings. The other guy had closely cropped hair, steel-rimmed glasses, and pasty skin while the girl had spiky black hair and the look of someone who'd been brutalized since they were young. All were broken, and perfect for Endersley's plans.

I committed the three faces to memory and was about to trawl back further into his recollections when I felt a spike in his heartbeat.

Go, an icy voice whispered in the center of his mind. *Now!*

I opened my eyes as Adams head butted me in the face.

Before I could recover, he tore away. Astrid began to go after him but I grabbed her arm, pulled her in and held her tight because I knew, with blood chilling certainty, what was coming.

A train clattered round the bend and Adams ran full tilt to meet it. There was a sickening thud, a squeal of wheels and a flash of light in the darkness.

49

We ran back through the tunnel, eager to clear the subway before the place went into lockdown. The train had come to a stop with half of its length in the station, the other half still in the tunnel. We moved fast and slipped through the ghoulish crowd of onlookers as they held up their cell phones to capture the morbid scene.

"That was unfortunate," Astrid said, as we emerged onto the sidewalk.

"I feel for the train driver," I said. "As for Adams, it was no loss."

We found Samuel leaning against the bus shelter, his attention split between the Three Horses Tavern and the little old lady standing beside him. She'd clearly warmed to his charms, and she laughed loudly at whatever it was he said. As we approached, she looked us up and down and made a comment about him keeping dark company.

"They're good friends, Edith," Samuel said, "even if they do look a bit odd."

Edith ignored us as she dug into her purse and handed Samuel a dollar.

"What's that for?" he asked.

"For the music," she said and nodded towards the bow he'd disguised as a guitar case.

"I didn't play any music," Samuel said as he tried to hand back the dollar.

"Oh, but you did. Your voice is a beautiful song, young man." Edith waved the dollar away, fixed Astrid and I with a suspicious glance and climbed aboard the bus that had just pulled over at the stop. The colorful banner plastered on its side featured a sparkling cluster of bright, cheery snowmen. The ad was for the Winter Festival and a cold pang passed through me. Would this become yet another date on a long list of infamous acts of violence and terror? No. I wasn't going to let that happen.

I grabbed my phone and called Haskins while Astrid told Samuel about the Adams situation.

"Rook," Haskins said with his customary irritation.

"Adams is...down."

"I heard there was a fatality on the subway. The call just came in. I figured with the proximity of the station to his tavern, and the fact that you were on his case..."

"There was nothing I could do. He ran down the tracks. But that's not why I'm calling. Grab a pen and paper. I've got a description of the bombers." I said as I proceeded to give him the details.

"Bombers?" Haskins said. "You never said anything-"

"They've lined up shooters as well." I filled him in on the entire sick plan. "But we're going to stop them. It's not going to happen. Now, circulate those descriptions."

"I'll get this out right away." Haskins said, "even though what we should be doing is shutting the festival down."

"We went over this, they'll just plan another attack and the chances are we won't know where. This man is not going to give up, we have to stop him." I glanced at the families on the bus as it pulled away and wondered how many of them were heading to the festival. "Okay," I said. "How about this; if we haven't tracked the suspects down by ten, we shut it down."

"I guess," Haskins said, "but I'm going to have submit a report on this. You know that, don't you?"

"I do. But tell them what I said, this is our chance to nail these bastards for good. Before they vanish and commit their atrocities elsewhere."

"Right." I could hear Haskins' conflict as he hung up and I understood it. The whole plan was a gamble and one that might literally blow up in my face if I got it wrong. Any innocent blood spilled would be on me. But what I'd said was true. If the Festival was closed down Endersley would order another assault, and that could mean even more casualties. I checked the time. Eight twenty three am. Just over ninety minutes to find three bomb-toting assholes and a truck full of shooters.

"What are you thinking?" Samuel asked.

"That we need to find Endersley's crew, and fast."

"He might well have used spells to conceal the bombers," Samuel said. "That's what I'd do."

"Yeah, me too," I said. "But while that might work on the blinkered authorities, it's not going to work on us. And... it could actually simplify things if we only have to look for people who are cloaked. Come on."

We arrived at the long stretch of the boulevard where they held the festival every year; five blocks lined with restaurants and shops, each of them vying for attention from the masses that were about to descend. In fact, the crowds were already beginning to swell, the coffee shops and diners were crammed with people, and kids wearing reindeer antlers, elf ears and tiny Santa hats. I would have considered it a cheerful sight if it wasn't for my knowledge of Endersley's plans, and the devastation it would bring if it came to fruition.

"Is there any way I can share the memories I stole from Adams; the images of the bombers and Slater?" I asked.

"Yes, I can take them, if you'll let me" Astrid said, "and I can pass them to Samuel. But I'll warn you, it's going to feel... strange."

"Let's do it," I said, as I scanned the crowds and glanced at my watch once more.

Astrid embraced me, her grip tight and warm. She looked up at me and as our eyes locked her pupils dilated. I felt myself flush. It wasn't what I was expecting, and I began to...

... a cold shudder passed through me. She was inside my head, a sensation I knew perfectly well thanks to my dark other. Memories began to flash through my mind without me summoning them and I watched passively as she rifled through those private things like a burglar. My dark other began to stir, detecting the invasion. He rose from the depths of my being, his anger and outrage charging through me...

Stop with the darkness, Morgan. Stop tapping into cursed magic. I want you to be you. Not someone else.

Hearing Astrid's voice in my head broke my other's pull. She released me and stepped away. "I'm sorry," she said.

"Did you get what you needed?" I asked, doing my best to sort through the feeling of intrusion and the words she'd whispered to me.

"Yes," Astrid said, "Samuel, come here."

I was struck by a sharp twinge of jealously as he embraced her, just as she'd embraced me. Then he gazed into her eyes blankly as she shared the information she'd taken from me. I glanced back through the crowd, searching for anyone using magical cloaks to disguise themselves. The tell was pretty simple, a glassy aura that was a dead giveaway.

"Okay," I said, as Samuel broke their embrace, "we know who we're looking for, and we've got," I checked my watch once more, "almost an hour to find them. No pressure then." I delved into my bag, pulled out a spare phone I'd picked up at the armory, and handed it to Samuel. Astrid held up hers and read out the number as he entered it into his phone. "If you see anything, call and I'll do the same. And," I paused as I looked at each of them in turn, "take care. Okay?" I smiled despite feeling sick. It felt like everything was about to go seriously wrong.

"You too," Astrid said, before striding into the crowd.

"We'll find them," Samuel said. His tone was light but I could see he felt almost as ill as I did. I nodded, and we split up.

There were people everywhere I looked. They wore winter hats, sipped cocoa and coffee, and their breath steamed the air as they checked on their little ones, their eyes bright with anticipation. All of them perfectly oblivious to the horror that was planned. I wove my way through the crowd as the buzz of their chatter filled the air.

The roads and intersections were barricaded off, which meant I had little option but to remain in the thick of the gathering revelers. Now and then police cars cruised down the empty street, and stony faced cops gazed from their windows. I hoped Haskins had managed to brief them and I was just about to search a row of food vendors when a series of screams pierced the air.

50

I raced toward the screams, my hand reaching for my holster, only to discover they weren't cries of terror but cries of delight. I watched as kids leaped up and down in a bouncy castle decorated like a snowy ice palace and a little girl smiled at me. Her grin faded as she continued to meet my eye. I tried to smile in return, but it didn't seem to help so I walked on past long tables covered in scarlet cloth edged with white trims. They were piled up with canned goods, bags of produce, bottled drinks and holiday candies. The donations continued to amass as people in the crowd stopped by with their contributions and volunteers rushed to pack up the groceries and load them into vans heading for local food banks. It made me think of the succubus Kitty's jaded remark.

It never ceases to amaze me how fickle blinkereds are. It's like there's an ocean of darkness bubbling below the surface, and all it takes to bring it flooding out is one little scratch.

She was wrong. Yes, a hidden darkness lurked below the facades of some people, but not all of them. And this gathering was proof of that, and the realization made me more determined than ever to stop Endersley. I waded through the throng until my phone began to rumble in my pocket. I leaned over a short-fenced barrier and took the call.

"We nabbed one," Haskins said. "Didn't look anything like your description, not at first, but one of my guys spotted some wires hanging out of a backpack and-"

"What does he look like?"

"He... uh. Well, he changed. At first he looked like a Chinese guy in a business suit but then he changed real fast. Blue hair, a face full of metal. And he ain't talking."

"There's a good chance his mind's been tampered with, so he might not be able to speak. Good work, Haskins."

"What about you? Anything?"

I heard the fear and desperation in his question. I felt it too. "Not yet, but we're working on it." I hung up and watched three cop cars race by, their lights flashing quietly as they escorted a van with tinted windows.

That left two more bombers. Plus the shooters, but from what we'd gleaned it didn't sound like they were going to act unless the bombs went off. Not that I was banking on that. I glanced around the crowd, scouring it for magical cloaks among hundreds of faces. The din of conversation and the proximity of the people began to feel more and more overwhelming as I desperately scanned through them.

I needed more clarity and focus. I grabbed a handful of crystals and shivered as their energy ignited my senses. It was almost too much to contain.

As I fought to control the swell of magic, my dark other stirred. I felt him watching, waiting to slip into my consciousness. It was unsettling. I moved through the crowd, clearing another block and spotted a few Nightkind cloaked as blinkereds. They saw me too and judging from their odd reactions they'd probably committed a few petty crimes already, but that wasn't my concern... there!

A glassy shimmer and behind it steel-rimmed glasses and darting eyes set in a pale, sickly face. A backpack, and a Winter Festival tote bag stuffed to the brim. He gazed at me, our eyes met and his mouth fell open. Then he turned and shoved through the crowd. I ran after him and fought my way through, knocking people aside, barking apologies as I went.

The man stopped for a moment and his hand strayed to his jacket.

Shit. Was he going to detonate? He glanced around, disappointment on his face. The crowd was thin here, much less of an impact than he could score elsewhere. I read all of this in his face and more. And then his eyes narrowed as he spotted an alley and ran for it, his backpack wobbling over his shoulder.

I raced after him but the gap between us began to grow. He was fast. Faster than me. Even weighed down with bombs and who knew what. I reached for my gun but held off. If I shot there was a chance I could trigger the explosives.

The energy from the crystals bubbled through me, seeking an outlet. I thought back to Talamos Gin and the black fire I'd summoned. I could do it again, I still had the knowledge I'd absorbed from him.

I dismissed the words Astrid had whispered inside my mind and summoned the fire. They appeared like tiny black feathers billowing in the palms of my hands. I ran on, ignoring the stitch in my side as I focused on the flames. They began to grow, swell and merge into dense orbs of fire. I threw them. They shot past the bomber and hit the wall at the end of the alley. The flames erupted over the brick walls and spread along the ground toward the bomber in a torrent of fire.

He jerked to a stop, glanced my way and then back to the conflagration.

"That's right," I shouted. "There's nowhere to run."

Ice-cold fury seeped through me as he took a step my way, then back to the flames. Finally, he turned to me. "Please!" he cried.

His panic had overridden whatever magical programming Endersley had installed in him. He set his bag down, pulled the backpack off and laid it on the ground.

I drew my gun and forced my fury down to a simmer as he held a hand out my way, as if trying to hold me back. Then his terror seemed to get the better of him and he ran and leapt over the flames.

He cleared the first wave and landed in a patch of smoldering ground, but within moments the flames began to swirl and sweep toward him.

As they closed in, the sounds that followed should have made me nauseous, but instead I caught myself reveling in his torment. I forced myself to shake the feeling off, to shun this new sadistic darkness as I raised the gun and ended his suffering.

His body fell as the flames surged around him like a twister, consuming him where he lay and filling the air with the stench of burnt flesh. Once their fuel was spent, the flames begin to flicker and soon they vanished into the ground, as if returning to hell.

I felt sick as I rang Haskins. "The second one's down. The other male," I said. "His pack's still in the alley. Send your bomb squad in, I'll text the coordinates."

"So one more to go," Haskins said, "you got twenty minutes, if we don't find her I'm shutting the festival down. You-"

A beep sounded on the line. "Someone else is calling. This could be our lucky break, I gotta go," I said as I hung up.

"Morgan." Astrid was almost breathless. "I see the girl. She's right in front of me."

"Where are you?" I asked.

"Near a tavern called The George and Dragon, there's a Japanese restaurant next door and-"

"Perfect, I'm two minutes away. What's she doing?"

"Lurking by a playground filled with children."

What better place to detonate a bomb for anyone looking to spark a war between the blinkereds and the magical community? Sick fucks. "I'm on my way. Stay with her." I ended the call and texted my coordinates to Haskins as I turned my back on the smoky charred remains and headed out of the blackened alleyway.

51

I phoned Samuel as I fought my way through the crowd.

"Morgan?" Samuel's voice was faint amongst the crackles and distortion and I could hear the wind screeching behind him.

"Two down. And Astrid's just found the girl. Where are you?"

"The rooftops. I thought a higher vantage point might…" Samuel tailed off.

"The girl's at a playground near a tavern called The George and Dragon. Find it and cover us from the roof. And if you see the girl reach toward her bag or… Samuel?"

He was silent, but I could still hear the wind blowing in the receiver. And then he said, "Oh," and the line went dead.

Shit. I called back. It rang and rang but there was no answer. I ran on, praying it was only a dead battery and that he'd be joining us soon, because we were going to need all the help we could get.

Fighting through the crowd was nearly impossible so I vaulted over the barrier and raced down the street, ignoring the cop that started shouting at me. I ran so hard the blinkered crowd became a blur of faces and sound. A police siren whooped, and I glanced back to find a patrol car barreling toward me on the wrong side of the road. I leaped over the fence and vanished into the crowd.

Finally, I turned the corner and spotted The George and Dragon. I raced past it toward the small park beyond. The cool air was scented with cotton candy and hotdogs and chimed with holiday tunes. Trees twinkled with brightly colored lights as families waited in the soft yellow glow of a mini Ferris wheel that had drawn in the crowd. I scanned the scene but no one stood out among the revelers or the carnies dressed as snowmen and elves.

I looked again and… there.

Along the fence. It took a moment to see past the polished illusion of a lanky woman wearing ski pants and a tall furry hat, to the girl hidden below. Her hair was black, greasy and spiked, and dark smudges underscored her eyes. She leaned on the barricade, her backpack hanging over her shoulders and a full harvest bag by her side.

I watched as she pulled her phone from her coat, peered at it, and put it back into her pocket. Moments later she did the same thing again, and then she glanced away as a couple led five small children toward the midway like a row of ducklings. She watched them pass with a subdued, vacant gaze. Drugs. She was high. But there was guilt as well. Guilt and doubt.

Two things I could work with.

I looked past her and spotted Astrid lurking under a nearby beech tree. She held her phone, pretending to read it, but her full attention was on the girl, and then she glanced at me as I called her.

"You see her?" Astrid answered.

"Yeah, I see her. Can you get closer?"

She nodded and glanced to the rooftops across the way. "Where's Samuel?"

"I don't know. He might have problems. We were talking and his phone cut out."

Astrid nodded. "We'll get to it as soon as we've dealt with her. What's the plan?"

"Get the bags away from her. Evacuating the place is too risky, it might set her off. I'll see if I can talk to her, try and lead her away from the fair. If that doesn't work I'll signal you. If I do, cut the straps off her backpack and run. I'll grab the bag at her feet and be right behind you. Pass the pack to me and I'll get them the hell out of here. She looks like she's strung out, but she could have a handler watching nearby, and there might be a remote detonator. Which means I'm going to have to move fast once I have the bags."

"Where are you taking them?"

"Across that street. There's a plaza a couple of blocks away. It should be empty seeing as everyone's here. Once I have it secure, I'll call Haskins, his people can deal with disarming the devices. Just keep an eye on the girl while I'm gone, don't let her go anywhere. I want to question her before we hand her over to the cops, find out what she knows."

"Got it," Astrid said. Then she paused and gave me a tired smile. "Be careful."

"You too." I gave her the best smile I could muster and slipped the phone into my pocket as I checked my watch. Quarter to ten. Haskins would be calling for his evacuation soon. I strode toward the girl and nodded to her. "Hey, do you know when the festival's starting?" I asked. "I thought it was supposed to get going at ten."

"Eleven," she said. Her voice was flat and low and her eyes darted over me. They were red and smeared with mascara.

Clearly she'd been crying, but there was a detachment in her body language, like she was somewhere else entirely.

I watched from the corner of my eye as Astrid moved closer.

"Can you like, go away?" the girl asked. She gave me an irritated, dismissive look and one of her hands began to stray to her pocket. I needed to distract her, and fast. I held her gaze and gave her a glimpse into the darkness within me. The listlessness left her eyes. "Endersley sent me," I said, glancing around like I was making sure no-one was listening.

"I didn't see you at the mill."

"I didn't see you either," I said. "Seems Endersley kept us in the dark about a lot of things. Listen, he sent me to check up on you, make sure you're going through with the plan. You look freaked out. You need to focus on the job, it's almost time."

The girl pulled her phone and I watched closely as the full scale of the horror seemed to dawn on her. "I don't know…" She glanced around at the kids behind her. "I can't…"

"You want me to take over?" I asked as I waved the tip of my fingers to tell Astrid to back off.

"Yeah," the girl said, "you do it. I can't." She reached for the strap on her bag.

"Careful," I said. "You don't want to call attention to us."

Slowly she removed the backpack and held it out to me. "Thank you," she said. I let my hand brush hers as I took the bag, and held her gaze in mine, befuddling her as I read her, fast.

Her name was Tiffany and her boyfriend, the guy with the blue hair and piercings, was David. He was the one who'd found them the job, and readily accepted it in exchange for a shit ton of heroin. Most of which they'd already smoked. In between the highs, David had outlined each and every reason why they should do the job and blow up *the whole fucking city*. He hated the place, hated everything, as did Tiffany. Most of their lives had been spent being ferried from one foster care home to another, plucked from one hotbed of abuse into another. Over and over again through their childhood and teenage years.

And then they'd met Slater. He'd supplied the drugs they'd sought out, and groomed them, sowing the seeds of this plan in their minds. And once they fell for his bait, he'd handed them over to Endersley, who'd used magic to strip away their frayed psychic defenses. He'd also made them go cold turkey these last two days, while soothing the pain of their nagging withdrawals with his potions. Having them clean had made it easier for his magic to reformat their minds so he could install his *malware* into their brains. It had worked but this morning when Tiffany had stopped by to see her foster mother to say goodbye, she'd found the almost forgotten remains of a wrap of heroin in a hidey-hole in her old bedroom. There hadn't been much, but it was enough to take the edge off Endersley's programming...

I rifled through her thoughts until I found what I was looking for. There was more coming. The night before last Tiffany had gone outside the mill for a smoke and overheard a conversation between Endersley and Slater. The bombs and shooters weren't the full plan. No, the full plan included medics who were going to inject victims with the virus, potentially infecting hundreds in one fell swoop.

That was the reason for the carnage... to seed the disease far and wide.

Tiffany flinched as I pulled my hand away from hers. She stared at me, her eyes almost accusing, like she knew what I'd done. "Are you going to stop it from happening?" she asked, her gaze filled with pleading. "I... I don't want people to get hurt. Not really."

"Yes. Just release the bag, carefully."

She sighed as she let the strap go. It was heavy. I hoisted it over my shoulder and held out my hand. "And now the bag," I said. She reached down and as she gave it to me a red light began to flash inside.

Shit. It seemed the bomb was rigged to make sure it was handled by Tiffany, and Tiffany alone, and we'd just tripped it.

I ran through the park, knocking people aside as I leaped over the fence into the street, the pack weighing down on my shoulder as the lights in the bag flashed brighter and brighter in the wintry gloom.

52

A police car shot out of an alleyway as I ran across the street. The squeal of its siren was loud and high and the cop's face paled as he looked from me to the backpack and then to the bag in my hand. He hit the brakes and began to climb out. I held his gaze as I moved toward him, befuddling him before seizing his wrist and overwhelming his senses long enough for me to run unhindered.

I raced along the deserted sidewalk, away from the merriment of the festival, and turned down a side street. The lights inside the bag were lit up like a Christmas tree and I wondered how long I had…

Parked cars and dark office buildings lined the still quiet neighborhood, and then my gaze fell on the gated subway station.

"Damn it!" There was a sharp pain in my arm as the bag suddenly grew impossibly heavy. Another enchantment.

I grabbed a crystal and used its magic to counteract the spell. It helped, a little. I ran on, the backpack slipping on my shoulders as I struggled with the bag's deadweight and watched the lights inside blinking faster and faster.

I kicked the locked gate that blocked off the subway entrance. It rattled but held firm so I pulled my gun and fired, annihilating the deadbolt with a single shot.

With a grunt I pushed it open and slipped the backpack into one hand as I struggled with the bag in my other. It felt like they were filled with concrete and my arms began to tremble as I drew them back.

"Come on!" I cried, putting everything I had into swinging the bombs forward to hurl them down the stairway.

They tumbled through the air as if in slow motion.

I turned and ran down the street as I waited for the…

BOOM!

The ground rumbled, the force of the blast threw me off my feet, and the world turned fiery red. Light flashed off the surrounding cars as a wave of heat drove me forward. I pulled my coat around me as it launched me through the air and slammed me into the ground. The surrounding cars shifted, groaned and burst into flames, one after the other in what felt like an endless chain reaction.

Then another blast roared followed by a sound like a thousand shattering windows. The second explosion shook the ground, even more violently. Slivers of glass tumbled around me in a deadly glittering rain and I cried out as something crashed down on my legs.

I waited for the devastation and fury to settle. Seconds felt like minutes but slowly the rumble faded and the piercing shrieks of alarms and sirens filled the void. I pulled my coat from my face and peered out.

The road was awash with shattered glass and brick, splintered wood, and crumpled, twisted burning cars. Black smoke and dust choked my lungs as I climbed to my feet and peered down at the street sign that had fallen on me.

I looked back at the subway. The fence surrounding it had

been mangled into a crumpled mess of scorched jagged metal. Thick black and grey smoke streamed from a gaping hole in the ground that looked like the doorway to hell. I clamped my coat to my mouth and staggered back along the street, my body riddled with jarring pain.

A fleet of squad cars appeared at the end of the block. I grabbed a handful of crystals, the stones cold and smooth against my grazed palms as I used their magic to render myself unseen. I reached the corner and limped past the stunned cops as they stared up at the smoky inferno.

The festival had erupted into mayhem. People ran and scattered, parents dragged their screaming children behind them and the faces I saw were filled with panic and horror. Some stood dumbfounded and the fires blazing in the buildings behind me reflected in their eyes as I made my way through the crowd.

"Morgan!" Astrid ran up and threw her arms around me. I ignored the shooting pain and embraced her. When she glanced at me her eyes were wet with tears. She reached inside her cloak and handed me a small blue bottle.

"What's this?" I asked.

"It'll help heal you. And take away some of the pain, temporarily."

She watched as I drank the viscous liquid down. It tasted of clove and pepper and a deep warmth passed through my system.

"What now?" Astrid asked.

I nodded to Tiffany, as she leaned on the barricade, staring at the drifting smoke. "I wanted to interrogate her, but there's no time. Find a cop and tell them to take her to Haskins. Have you heard from Samuel?"

"No."

"Damn." I shook my head. "I hope he's alright. Keep

calling him. I need to get a line on those shooters and fast." I vaulted back over the barricade. The scene was pure chaos. Black vans and ambulances shot past and then screeched to a halt behind the knot of police cars blocking the street leading to the smoldering subway station.

"Hey!" a cop yelled and strode toward me. I glanced back at his motorcycle, the key gleaming in its ignition. Perfect.

"Stop," I said. His brow creased, but he did as I commanded, his senses confounded. I placed a hand prickling with magic on his shoulder and gazed into his eyes. "That girl over there" I said, nodding to Tiffany, "there's an APB out on her. Notify Detective Haskins immediately."

He nodded as I walked to his bike, jumped on, fired it up and gunned it.

I swept off through the smoke and lights, weaving past the pandemonium as I searched for the second wave of attackers.

53

There. I slowed as I spotted a courier truck in the middle of a side street with men jumping out of the back. It was the same vehicle I'd seen in the memory I'd stolen from the magician.

I paused at the top of the block and watched as the men stood in a rough line. They were holding assault rifles and one of the hired guns, a tower of muscle and thuggishness, turned and held my gaze. He reached into his pocket and held out a phone, glanced from it to me and then back to the phone as he elbowed the guy next to him, as if comparing the picture. This was starting to feel like the auction house all over again, another set up. I grabbed as many crystals as I could fit in my hands, held them tight, and absorbed their energy.

The rush of magic that flooded through me was so intense I nearly blacked out. I let out my breath slowly, releasing some of the tension as the spent stones fell to the ground.

My senses raged with power and the world turned brighter, clearer. When I glanced back to the men they were all looking my way, including Slater. The energy crackled through me. My limbs trembled and my heart pounded as I fought to contain it, to focus.

I armed myself and buttoned my coat, hoping whatever power it held within its magical fabrics was still working. Then I twisted the throttle and Slater and his men raised their guns as the bike revved and I went roaring toward them.

I closed the distance between us in a blur of brick and glass as I focused on the men ahead of me. Two of them started shooting but their bullets zipped past me. I returned fire, taking one down, and then the other. Their blood misted the air as I sped past.

A steady stream of rounds followed. They pounded the back of my coat and one zipped by so close to my head, I heard its whine in my ear.

I braked, leaped off the bike, and ran for cover behind a blue steel dumpster.

The crack of gunfire echoed off the buildings as Slater and his men strode my way, their muzzle fire flashing in the gloom. I ducked behind the huge container as a round of bullets pinged off it and glanced up to the rooftops, hoping to spot Samuel, but there were no arrows, no backup.

I pulled a small mirror from my bag and angled it out toward the street. There were five of the bastards left. Slater was in the middle, reloading. I swung around and took one down with a bullet to the head.

Slater jerked his rifle my way. I ducked back as a volley of bullets rattled the battered steel box, and then I pushed the hulking thing away from the wall and ran low, taking cover behind a sports car. Within seconds it was riddled with holes and its windows were reduced to tiny cubes of glass gleaming on the asphalt. I had less than thirty seconds before Slater and his goons would be on me. I forced myself to take another deep breath and refocus.

The magic pulsing through me was still almost more than I could handle. I glanced around as I willed my heart to slow and caught sight of myself in the grey tinted windows of the building across the way. My reflection was ghostly, drawn out. It gave me an idea.

My hands shook as I rallied the crystal's power and created an apparition of myself. The projection materialized beside me in a half crouched stance, and then its brow furrowed as its nervous, exhausted eyes looked me over.

All in all a perfect facsimile.

I sent him out into the middle of the street, his illusory gun raised as he charged toward Slater and company.

They fired and I seized the opportunity to take two down before Slater and his remaining goon realized what had happened. The magic I'd used for the illusion had taken almost everything out of me, and I found myself deeply fatigued.

Help us! I yelled to my other as bullets ricocheted off the ground around me.

I might. If you give me control. For good, he replied.

Never.

Then we die together.

Fuck him. I'd rather die in this cold street than become a phantom in the recesses of his mind, forever subjected to his dark tyranny. I leaped up and fired, taking down Slater's remaining henchman.

That was my final round.

Slater fired back; a bullet skimmed the side of my head and another punched my chest. Slater was on empty too. He dropped the rifle, pulled a Bowie knife from his jacket and ran toward me. I unsheathed the sword of intention, reveling in the glint of fear in his eye as he slowed and backed away.

"Seems you're screwed," I said. "Now, what do you think

would stop a guy from plucking that last good eye of yours out before running his sword through your heart? Because I'm tempted. Really, really tempted. But I also like the idea of you rotting in jail. You were a big man in prison from what I've heard, but I guess you found out there's always someone bigger. And you're not as young as you were, which'll make things interesting. Yeah, I think it'll be more fun to hand you over to Haskins. He'll make damn sure you get a good long lease on your new cell."

Slater clutched his knife as he continued to back away, glancing from side to side while assessing his options. "We have your friend," he said. "You know, Robin Hood with the bow and arrows. Caught him up on the roof. Killed two of my men, before the others got the drop on him. Put your sword down and you'll get to see him. Maybe even in one piece."

"Where is he?" I lowered the sword but gripped it tightly.

"He's gone off to take a little quiz at the mill. Now drop the fucking sword."

"No." Sparing Slater would do nothing to help Samuel. I walked toward him, my rage igniting as I considered what he'd planned to do this morning. "You sick son of a bitch. There were families, children…" My blood felt like it was on fire. I fought to contain the darkness inside me as the remnants of the magic I'd stolen from Talamos Gin bubbled up. Astrid had been right, taking other people's magic hadn't been a brilliant idea.

I strode toward Slater and as he looked into my eyes he dropped his knife and held up his hands. I felt the impulse to swing the sword, open a deep and bloody gash in his throat, then watch him bleed out before me.

And I almost did it. *Almost.* But at the last second I punched him in the face and felt his cheek bone shatter below my fist. He fell and barely had time to cry out before I clocked him with the pommel of the sword, knocking him out cold. I grabbed his wrist, plunged through his unconscious mind and got the location of the mill. Then I grabbed my phone and called Astrid. There was no answer so I hung up and rang Haskins instead.

"Where the hell are you, Rook?"

I glanced up at the road sign. "Wilson Street. Slater's here and the shooter situation's been dealt with. Get your people to look for ambulances. Search them, make sure they're being driven and staffed by authentic medics."

"Ambulances?"

"Yeah. I'd help you but I have something else I need to take care of." *Urgently.* "Did Astrid-"

"Astrid? Is she that hokey broad you were hanging around with?"

I swallowed my first response. "Did she hand the girl over?"

"She did, but the little bitch wasn't carrying any bombs. I assume it was you who set them off?" Haskins asked.

"They were rigged, there was no choice."

He gave a long sigh. "I guess you did what you had to." He sounded thankful, even if he didn't say it.

"Is Astrid still with you?"

"No. The last I saw, she was being helped into an ambulance... oh."

"Did you see where it went?" I asked. My heart began to race and the adrenaline coursing through me made me feel sick.

"No. It just took off."

I thought back to the thug I'd seen with Slater. The one who had checked his phone as he'd stared at me. They'd been looking for us. Hunting us. "I gotta go, Haskins," I said.

I called Astrid and Samuel again. Nothing. I gunned the

engine and took off, roaring back along the streets as columns of thick black smoke rose up over the city.

54

The old steel mill was a rusting grey blemish that rose like a barb from an expanse of wild grassy land. A guard house and gate blocked off the long potholed road that led to the sprawling cluster of buildings, so I headed toward a rural bridge spanning the brown river snaking around the back side of the property. The river was quiet, no boats, no people, no witnesses.

I raced down the dusty towpath that ran along its tall grassy bank. The handlebars juddered against the rough stony ground and the rushes grew thick where the river drew up behind the mill. I pulled over and climbed the bank, my telescope clutched in my hand.

A tall chain-link fence ran around the compound and a few figures were wandering the yard. The restless. It seemed Endersley had them prowling around the place like guard dogs. Beyond the zombies, a row of blast furnaces and coal heaps ran along one side of a huge brick building. A corner of its corrugated roofing had blown away and there were several gaping windows that looked like they'd been glassless for years. I swept the telescope up the colossal furnace tower that loomed over the building and found a sentry posted atop it, rifle in hand. Thankfully, they seemed to be keeping watch over the gate in the distance.

I ran through the long grass, keeping low as I approached the fence. The shaky chain link rattled as I climbed and flung my coat over the loose coils of barbed wire. I looked around quickly then clambered over, clinging to the cold post on the other side as I tried to free the sleeve of my vital armor from the rusting snags.

As I reached the ground and turned to brush off my hands and slip the coat on, I caught movement in the shadows of a nearby shed. It was one of the restless. I pulled my gun as it came at me. The hammer clicked as his dead eyes met mine. Shit, I hadn't reloaded the damn thing.

The zombie hissed and ran at me with unnerving speed. I pulled the sword of intention, lopped his head off and stumbled past his twitching corpse, and was so preoccupied with Endersley's sick handiwork that I failed to hear the others lumbering up behind me.

I spun around to find a gaunt, haggard old woman looming in, and three more not far behind her. There was no time to raise my blade. She lunged. I shoved her away, but she grabbed my arm and dragged me down with her as she fell. The others leaped, their bodies eclipsing the light, their faces ruined and feral.

My sword was lost in the tangle of bodies. I let it go and pulled the mhudambe dagger. The blade slipped through the snarling pile like it was nothing but soft grey snow. The restless woman snapped but her grip loosened as I plunged the knife into her skull. I shouldered her away and kicked back another. Then a hand caught my throat, and began to squeeze, the grip powerful and relentless. I head-butted my attacker and brought the knife up through his chest. His eyes grew wide and he groaned as I pulled the knife up through his flesh and bone, cutting away the last of his life.

I scrambled to my feet, grabbed my sword and sheared off their heads.

My hand tightened on the grip as I glanced toward the brick building and thought of finally reaching Endersley. It was time to end him. But first, the sentry.

I stormed toward the rusting ladder that ran up the side of the tower, dropping my bag as I hoisted myself up onto the first rung. The wind blew hard and the sky above me was a swirling mass of blues and grays. I didn't look down, I just scaled the creaking, moaning structure, one bruised and aching hand after the other.

As I reached the top, the tinny din of voices wafted around me. A guard sat on a platform across from the ladder, his legs dangling over the side and his weapon resting on his lap as he watched a video on his phone. By the time he knew I was there I had his rifle in my hand and the barrel pointed at his head. He was an older man with broad shoulders, long oily hair and sallow eyes, but then I saw he wasn't entirely human. "Give me my fucking gun," The were-beast growled. He sounded angry, as well as afraid, but not of me.

"Where's Endersley?"

His eyes flitted to the building below, answering my question. "Getting ready for another barbecue." Spite seemed to override his concerns and a slow, mocking smile broke upon his lips.

"Barbecue? Well, clearly you're dying to explain, so here's your chance."

"Just the same old same old. He's cooking up some blinkereds." He gave a toothy grin but the nervousness returned to his eyes. Things had gone wrong here. Most likely after the strike on the Winter Festival had gotten screwed up. I imagined Endersley was furious, Stroud too.

I prodded the gun harder into his forehead. "Why's he killing blinkereds?"

"He runs his tests, and the ones who don't work out get cooked."

"Why?"

"For shits and giggles." He was trying to antagonize me, and it was working. His eyes flitted to the rifle and he moved fast as he tried to snatch the weapon away. I yanked it back, twisted it, and smashed the butt over his head, knocking him out. I'd have put a bullet in him if my next move hadn't required stealth. Instead I propped him up so it looked like he was still keeping watch.

I glanced down to the yard around the mill. Three ambulances were parked out front, which meant at least some of Endersley's people had escaped the festival. I climbed back down the ladder, threw my bag over my shoulder and made my way around the brick building to find a way inside.

The sky had darkened, giving me shadows to hide in. A few restless still stumbled through the gloom, but they were easy enough to evade. I found a side door with a half broken lock and finished the job with a quick spell. As I pulled the door open, its squeal echoed through the cavernous interior.

A bright orange glow flooded the far end of the building highlighting the hulking, rusting machinery that filled the main floor. I slipped inside amid the relentless roar and hiss of the furnace, taking cover among the shadows as I caught sight of someone.

I watched as they flitted across a long raised platform near the fiery light and stooped over a line of workbenches. Endersley? It had to be. Those mad, jittery movements couldn't belong to anyone else.

I was poised to bolt up a ladder to the gantry above when I heard voices coming my way. Two guards, rifles slung over their shoulders. Neither had seen me but I grabbed a crystal and cloaked myself as I stepped back into the murk. As they neared, I took them down and dragged them out of sight. Then I climbed up to the gantry and made my way across, sticking to the shadows as I went.

It was only as I neared the platform that I saw Astrid and Samuel kneeling with five blinkereds. All of them had their arms chained behind their backs but they seemed okay and I was filled with relief at the sight of my friends. They seemed to be watching Endersley as he hunched over the workbench and gazed through a microscope. He was ranting to himself, his voice high and wheedling and the bastard looked even rattier in the flesh, with those protruding eyes and mop of wiry grey hair. He sighed and muttered as he grabbed a syringe. "Who's next then?" He called, before glancing up to the yawning darkness above him.

But it wasn't darkness. It was a huge canvas filled with swirling black paint.

A portal.

I shuddered as my dark other slithered and pulled at my consciousness before shrinking away. He'd been so still and withdrawn that his sudden resurfacing startled me. I glanced back to Endersley, conflicted. I had the rifle I'd seized on the tower, and a clear shot. But the canvas was churning darkly and the ridges of black paint upon its surface were slowly glimmering.

Stroud was coming. I could feel it. And Endersley could too, judging by his rising panic as he stooped to scrawl into a notebook. I clambered over the gantry, hung and dropped to the platform, the roar of the furnace masking the din of my landing.

I ducked behind a blackened crucible and peered out, making sure Endersley was still distracted, before darting into the gloom on the other side. Both Astrid and Samuel had seen me, the blinkereds too, but no one stirred.

"Help is on the way, we'll get you all out of here" I whispered as I crept behind the blinkereds. "Just stay still and quiet." I crouched behind Astrid and Samuel. They kept their eyes on Endersley as he continued to mutter to himself at the workbench.

"You okay?" I whispered.

"Warm and toasty," Samuel replied, but as he continued there was no humor in his voice. "I'm sorry, Morgan. They got the jump on me. There was too many of them. Plus they had a lot of guns."

"It's happened to the best of us. How about you, Astrid?" I whispered.

"I'm angry," she said. "Really fucking angry and ready to shed some blood."

"Good," I said as I laid the rifle down, grabbed one of the last crystals from my bag and tried to turn the lock on the chains to rust. "This isn't working"

"Yeah, we weren't able to conjure our way out either." Samuel whispered "If you've still got that wicked dagger, this would be a good time to use it."

He held his bound arms up as I pulled out the blade and slipped it through the heavy chains. "Is that better?"

"Yeah and just in time." He stretched his arms and kept an eye on Endersley as I cut Astrid loose. "Stroud's on the way. He spoke to Endersley earlier via one of the blinkered corpses. And the gods know there were plenty of them for him to choose from. Enderley's been on a spree, killed at least a dozen since we arrived. Some went into the furnace, some were injected and turned restless. I want that bastard's head."

"You'll have it. Just-"

A crackling, hissing static filled the air and the thick ridges of paint upon the canvas began to undulate and peak like a turning tide.

Stroud was coming.

55

The painting shimmered and tendrils rose like smoke from the edges as the pigments within its framework churned and writhed like a pit of snakes below a moonless sky. A heavy rumbling filled the mill, the din so deafening it almost seemed the world was caving in.

Endersley turned to the canvas, his twitchy fingers pulling at the ends of his sleeves and his face filled with nervous anticipation. Then he folded his hands submissively before him as two forms emerged from the center of the dark abyss. One remained hulking and indistinct while Stroud's face appeared as pale as freshly fallen snow against his scarlet frock coat.

I moved into the shadows, pulled the dagger from its sheath and crouched down, biding my time. As I waited to spring, Stroud's companion came into focus. It was a colossus encased in armor. At first I took him to be a giant knight, and then I saw the cloudy corpse-blue eyes. A hexling. A towering armored hexling, that stood ten to twelve feet tall.

Stroud turned to Endersley and his face bore a dark, furious expression. "I saw your *grand scheme* unfold in the city.

Watched it through the eyes of the dead. There should have been hundreds if not thousands of eyes to peer through, but the only conduits I could find were the ones Rook and his friends had left in their wake."

"I have them." Endersley's lips twitched into a smile as he nodded towards Astrid and Samuel. "Right over there."

Stroud barely gave them a glance. "You may have his companions, but you do not have Rook. And now the blinkereds are stirring like a nest of copperfangs. They know something's happening, they sense it. But we needed an outrage to tip them to outright war. And you failed to provide it."

"The restless will take care of that-"

"Your methods are not working. The blinkereds are armed to the teeth. We'll need them to turn on the magical community, and for the magical community to turn on them. The meager number of restless you've managed to raise will not inspire the conflict. The blinkereds need to be pushed to war. These are a people who have been abused and milked like cattle by their masters for centuries, yet the vast majority of them haven't even registered it. We needed an outrage, a massacre to get their blood up."

Endersley swept a hand toward his makeshift laboratory. "I'm on the verge of something big. Something that should cleanse this world come what may."

"What is it?" Stroud asked, his ghostly face filled with mocking dismissal.

"A means of making the disease airborne." Endersley glanced back to the shackled people. "My recent tests have all been promising. *Very* promising."

As Stroud turned to glance at the chained blinkereds, his eyes passed over mine and he froze.

Fuck.

I stepped into the light, dagger in hand.

"Rook!" Endersley said. "He's-"

"Here," Stroud finished. He floated across the platform, his approach silent as he glared down at me. "And what is this?" he asked, his eyes on the dagger, his tone more curious than afraid.

"Your demise," I said, "I'm going to kill you." Terrible, almost uncontrollable anger consumed me as I faced the *man* responsible for the vile deeds that had befallen all that I'd held dear. Here he was, the monster that had propped up Wyght and the misery she'd inflicted on so many. The man who had Tom killed in a derelict tunnel reeking of stale piss. The man who'd had Hellwyn destroyed right before my very eyes.

"I don't want to hurt you." Stroud's spectral eyes locked on mine. They were dangerously hypnotic, like gazing down from a rickety bridge and being filled with a terrible yearning to leap. Slowly his darkness began to insinuate itself in my mind...

He pointed his ghostly finger but kept a careful distance as he spoke. "You don't want to harm me, Morgan. It would be a mistake. Just as a young boy being dragged to this vile world was a mistake. But then the knight, Tom, was no stranger to errors. Indeed he made one after another, but the most atrocious of them was his decision to follow the Queen's command to slaughter me and everyone I loved. But in the end," he smiled, "it seems he failed there too, didn't he my son?"

The word struck me like a wrecking ball and the room seemed to spin. I felt sick, deathly ill and yet this realization wasn't a surprise, not fully. There had been a part of me that had known all along. While the truth had been locked away, it seeped out over the years, manifesting as odd dreams and visions. It was a secret knowledge that belonged to my dark other and he'd held it close and hidden; he was Stroud's son. Which made me... what?

"You're wondering who you are?" Stroud asked. "Let me solve the mystery for you, Morgan. You're but a splinter of my son's soul. A fragment of his mind. You're the heroic persona he clung to when he was afraid. When the arcane truths I revealed to him as a child were too much for his young mind to bear. The side of him that rose up when he wished to deny his true unfettered nature and retreat into himself. You're not real, Rook, you're even more of a phantom than I am. An aberration that surfaced when my boy was ripped away from his world and was thrust into another. The split of a mind under great duress. You've had your time. You've fared as well as any covert parasite. Perhaps you've even served a purpose? For you concealed my young, inexperienced son's commanding spirit from this hobbling intolerant blinkered society. But now it's time for you to be expunged."

Move aside, my other roared, his demand forceful.

"I'm not going anywhere," I said. Stroud's revelations were cutting and they'd made me sick to my core, but I wasn't going to crumble. Aberration or not, my name was Morgan Rook. I lived, I breathed, I loved. And I was as real as anything else in this world.

I charged toward Stroud, dagger in hand.

The hexling's eyes flashed as it rounded on me, its heavy steps making the platform rattle and shake. It raised an armored fist, the mace in its grip glinting in the light of the furnace. I backed along the platform and ducked the swing of the brutal iron ball. It crashed to the metal floor and the platform buckled and jerked, throwing Endersley off his feet. He sprang up with an ax in his hand, his eyes feverish as they jumped from Stroud to me, and then to Astrid and Samuel still crouched on their knees.

The hexling swung the mace again, I dove aside and the chain whistled overhead as it cut through the air. Once it was clear I dashed forward, my dagger and gaze fixed on Stroud. He was within reach, and his scornful iciness was giving way to fear.

I lunged at him, intending to sever his throat a second time...

No!

My other struck so hard he threw me from my consciousness. I watched as he stayed my hand before it reached Stroud, the dagger stopping just short of his ghostly throat. I tried to claw my way back into my own mind but he'd seized control. This was what he'd been biding his time for... conserving his strength to use against me in this moment.

I pushed back, wrestling against his psyche but his grip was like iron.

The platform shook as the hexling loomed and the shadow of its mace fell over me.

Stroud waved a spectral hand, commanding it to stop. He gazed from the dagger to his son. "Destroy it. Quickly."

I could only watch as my other leaped toward the furnace. *No!* I cried. I tried to shove him aside but his force was greater. We neared Astrid and Samuel as Endersley rounded on them, ax in hand. Samuel ran toward me then leaped away as my other thrust the blade, almost tearing through his chest. He followed through with a punch and I felt a flash of pain as my fist met Samuel's chin, sending him toppling to the floor. Astrid's gaze fell on the blade as she held Endersley back and I could see no one else could stop him as we strode toward the furnace, the roar of its heat growing in intensity.

No! I used everything I had to thwart his will as he raised my hand. For a moment I stilled it, but then he shoved me back and hurled the dagger. It sailed through the air, the orange flames gleaming on its pearlescent blade as it wheeled round and around and plunged into the burning coals.

What have you done! My rage boiled over as I shoved against him, grasping at the edges of my own consciousness. Finally I found purchase. He tried to shove me away but my anger overwhelmed his and I pushed back and took control.

But I was too late, the dagger was gone.

I dove for the rifle I'd hidden in the shadows, and shot Endersley as he swung his ax at Samuel. The bullet struck him in the chest and he staggered and toppled to the ground with a thud.

The floor rumbled as the hexling descended. Someone moved in from the gloom. Astrid. She'd recovered their weapons and threw Samuel his bow and quiver then pulled a knife from under her cloak.

I wheeled around as the light shifted and another heavy rumble filled the air. It was Stroud, drawing in darkness from the portal behind him. He placed his hands together and unleashed a stream of shadows at Samuel and Astrid. They leaped as one and rolled across the ground as the deadly curse obliterated the machinery behind them and unleashed a rain of dust from above.

Stroud continued to summon the darkness as his hands reached toward the corners of the room and their murky depths lightened as his powers grew.

His sights were locked on Astrid. I ran as the black tendril emerged from his hand. With a viper-like strike, it hit before I could reach her, and she cried out my name as she collapsed to the ground.

56

The torrent of darkness continued to stream from Stroud's hand. It slithered through the air like a serpent and drew back to strike Astrid again as she lay helplessly upon the floor. I leaped into its path, screaming. The icy darkness bit into me and everything went black, then my eyes flew open and a great chill shot into my blood as I gasped for breath.

Stroud had seized the spell and modified its intent in an effort to save his son, but he was too late. The malicious power was inside me and I could feel it snaking through my veins as it raced toward my heart. The pain was agonizing but I embraced it. I let it sink into my cells, drawing in its power just as I'd done with Talamos Gin's magic, so that I could use it as my own. Stroud watched, open mouthed. In awe.

His memories flashed through my mind. I saw him standing in a grove of trees, staring down at piles of bones. His cult slaughtered, his wife and son... or so he'd believed in that moment, all dead. The terrible agony churning within him was almost too much to bear. Then a slow, grave-cold call to vengeance whispered and nagged away at him, demanding an oath of devastation and retribution. It was every inch as keen as mine had been for Elsbeth Wyght. I truly was my father's son...

I slipped back into my own consciousness and watched Stroud's ghostly hands grow thick with shadows. The hexling moved to his side, protecting its master. I gazed back to find Samuel clutching Astrid's hand, she was almost as pale as Stroud, her face stricken and deathly. The sight of her broke my heart.

Samuel glanced past me to Stroud, his teeth bared, his eyes filled with a malice I'd never seen in him before. Its intensity chilled me to the bone. He clutched an arrow in his other hand and the point began to glow, as if it had been just pulled from the forge roaring behind him. He was hexing it, no... *they* were hexing it. I watched as the last of Astrid's magic slipped from her fingers into Samuel's hand. Gently, Samuel released her and notched the arrow in his bow string.

The hexling moved toward its master, but not fast enough.

Samuel let the arrow fly. It arced through the air like a comet, hissing as it shot toward Stroud. The hexling tried to block it but its armor was too cumbersome.

Pain and surprise passed like a cloud over Stroud's spectral face as the arrow passed through him. The strike wasn't fatal but it was clear he'd been wounded. His form flickered and the shadows in his hands withdrew. He threw a weak flickering curse at Samuel, but he stepped aside, and it fizzled off into the gloom. "Fucking coward!" Samuel roared. He strode toward Stroud and I joined him, my strength still hampered by his curse.

Stroud looked at us and I saw the flicker of fear in his eyes. Then he turned and fled for the portal as his hexling thundered toward us.

I summoned all the power of Stroud's curse into my palms and conjured a ball of black flames. It shot toward the writhing canvas but struck the creature as it leaped to protect its master. Then Stroud's pale form merged with the darkening shadows as he vanished into the rift.

57

The hexling was ablaze as it charged across the platform, its dead eyes fixed on Astrid. I confronted the creature, my sword raised as I tried to divert it, but it paid me no heed.

Samuel's arrows flew, glancing off its visor as I swung the sword of intention at its legs, trying to slow its descent upon her, but the blade was no match for its armor.

The shadow of the creature's arm swept across the floor as it swung its mace. Samuel rolled out of the way and the weapon smashed into the platform. He leaped to his feet and fired an arrow that slipped through a gap near the hexling's wrist. Its fist spasmed and the mace fell.

It seemed the arrows might be our best chance at downing it, if Samuel could get a clear shot. I ran behind it and clambered up its back clinging to a joint in the plating as I plunged the sword of intention between it.

The hexling faltered as I swung up to its shoulder, sheathed the sword, and pulled at its visor. It shifted, but not enough.

Give me strength I cried as the last dregs of Stroud's power swirled through my veins.

No my other growled as he surfaced, drew the remains of the magic into my hand and discharged it into the ground.

You're next, I said, *once I'm done with Stroud I'm coming for you.* He bristled with fury but it seemed his power was spent. But I had no magic to summon either, and no access to crystals as the hexling stormed toward Astrid.

It would crush her within seconds.

I grasped the visor with every scrap of strength I had left, and pulled. The metal bit into my fingers and it squealed as it slowly began to lift. I took a deep breath, gave it one final tug and it creaked as it shot open. Samuel stood over Astrid, an arrow poised. He fired and it struck the hexling's face.

It wasn't enough.

Enraged, the hexling stumbled on.

I pulled my sword, fixed my eyes to the joint at its armored neck, and swung hard. "Cut!"

The blade glowed bright as it sliced through the air, my every intent driving it. It struck the joint, sank deep into the giant's throat, severing its dead flesh and bone in a perfect stroke.

Its head stayed seated upon its lumbering shoulders until I kicked it hard and sent it hurtling to the floor with an almighty thump. The hexling's body toppled, one step toward Astrid, one step back.

It was going to fall.

I threw the sword down and grabbed the armor on its back as I dropped, pulling it backwards, and then leaped clear as it crumpled into a cloud of dust.

As I picked up my blade and looked back, Samuel was already on his knees at Astrid side. And then something moved in the corner of the platform.

Endersley was up, fumbling at his work bench. He turned, a syringe in each hand as he advanced on them.

The glow of my sword caught Endersley's attention. He wheeled my way as I stumbled toward him, his eyes filled with wild, maniacal fury. I was too shattered and broken to speak but the hatred I had for the man energized the sword.

"You should-" Endersley began. I swung the blade and lopped his arm off. It fell to the ground and before he could react, I had his hand in my grasp. I wrestled the syringe from his fist and plunged it into his chest.

"Enjoy," I said, before head-butting him in the face. He staggered back in a strange, staccato way. Then he grasped the syringe, pulled it out and threw it down. His face turned ashen and his entire body began to convulse. "My heart!" He clutched his chest and his eyes bulged. "It's stopping. It…" Blood tinged his eyes red, and he bared his ratty teeth as he toppled to his knees with a scream. The sound was horrific, but it added to the triumphant swell of vengeful fury that had me held in its intoxicating spell.

"Kill him," Astrid said, then she coughed violently as she lay cradled in Samuel's arms. Her face was as white as chalk and the torment in her eyes was enough to jolt me from my sick thirst to watch Endersley suffer. Then I realized she wasn't talking to me, but to Samuel. He laid her down gently, notched an arrow and let it fly. It struck Endersley's throat. He glanced around and tried to speak, then collapsed.

"He's infected," Samuel called to me, his face grim. "You'll have to decapitate him or he'll rise again."

I drew back the sword of intention and did as he'd asked. I felt no pleasure in the act, just a terrible emptiness.

"I'll find help!" I whispered as I knelt beside Astrid. Her eyes were fixed on mine and she managed a brief, weak smile. There was a mix of emotions in her gaze. Love. Anger. Fear … of me. She grabbed my hand as her body convulsed and I received a jolting glimpse of her condition.

She'd been cursed. The pain would have been unimaginable to me had I not known it once myself. And as I recalled the night that Wyght's witch had cursed me, I thought of Talulah. She'd cured me all those years ago. Maybe she could help, if I got Astrid to her in time…

My hands shook as I pulled my phone from my pocket and dialed Talulah's number. The phone rang and rang, and I choked as it went to voicemail.

58

My mind raced. I thought about driving Astrid straight to the shop, but Talulah might not even be there and there was no time to waste. It was clear by the weak, wandering gaze in her eyes that we didn't have long.

I racked my brain as I tried to think of anyone else that could help. There were plenty of healers in the city, but I had no idea who possessed the skills or knowledge to handle a curse like this. My thoughts kept circling around memories of the night I'd been cursed and as they did, I thought of the Silver Spiral. And then of Willow and her coven.

Seraphina!

I had no way of reaching her by phone but the old dance hall where the witches lived and worked wasn't far. Maybe they could help. It was a long shot, but it was all I had.

"What are we going to do?" Samuel asked. He spoke calmly for Astrid, but I sensed the panic churning below his words.

"The white witches from Temple Park, we'll take her to them. Wait here, I'll get a vehicle." As I rose to leave I spotted the cowering blinkereds, still chained alongside the furnace. One had passed out and the others stared up at us in abject horror. "Can you release them," I asked Samuel. "And help them forget this happened." He nodded as I scooped up the rifle and ran down the stairs.

There were still restless wandering in the yard outside. They spotted me and staggered my way. I had no choice but to take them down. I brought up the gun and shot three through the head. They dropped immediately but the next one continued to twitch and moan as he came at me. I swung the sword and decapitated him, ending the poor bastard's suffering. He blinked softly and the light in his eyes went out.

I ran through the yard toward the ambulances. The wind howled as I pulled the door of the nearest one open, climbed into the driver's seat and reached up to start it.

The keys were gone.

I held my breath as my hand clung to the ignition and my mind raced. There was no time, not for this. I kicked at the pedals. The crushing grief flew from my lungs in a screaming, growling shout, then my swimming head lolled forward and struck the steering wheel.

As I inhaled a charge leapt from hand and the engine roared to life. "Thank you!" I gripped the wheel, threw it into reverse and raced backward toward the doorway of the mill.

Together Samuel and I lifted Astrid onto a stretcher and secured it in the back of the vehicle before gently closing the doors. Samuel's face was as grave as mine as we climbed into the front. The ambulance lights flashed in the gloom as I sped down the drive, smashed through the security gate and raced toward the highway.

I switched on the sirens as we neared town. Samuel peered over his shoulder every few minutes to check on Astrid but neither of us said a word.

The old dance hall was on the outskirts of the city in a decidedly unpopular and disused part of town. How much of this was urban decay and how much was Seraphina and her coven's doings was hard to say. I pulled up outside and pounded on the doors under the old marquee. A spirited young witch opened them, saw my face and didn't need much persuasion to summon Seraphina.

She appeared moments later, her fast bright eyes reading me in a flash. "What is it, Morgan?" she asked, her usually kindly face solemn.

"Cursed. My friend's been cursed. She's in a lot of pain. It's bad."

"Where?" Seraphina asked.

With a snap of her fingers several witches rushed to her side and I led them to the ambulance. We stood back as they carefully unstrapped Astrid and carried her toward the building.

"Is she going to be okay?" I asked.

"Yes. We can help her."

"How long will it take?" I asked as I walked anxiously beside her.

"Three nights, that should do it," Seraphina said, "but you can't come in. This isn't for you."

I nodded. I got it. I leaned over and kissed Astrid lightly on the lips. Her eyes were still distraught, but a little of the cloudiness left them as she focused on me. "You'll be okay, you're with friends." I said. I placed my hand over hers and did my best not to wince at her ice-cold touch. I kissed her once more and then Samuel and I watched in silence as the witches took her inside and the doors closed softly behind them.

"What now?" Samuel asked as we stood on the still, empty sidewalk. I didn't know how to answer and turned my gaze to the bare brittle branches that stretched up toward the stars. It seemed autumn was long gone and the dark months had arrived. I glanced at Samuel and saw the apprehension in his eyes. He was wary of me and I couldn't blame him. I'd tainted myself with other people's magic, Stroud's included. And if that wasn't bad enough, somewhere within my mind lurked his wicked, spiteful son.

"Three nights." I whispered.

Samuel nodded but said nothing.

"Then we hunt down Stroud," I said. "And destroy him or die trying. But come what may, I'll never be his son. You know that right?"

Samuel looked me in the eye and gave a slight nod. "I believe in you, Morgan. You're a good man, for the most part. Let's keep that part of you alive and banish the other. As I said before, there are ways to do that, but not in this world."

"Whatever it takes," I said.

I walked toward the ambulance and called Haskins. "It's over," I said as he answered.

"You sure?"

"I can tell you where the bodies are."

"That won't be necessary. I'm already up to my neck in shit, Rook. The news crews are going crazy and there's all sorts of wild rumors and speculation flying around about what happened at the festival. You got any hocus pocus that'll dial this nightmare back a notch or two?"

I glanced at Samuel. "No. But I might know a man who does." I hung up and approached Samuel. "The story that the blinkered media's dishing out about the festival needs be quelled."

"I don't think I could persuade that many people, Morgan" Samuel said. "Not unless you can get them all in one place and make sure I have a shit-ton of magic at my disposal."

I shook my head, "You don't need to persuade all of them. Just one or two will do, as long as it's the right ones. Do that and the rest of the pack will follow." I flicked through my phone, looked up the local news channel and paused on an image of their lead journalist.

Samuel's eyes widened and he smoothed his mustache as his lips curled into a half smile. "I might just be up to it. Do you know where to find her?"

"She'll find you if we offer her an exclusive. We just need a convincing enough tale to catch her interest."

"Oh, I do pretty well with stories. Give me a moment or two and I'll conjure up something sparkly and marvelous." Samuel walked over to a bench, stacked his pipe and his eyes drifted to whatever scurrilous mind-palace he went to for plotting.

I called Dauple.

"Are you okay, Morgan?"

"No, but I will be. In a few days." I told him about the mill, the blinkereds who would need help, the corpses, and how to dispose of Endersley's work and equipment.

"I'm on it. But what about you? The Organization's searching for you, and so's the Council. You've stirred up a fire ant's nest."

"Then it's time to raze it to the ground," I said, then thanked him before hanging up.

A bitter wind shook the trees and sent the leaves on the sidewalk chasing themselves in rustling spirals. They made me think back to the visions I'd had in Copperwood Falls. Of Stroud leading a procession of the dead across a marble floor, and the scattering of leaves and dirt he'd left in his wake. At the time I'd thought it had been a hallucination brought on by the drugs they'd given me, but I was wrong. It had been a string of memories. My other's memories of his time in Penrythe, and of his father.

No, not *his* memories. *Our* memories; I was just as alive as he was. Even more so perhaps.

I felt him stir within me, a dormant force once more. One I was certain would rise against me given time. I shook my head as I caught my reflection in an icy puddle. "You'll be dead soon enough brother," I said, "I'm coming for you, your father, the Council and everyone else who brought the darkness to this world." I took a deep breath and released it slowly. "You'll see, it'll all go down like a house of cards. Whatever it takes."

Book 5: Morgan Rook returns in **The Shadow Rises**, the final novel in the acclaimed Order of Shadows series. Old Enemies. A battle between Worlds. The Final Confrontation. **Get your copy here:** https://kithallows.com/ShadowKindle

Want to know what set Morgan on his road to revenge before the events of Dark City? Read the free prequel story Dark Covenant today (and access exclusive Kit Hallows stories) right here: https://kithallows.com/DarkCovenant

READ ON FOR A FREE PREVIEW OF
THE SHADOW RISES

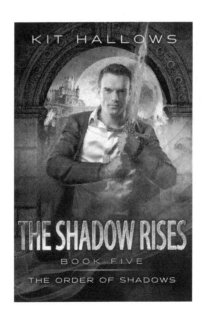

THE SHADOW RISES CHAPTER 1

Snowflakes swirled like volcanic ash through the dark evening sky. They looked grey and intricate as they drifted down in the late November moonlight. It seemed winter had arrived early.

I fastened my coat and blew a warming breath into my hands as I glanced from the slow, frigid lapping waves along the shoreline to the silent, empty dockyard. "Where are you Dauple?" I muttered, wincing as the breeze stirred up another fetid whiff of fermenting seaweed and dead fish.

It had been less than an hour since he'd called, pleading with me urgently to meet him in this forlorn corner of the city. I'd already had important plans but I'd never known him to ask for help, not if it wasn't truly serious. His voice had been riddled with fear and desperation yet something in the way he'd spoken had almost made each word sound as if he'd been reading it from a script. "What's the problem?" I'd asked. He'd muttered something about a demon and the phone went dead.

As I stood alone, waiting in the dark along the eerie, desolate beach, I wished I'd taken Samuel up on his offer to come with me.

We'd been planning on meeting Astrid as she left the care

343

of the witches. Then I got the call. Making sure at least one of us was there for her had seemed far more important, and if I could have figured out a way to have been there myself, that *one of us* would have been me. But at least I'd been able to speak with her for a few moments the night before. It had been great to hear her voice and she'd assured me she'd fully recovered from Stroud's vicious curse, much to my relief.

A growl issued from the gloom, breaking my thoughts, followed by a clatter like falling tin cans. As I walked toward the din, a starved, mangy dog ran past me and vanished into the murk. A false alarm.

I trusted Dauple implicitly, but something about this situation was beginning to feel very wrong. Like I'd walked into a trap... I shivered and blew another fleetingly warm breath into my hands. A slow wave broke upon the shore and I turned back to regard the old pier where Dauple had told me he'd be. I'd already checked it for signs of him, but there'd been nothing definitive. No bodies, no signs of a struggle, just the slow, relentless lap of the tide and a nagging sense that Dauple had gotten himself into some serious trouble. I pulled my gun and checked the chamber, as if the round might have somehow magically vanished since I'd last looked. It hadn't, it was locked and loaded, and my sword was still secured under my coat.

So why did I feel so strangely vulnerable?

"Come on, Dauple," I whispered as I turned back and headed toward the dry dock. As I made my way up the beach, the rusted remains of a fishing boat towered overhead and I took care to avoid the tangled nets strewn among the abandoned anchor and engine parts.

Thud.

The echoing din came from the vast gloomy structure in the

boatyard ahead, and was followed by a rattle of chains, and a voice crying out, its tone high and strained.

I dashed through the narrow path between the rows of dilapidated vessels stowed in the dry dock, moving as silently as I could.

When I'd checked the tall hangar-like structure earlier, it had clearly been locked down for the winter, but I paused as a flash of light came through the high barred windows on one side of the building.

Someone was in there.

I tried to call Dauple but his phone went straight to voicemail.

Clunk.

Something shifted behind me and I spun around, my breath frosting the night air and obscuring my view.

Was someone lurking by the skeletal remains of the old trawler? No, just a trick of the shadows and snowfall.

I turned back to the building and checked the doors. They were still locked. I pulled a crystal from my bag and dissolved the locks to rust. Pushing the door open, I swept my gun to the corners before stepping inside. The place was crammed full of boats, their silhouettes gave the place the air of a maritime graveyard, adding to the already sinister atmosphere.

"No!"

I glanced up, and followed the voice until it was abruptly cut off.

A gleam flashed in the murk above, like a small pair of flashlights held close together, but it was far too intense to have been powered by any battery. I inched forward, checking the floor for obstacles, my gun held before me. Then I paused as another muffled cry rang out, followed by a groan that very much sounded like Dauple.

Someone whispered, their voice a low, insidious hiss. It put me in mind of… rattlesnakes.

A metal staircase at the end of the hangar led up to a narrow platform that ran around the circumference of the place and there… two silhouettes, one crooked and hunched over, the other tall with fiery glowing eyes…

Rhymes.

I swept my gun up but eased my finger away from the trigger. I couldn't shoot, not without the risk of hitting Dauple. I had to lead Rhymes away from him.

"You've kidnapped the mortician, Rhymes? What are you after?" I called, my voice echoing in the emptiness as I glanced back to make sure there weren't any other agents concealed in the darkness.

"Just you, Morgan," Rhymes called with a soft hiss. He sounded at ease, happy even, as if he was about to tell me some good news. "Show yourself."

"No. Not until you let Dauple go."

"Why would I give him up?" Rhymes asked, his voice almost playful.

"Because he's one of us."

"Is that so?" Rhymes asked. His voice was worryingly close, even though he hadn't moved. "Do you know, I'm not so certain he is. You see there's been a bit of a shake-up within the Organization. New blood to replace the old after our cull of those who were loyal to compromised elements, like your friend Erland Underwood. And of course rogue agents, such as yourself. You do realize you're still wanted for the murder of that poor old man, don't you?"

I kept my silence as I moved through the gloom and ducked behind the ruins of a trawler for cover.

"Why have you gone so quiet, Rook?" Rhymes asked, "Are

you trying to sneak up on me?" He laughed. "I'd advise against it if you want to see your friend again."

Dauple's scream was unhindered now. "Please..." he cried, and then his voice was cut off.

"I asked you politely, Morgan," Rhymes called. "Don't test my patience."

"Come on down, I'm happy to talk," I said. I was close enough to the stairway to see the obscured glow of Rhymes' eyes from below his customary shades and wide-brimmed hat. He chuckled and lifted his glasses to shed some light on Dauple's bruised and bloodied face.

"Run, Morgan!" Dauple cried. "Go!" Then he whimpered as Rhymes poked a black gloved finger into his throat.

"Hush, you silly little corpse disturber," Rhymes hissed. As he turned back toward me shadows danced across his face, unaffected by the blazing light of his eyes. He smiled, revealing stark white teeth. "This was fun, but I'm beginning to find myself growing irritable, Morgan. Reveal yourself before I bite off your friend's hooked nose and force him to eat it."

I stepped out from behind the trawler and Rhymes reached into his long coat faster than a striking snake, sweeping his revolver my way. With a flash, gunfire roared in the gloom and I heard the bullet's piercing whine just before it hit me.

THE SHADOW RISES CHAPTER 2

I stumbled back into the boat as the round struck my chest. My coat absorbed most of the impact, but it still hurt like hell. Then Rhymes' gun roared again as I dove behind another boat.

Bright light from a handful of crystals filled the gloom as I consumed their power and fragments of wood flew past my face as another bullet splintered the hull.

I forced myself to slow my breath and focus. In one swift motion I swept around the bow, zeroed in on the light of Rhymes' eyes and took aim. My bullet clipped his arm. He cried out, dropping his gun. It clanked along the metal landing and fell to the ground with a thud. Rhymes recovered fast and loped toward Dauple who was trying to shuffle away.

"No, no, no," Rhymes said as he snatched Dauple up, spun him around and stepped behind him, using him as a shield. The light of his eyes lit Dauple's harried face as Rhymes grinned down at me. "Another shot, Morgan? Go on. Who knows, you might get lucky."

I shook my head and ran across the hangar, scooping up Rhymes' gun as I went. I realized my error as the temperature dropped and the world around me darkened far more than it should have. The gloom rumbled and darkness crawled at the edge of my vision. I spun around.

Rhymes loomed, right before my eyes, his teeth blazing in a sick white, psychotic grin. He swept a gloved hand toward me and a flash of silver caught me off guard.

I jumped away as his flick-knife caught the fabric of my coat, causing it to crackle and flash with blue light.

"Ah," Rhymes said, as he stepped back and tensed to pounce again. "I've heard tell of your magical coat. What a wondrous gift!" He removed his sunglasses, dousing me in a blinding glare as he prepared to strike. I fired, but the bullet ricocheted in the distance.

I threw a punch. It connected with cold, taut flesh. Rhymes groaned, and I heard the scuffle of his shoes as he leaped toward me. I clasped my hand over my face, shielding myself from the glow and fired again. This time he cried out and his eyes flickered like bulbs on a faulty circuit. Before I could shoot again, he grabbed my hand and twisted. My gun clattered to the floor. I stumbled back, pulled the sword of intention and held it between us.

Rhymes clasped a hand to his side, his fingers slick with green-grey ichor.

I leaped forward, taking a stab at his heart but he evaded me and seized my wrist. He lunged fast, trying to bite my face. I head-butted him, wriggled free and hobbled out of reach.

Rhymes' eyes grew brighter. He stared, his gaze loitering at my chest.

A whiff of smoke filled my nostrils. I looked down. The smoldering glow of his eyes was focused, right where my heart was. I brought my blade up flat and gave it a refining twist, reflecting the fiery light right back at him.

Rhymes howled and blundered back. I closed the distance between us and lunged. The sword tore through his chest. He grabbed my hand and held the blade steady. His eyes were dimmer now, and instead of flinching away from his gaze I began to absorb the powers he had hidden within.

Snapshots of his life appeared in my mind...

The squalid apartment in which he'd been brought up, as a stranger in an alien world. The cry of his mother's voice. She was a bent, broken blinkered woman, and his father a demon, scales and all. I caught glimpses of the abuse Rhymes had endured as a child, spurred by his father's refusal to accept his half blinkered bloodline. The cruel games, the casual sadism, the beatings so routine and consistent they almost became mundane.

Until the night his demonic father had gone too far and finally broke whatever humanity Rhymes had had left within him. And after the torrent of mad fiery fury had consumed Rhymes' soul, it had burst forth from his eyes as he'd slaughtered his parents, daubing the walls with their remains.

I broke his gaze as I continued to drain away his powers.

"You're stealing my essence," Rhymes said. His eyes flickered again. "How?"

"It's my new party trick," I said. "Like it?"

"No one does that," Rhymes stepped away and retreated to the shadows. "No one."

"Seems I do," I said. A flash of sadism surged through me as his eldritch power coursed through my veins, teeming alongside the darkness I'd stolen from Stroud and Talamos Gin. I felt my other shiver. The sensation was exquisite, I almost enjoyed his discomfort as much as the growing terror on Rhymes' face. And to think, I'd actually feared this demon once, not so long ago.

The gloom began to build around Rhymes. It was a darkness that could not legitimately exist, not in this world. I summoned the magic racing through me and cast it, forming black flames that danced upon my palms, drawing Rhymes' gaze. "That's right," I said. "I'm going to show you some real power."

The darkness surrounding him drew in, swaddling his form like a blanket. He was about to move, and fast.

I hurled the fireballs.

One raced by his head, roaring into the yawning gloom. The other streamed toward his face. He threw up a hand and screamed as the flames struck his gloved palm and caught the side of his face alight.

He cried out, uttering words of power as he began to fade into the darkness that drew around him, spinning faster and faster, like a whirlwind. It formed a shadowy column, still alight with black flames, as it rose up and settled upon the platform above. Right next to Dauple.

Dauple's eyes grew wide as he watched the spinning black pillar spit out Rhymes.

He staggered along the platform, as the devil clutched one hand to the wound in his side and fumbled inside his coat with the other.

I ran, taking the stairs two at a time, reaching the platform as Rhymes lurched toward Dauple, knife in hand. Before I could close the gap, he seized Dauple and held the blade to his throat. "Stop, Rook," Rhymes growled, "stay back."

"You hurt him, and I'll eviscerate you and everything you hold dear," I promised. "Let him go. Now!"

Before I could move, Dauple began to squirm. Rhymes clasped him harder, but Dauple's hand struck the wound in his side, causing the half-demon to scream with agony. He released Dauple and his pointed white teeth gritted in pain, but as Dauple staggered across the platform, Rhymes brought up the glinting knife clutched in his black gloved fingers.

Before I could move he threw it, and I could only watch as

the blade spun around and around, handle to tip, tip to handle in a grim shimmering circle.

Thunk!

It hit Dauple square in the back. He froze before he fell, and gave a strangled gasp that vanished into the gloom.

THE SHADOW RISES CHAPTER 3

Rhymes grinned at me as he clutched his wound and shuffled back toward the wall. Then the darkness enveloped him, and he was gone.

I ran to where Dauple lay, the bloody knife protruding from his back. His hands were sprawled before him, gripping the platform as if it were dear life itself.

"Hold still." I clasped the hilt and carefully, slowly, drew it out. I examined the blade for inscriptions, runes or hexes. It seemed to be a normal weapon, except for a slight discoloration of the metal, which suggested it could have been tainted with some kind of toxin.

I set the weapon down, pulled back Dauple's coat and ripped open the hole in his shirt, revealing the wound. My medical knowledge was limited but it seemed clear, by the spasms passing through his body, that his injury was serious. *Very* serious.

He groaned as I delved into my bag and pulled out a vial of healing water. I poured it over the wound and tried to bandage him up. He cried out as the cloth touched his flesh and his fingers gripped the metal struts. "No good," he said.

He grimaced and turned onto his side before I could stop him. "Poisoned. Maybe Cyamorth. The wound's mortal." His teeth were stained with blood as he added, "I've seen it before."

"I'm not going to let this happen..."

Dauple shook then convulsed with such force he flipped onto his back. His eyes grew wide as he stared up at the ceiling. "Not long," he said.

"I..." I gripped his hand and fought back my tears. Despite his strangeness and grotesquerie, he'd been one of the few people in the Organization who had been loyal. And while he was mildly insane and undeniably odd, he was my friend. I wasn't going to give up on him.

He was dying. That was as clear as day, and I didn't have a cure but a thought, a memory, shot through my mind. The dealer from Copperwood Falls, the one I'd pursued into death's domain. "I saved someone before," I said. "I can do it again. But... I don't have any black crystals."

Dauple gave a bittersweet smile. "I do."

"Really?" I asked. "You said you were addicted. I thought you'd quit?"

"Yeah. I... carry one to remind myself that I have power over it. That they don't rule me."

"Where?"

"Chest pocket. Close to my heart." Dauple grinned but his eyes were beginning to roll back. He was fading fast.

I reached into my bag and grabbed a handful of crystals and used their energy to cast a protective spell around, in case Rhymes returned. Motes of golden light shimmered in the surrounding air as the shield manifested. It wasn't perfect, but it would do.

My hands were shaking. I took a slow, deep breath as my prior, nightmarish experience with the black crystals leapt to the forefront of my mind. Forcing my apprehension aside I reached into Dauple's shirt pocket. He shuddered, coughed and squirmed but I found it; a small leather pouch, bound with an enchantment to seal in the dark magic. Its embroidered inscription read:

RIP 2001 - 2006

Presumably the years he'd lost to his addiction. My fingers tensed as I loosened the knot and reached inside. A jolt of power rushed through me as I brushed against cold, polished stone. Then I pulled it from the bag.

The shard was long and jagged and its blackness shimmered like a trail of coal dust on a moonlit night. A low hum thrummed from the stone; a shattering echo of the suffering that had been inflicted on the poor soul who's life force had been stolen when the crystal was charged. The resonance of pure, black evil.

The stone pulsed like a living thing as I wrapped my fingers around it and drew in its power. The magic scorched my skin, my blood, and my very cells. I shuddered as it flooded me with malevolent power and my dark other shivered deep within.

"God Damn it!" I cried, as the power from the stone collided with the black magic I'd stolen before, turning everything to darkness.

What had I done? What would I become? I forced the thoughts from my mind as Dauple gave a final gasp, gripped my hand, and slipped away.

THE SHADOW RISES CHAPTER 4

The platform faded around us as I gripped Dauple's lifeless wrist and heavy clouds of darkness whirled in thick plumes of black and gray as the world lost its substance.

I grasped the sword of intention in one hand and willed it to travel with me.

The mist swirled faster and faster and when it broke, we were in a strange, incorporeal limbo. An icy breeze scented by deathly things blew around us. I clutched Dauple's cold fingers in my hand and as the swirling gloom shifted we passed from our world to another. The mist continued to churn and I caught glimpses of the golden motes of light gleaming along the shield I'd conjured with Rhymes' power.

Slowly, the fog thinned revealing heavy black stone walls that reached up into the boundless shadows above. As my consciousness settled into this gloomy new place, light from a row of dark candles twinkled from a line of hollows carved into the wall of the corridor. I checked Dauple hoping something, anything, had changed but his eyes were sightless and his body still.

The air grew icier as I stepped out from under the magical shield, and a ripe hollow breeze laced with the scents of carrion, must, and rot wafted past me. Voices whispered along the short corridor and I followed them to a chamber with the statue of a cowled woman surrounded by clouds of green-tinged light.

I'd seen her stony countenance before, as well as the circle of seven swords that were laid upon the ground near her gray feet. As I stooped to examine one, I noticed a short tunnel in the wall and followed it to an immense room filled with corpses. Some lay on stretchers, some on stone plinths, and around them were figures dressed in black silken robes.

Bright blue fire flickered in a nearby brazier. I stepped toward it in the hopes of finding some warmth but my movement drew the gaze of a man attending to the corpse of a shriveled old woman. He was tall and powerfully built and his brow lowered as he moved toward me.

I turned and rushed back to Dauple.

"Who are you?" the man called as he followed, his accent heavy but its origin unfamiliar. "Why are you here?"

"I need help," I said, and nodded to where Dauple lay, "my friend needs..." The man shoved past me and reached for Dauple but hissed and withdrew amid a burst of golden light as he struck the shield.

"What is this?" the man demanded. He drew a sword he'd had been concealed beneath his robes. "Remove the spell, he must be anointed."

"No."

"Are you denying us our duty and purpose?"

"He doesn't belong here," I said, "not yet at least. He has to come back with me."

The man shook his head. "Return to where you came from. Now, while you still can."

"I'm not leaving him here, he's not ready."

"You're dictating the laws that govern mortality now, are you?" The man raised his blade. "Go back. This is your last chance."

"No." I pulled the sword of intention. "Not until you help me wake him."

The man's eyes glinted as he examined me closer. "You're the one, are you not? I've heard tell of you." He reached for the disc of bone suspended on the silver chain around his neck and rubbed its center.

The circle of swords that surrounded the statue glowed and the air in the chamber flickered as an ethereal figure slowly materialized in its midst.

I saw the raven black hair and I knew it was her, the priestess I'd encountered the first time I'd come to this place. Her eyes narrowed as they focused on me and she hissed as she stepped from the circle. "You've returned," she said as she pulled a sword from the sheath by her side, "that was a grave mistake."

"It wasn't like I had a choice," I said, doing my best to appear unfazed as I gestured to Dauple. "He needs help, this is not his time."

"That's not for you to decide, otherworlder," She nodded to the man and they raised their swords.

I brought my own up and stepped toward her. "We've danced this one before. I'm happy to do it again if we must, but I'll hurt you. You and anyone else with ill intent toward my friend. But if you heal him, we'll leave in peace."

"We are not healers." the woman said, her words filled with scorn. "We merely attend to the dead, and that man," her eyes flitted to Dauple, "is dead. He belongs here."

"That's not true," I said. "I left here with someone before, you remember?"

"No. You abducted him against his will and escaped, but you won't manage it again." She nodded to the man beside her and he traced a finger around the disc of bone at his neck. The air shimmered above the circle of swords and another robed figure emerged, a lean and well armed man. As he stepped forward, another man emerged and then a woman, and soon the corridor was blocked.

I held my head high, conveying a confidence I didn't feel.

One of the men, gaunt and elderly, approached Dauple. He reached for him but withdrew his bony hand as the shield shimmered and singed his fingers. I'd used almost all the magic I'd had casting the spell; it was still holding, but it would only last so long.

I took a defensive step back as a slight priestess with bright eyes thrust her blade at me and tried to twist the sword from my hands. I tightened my grip on the hilt and took a step forward, disarming her then gripping her by the throat. I gazed over her shoulder toward the woman with raven hair. She watched keenly, her eyes unreadable.

"I'll kill her." I said, "along with the rest of you, I promise. You're priests, not warriors. That's plain enough to see."

"You know nothing of us," the woman with the raven hair said. She strode forward and swung her sword, forcing me to meet it. I released my hostage as I deflected the blow. Sparks flew from our locked blades and the dark priestess stared me down.

I stepped away, breaking eye contact. "That's not true," I said, "I know at least one thing about you."

"What?"

"That you're looking for my father. When we first met you told me he'd cheated you."

"He cheated our master."

"And you want to find him." I said.

"We *will* find him. Just as we'd have found you, given time."

I lowered my sword and offered my other hand. "Morgan Rook."

"I know who you are." She gave my hand a dismissive glance.

"And you are?" I asked, doing my best to seem at ease with the throng of deathly priests surrounding me.

"Temperance, not that my name is any concern of yours. Now, my brother offered you a chance to leave, and you refused it, which means you will remain within our domain."

"Not without a fight," I said, "and judging by your attempts to subdue me so far, I'm guessing combat isn't your strong point."

"Don't be so certain," Temperance said. "You've invaded a sacred space, and this violation will not go unpunished."

"Of course not, but there are many ways to repent." I said, noting the whisper of their robes as they surged toward me. I held my sword out, glad for the crackle of fire fizzling around its silver blade. "Let's think about this, before things get bloody and painful. You'd rather take this man, who has done nothing to you," I gestured to Dauple, "as well as myself, instead of Rowan Stroud, the man who cheated your master. Is that right?"

Temperance held up a hand and brought the other priests to a halt. "We'll get Stroud eventually, and in the meantime we'll have his son."

"*Eventually?* Don't be so sure. Are you aware he's a shade?" I said, "A phantom caught between life and death. I expect he can remain in that state for as long as he chooses and there's nothing you can do about it, or you'd have done so already.

Why wait around with your hands tied when I can deliver him directly to you?"

Her gaze continued to bore into mine, but her sword lowered. "Where is he?"

"Right now? I'm not entirely certain. But I'm on his trail and I'll find him quicker if you don't hold me up. So what will it be? Would your master prefer two mediocre corpses, or Rowan Stroud?"

"If it came down to a choice, he'd want Stroud. But how can you possibly deliver him to us?"

"I intend to kill him."

"Why should I believe you? You stole from us before and fled like a thief in the night."

"True," I said, "but I keep to my word."

"*If* we agree to your terms, you'll deliver Stroud, with no games or trickery?" Temperance asked. "On your life?"

I could see her naked ambition and the urgent need to serve and please her master. I could have used it to my advantage and lied, but I didn't. "Yes, but I'll be honest, I don't know how long it will take. I could find him tomorrow, or it could be in years to come. But I *will* find him. Or perhaps he'll find me; after all, I have something he wants."

"The other within you," Temperance said, and as I saw the flicker of apprehension in her eyes, I realized *he* was probably the only reason I was still alive.

"Exactly." I sheathed my sword. "Now let's make our deal, heal my friend and let him leave with me and I'll-"

"Him?" Temperance bared her fangs. "He's dead. He belongs here."

"No, I'm taking him back, he belongs in the blinkered world with me. Restore his life, there's more than enough power within these blackened walls to get it done."

She stared at me for a moment, before giving a slight nod. "Very well, but you must remove the shield."

"Sure." I hid my relief. The spell fueling the shield was moments away from collapsing anyway. I made a show of sweeping a hand over it and withdrawing the magic. Then the air twinkled with golden light, as it melted away.

Temperance inspected the wound in Dauple's back, placed her fingers over it, and began to hum in a low, off-key tone. The other priests and priestesses' joined her, filling the passage with a sedate, ominous chorus that shifted from discordant to deeply melodic. It was the sound of angels and second chances. The mysterious rhythm of life welling up and blooming. A sacred song I should never have witnessed, but was glad to the deepest depths of my heart that I had. Slowly, it swelled and built into a crescendo that was so raw and beautiful that it brought tears to my eyes and I let them fall.

I watched in silence as Dauple's flesh knitted itself together and soon the wound was sealed. Temperance turned him onto his back, and leaned over to kiss each of his eyes, before placing a hand upon his chest.

Dauple coughed and grimaced, gritting his blood-stained teeth. His eyes opened, and he stared at the ceiling with a grave look. And then he gazed from Temperance to me. "What…"

"Everything's okay," I said. "Just stay still."

Temperance's fangs protruded from her lips as she turned my way. "Take him back with you and don't let us down. Because if you do, I'll destroy the spirits of those you've loved the moment they appear before me."

I nodded as I took Dauple's hand and using the last of the black crystal's power, willed us to pass out from the charnel realm back to the blinkered world. The stones blurred and ran like ink as Temperance's eyes locked onto mine. And then they vanished amid billowing columns of smoke as we passed into the terrible limbo between places.

"Where are we?" Dauple asked.

"Nowhere." I gripped his hand and focused my thoughts on the shipyard. The air wavered and the last of the morbid scents disappeared as we found ourselves kneeling upon the platform once more. Dauple breathed deeply and took a moment to gaze around before turning to me. "I was dead wasn't I? Right here. And you saved me." His eyes glinted with tears.

"Never mind that." I clapped his shoulder. "Just get yourself out of the city. Find somewhere safe to go to, somewhere no one knows. Okay?"

"Okay." Dauple gave me a weak, yet almost beatific smile, as he added, "I've been meaning to visit my brother for a while now."

Brother? There was two of them... I suppressed a shiver. "I didn't know you had a brother."

"Yes, Alfred. He lives in the north. Not too far from the city, but far enough not to be noticed."

"Good. Go there, keep your head down and tell Bastion to do the same, if you haven't already."

Dauple gave me a curious look. "Bastion's gone, Morgan."

"What do you mean gone?"

"They were going to *fire* him. Humble sent Osbert and a pair of mercenaries to bring him in. I warned Bastion, told him to flee. He left at once, along with Madhav."

"Good," I said, "although I really need to restock, and sooner rather than later."

"Snarksmuth's taken over the armory now."

"Has he?" I reached into my bag for my remaining crystal and soaked up its power. "I can deal with that little shit, you just get out of here, okay?"

"I will. But where are you going?"

"I'm going hunting. For Rhymes, Stroud, Lampton. Every last one of them."

To read the rest of Ender of Worlds visit https:// kithallows.com/ShadowBook

DARK COVENANT

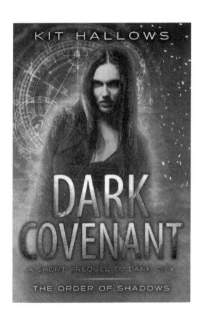

Get your free copy of Dark Covenant, the explosive prequel to Dark City, as well as exclusive access to my mailing list for author updates and free Urban Fantasy stories by visiting: https://kithallows.com/DarkCovenant

ALSO BY KIT HALLOWS

The Order of Shadows Series

Dark City

Midnight Falls

A Game of Witches

Ender of Worlds

The Shadow Rises

Myth Bane

Short Stories

Dark Covenant (Newsletter Exclusive)

The Ghost's Story

AFTERWORD

Thank you so much for reading Ender of Worlds. If you enjoyed the novel I'd be incredibly grateful if you could spread the word by leaving a short review on Amazon!

Thank you & best wishes,
Kit Hallows

ABOUT THE AUTHOR

Kit Hallows was born in London, England and now lives in the United States. Kit spends most his time dreaming up tales of urban fantasy, occult horror and magical adventure. Currently Kit's planning new stories and adventures in dark magical worlds.

Join Kit at kithallows.com and sign up for exclusive reads.

For more information
kithallows.com
kit@kithallows.com

Made in the USA
San Bernardino, CA
19 June 2020

73726281R00234